DIY Publishing

Grow House

Buz Etheredge

Hello Everyone;

I hope you enjoy *Grow House.*

Have you ever felt you had the world by the tail on a downhill pull and suddenly, the fan blades became very messy?

Maybe it was a random event that rocked your world. Or a series of poor decisions that had caught up with you. Possibly the warm water you safely steeped in for ages had suddenly begun to boil.

It happens.

Not personally challenged by the status quo, I chose to play Corporate *Frogger,* hopping across the four corners of North America in the pursuit of a paycheck. And I figured, being a moving target was the best way to avoid getting squished. No moss grew on this stone.

Along the way, I was fortunate to come across a large pallet of characters...all acting out their parts in the unscripted plays that inspired the journey of the Henderson's.

So, what did I learn?

We all respond differently to the random hands we are dealt. And, no level of intellect, education, wealth or status has a corner on rational behavior.

As Kenny Rogers sang, it's not so much about the cards but how they're played. To that I would add, being able to find some humor when the cards do not come our way...or when we do something utterly stupid.

I had mulled over the theme of *Grow House* for a while. But the decision to move forward came to me at a friend's Festivus party. You Seinfeld fans know what this is all about. So, I wish to give a shout out to Joe and Joyce Provissiero and fellow Festivans for inspiring me to quit mulling and start writing.

For starters, I attended a writing workshop by author Lauretta Hannon. Having been presented the Cracker Queen's coveted red lipstick tube, I knew I was on my way. I then reached out to my friend Nikki Moustaki, an accomplished writer and animal advocate. Fortunately, she introduced me to her editor Leonard Nash. I give thanks to her for opening this door and to Leonard for his brutal critiques and wise counsel that hopefully advanced my capabilities.

I give a special hats off to all the friends and frenemies, jerks and goofballs that have given me so much rich material from which to harvest.

To my loving wife of 40+ years and our wonderful boys, I so appreciate your support, patience and willingness to grow, learn and love. It is to you I dedicate my effort to bring some laughter to the less serious side of life.

Buz

Buz Etheredge

To Peg, Will and Wade

5

Chapter 1

Three's Company

Keeping an eye on the car inches in front, Sandy Henderson advances her radio for updates on the convergence of massive weather systems. Despite the warnings, she is determined to catch the last day of The Mart to secure supplies for her design and decorating business. Crawling along, she hopes the weather will hold for the twenty-five-mile trip home to Marietta. Unconsciously she nibbles at a bleeding cuticle. Her concerns heighten as ice pellets crackle against the windshield. Barely out of downtown Atlanta, she finds her two-wheel drive Ford Explorer unsuitable for the conditions.

Stalled behind a line of vehicles, she clutches her phone against the steering wheel and texts updates on her worsening plight. Newscasters offer a possible haven six miles north. With the rear tires having no traction, she abandons her vehicle at roadside. Having decided to hike to the refuge, she zips up her nylon parka, dons the hood, and straps on her shoulder bag. She curses herself for choosing form over function as her leather soled booties splash into the semi-frozen slush.

After ten minutes of stumbling past idling cars and trucks, a SUV pulls alongside. The window rolls down and a young girl hollers out, "Hey, want a lift? I've got four-wheel drive."

Inside the warm cabin introductions are made. "Hi, I'm Sandy. I really appreciate this."

"No problem. I'm Abby. Don't know how far we can get. We'll be fine if this single lane stays open. How far you going?"

"They've got a refuge set-up at the CEPAC. With the sound of things, nobody's getting anywhere they want to tonight. How about you?"

"I was trying to make it to Nashville but I'm afraid that's not going to happen."

The SUV moves through the narrow lane for a short time before coming to a halt. Looking around the sloping bend, Abby sees hundreds of tail lights stretching to the horizon. "Sandy, there's hardly any movement for miles and I only have several gallons left in my tank. I don't want to stall out in the middle of I-75."

"Let's hoof it to the refuge." Sandy suggests.

"Okay, I'll get off the bridge and find a place to ditch."

As Abby nudges forward, Sandy makes a call. "David. So glad I got through to you. Are we going to have the meeting tomorrow?"

"Of course not. The weather's shutting down everything. I've had HQ send out a notice. Where are you? Hope you're not caught up in all this crap."

"I'm right in the middle of it. I abandoned my car at Northside and hitched a ride. But now we're over the Chattahoochee, barely moving and running out of gas. So we're taking off on foot."

"You're leaving the car?"

"They've got a shelter set up at the Cobb Energy Performing Arts Center just a ways up the highway. We'll be fine. Have to go. The battery's about gone. Take care."

"Wait! The Chattahoochee? I'm at The Waverly about a block or so past the CEPAC. Come here instead. They're taking in travelers too."

"The Waverly? Are they going to let us crash in their lobby?" Sandy looks to Abby for approval.

"Yes. There's plenty of room. It's a lot nicer than the performing arts center."

"Are you sure, David?" Abby shrugs and nods approval to Sandy.

"Yes. Get off on Cumberland Boulevard and go west to Cobb Galleria and I'll meet you at the intersection and we'll come back here."

Sandy stuffs the dead cell in her bag and pushes open the passenger door. Freezing rain slashes her face as she steps onto to the trodden path. Abby is bracing against the left front fender as Sandy calls, "Abby, follow me."

After a torturous forty-five minutes, they reach David at the top of a long incline. He gives Sandy a brief hug and wraps a blanket around her shoulders. "Are you guys all right? Thought you'd never show."

Sandy pulls the blanket around her and chatters, "Other than not being able to feel my feet, I guess so. This is Abby. She picked me up a while back when my SUV got stuck."

David points up the incline and says, "Nice to meet you. We need to get moving."

Their shoes are no match for the slippery conditions as gusting winds blow rain and snow mix. With stinging faces and numbed extremities, they trudge toward the Waverly.

Outside the grand entrance, the scene is chaotic as horns honk and exhausts steam in the frigid air. David forces through the stragglers into the flooded lobby and pulls Sandy aside. "They're all sold out here but I have a room. You are more than welcome to stay."

Sandy exclaims, "What? You didn't say anything about us staying in *your* room." She takes off her knit cap and shakes the droplets of melting snow. "Thanks, but Abby and I'll just bed down in the lobby."

Sandy's mind races at the prospect of being in a room with David Stark--a recently retired NFL tight end. Of mixed parentage, the blending of Italian, African, and Euro Asian had produced an Adonis of good looks. She was instantly attracted to him while working on a children's car seat campaign. As Vice President of Secure America, David is coordinating efforts with her as a local volunteer. A big event was scheduled the next day in Marietta to kick off the state campaign.

Catching Abby's eye, David laughs, "That's crazy. You guys can't sleep in the lobby when I have a suite with plenty of room. And who's going to say anything? Safety in numbers, right?"

He whispers in Sandy's ear, "She was driving a car? Looks like she's thirteen."

Sandy shakes out the stinky blanket David has given her. "Just tiny, I reckon." She cocks her head. With a suspicious tone, she says, "So how big is your room, David?"

"Big, really big. The Presidential suite. Our Chicago office got it for me. The last one available. And, sorry about the smelly blanket. Smokey wasn't expecting to loan it out today."

"Smokey? Ugh. It does reek, but it worked for the moment." She looks at Abby. "You okay with this arrangement?"

"Are you kidding me? The Presidential Suite? Where's the key?"

"All right David. I guess we'll take you up on your offer. Glad Abby's with me."

Abby high fives her new friend. "Hell, yeah! That's what I'm talking about."

With two fingers, Sandy removes the blanket. Mocking her disdain, David rings it around his neck and points to the elevators. Reaching the top, he uses his security key to gain access to the penthouse level. After inserting the key card into room #1825, the green light blinks and they enter.

David draws back the expansive drapes, revealing the winter storm that is wreaking havoc on north Georgia. The sprawling suite is elegantly appointed and detailed to perfection. A gas fire warms the sunken living room. Large sectional sofas face the flat screen TV stretching across the mantel top. Adorned with flowers and fresh fruit, the dining room flows to a stocked bar and fridge. The over-sized master with king bed adjoins an en suite with a four person Jacuzzi and walk-in shower. A second room is fitted with a queen and full bath. The corner penthouse has panoramic views of the epic arctic storm system as it invades the Southeast from Arkansas to the Carolinas.

Abby spins around. "Shit, this is fuckin' on fleek! And to think only three hours ago, I thought we were screwed. Thank you so much Mr. Stark."

David flinches at Abby's profane inflections. "You're most welcome, and please call me David. None of us expected to be in this predicament when we woke up this morning. Just happy I can help. Maybe we need to change out of these clothes." Returning from the master bath, he tosses two plush bathrobes to his guests.

Abby wraps her arms around David, barely reaching above his waist. "You guys are so sweet to help me out. I don't want to spoil your evening. Hope I can get to my car tomorrow and be on my way."

David releases the grip of Abby's lingering hug. "Sandy and I are business associates, that's all. Let's see how the storm plays out. It looks like it's going to be pretty bad though."

Abby arches on her toes and kisses Sandy on the cheek. "I'm so glad we met. Are you sure it's okay?"

Sandy marvels at her beauty. As if she were a Pixar princess, Abby is crafted and proportioned to near perfection. Barely weighing ninety pounds, she strains every stitch of her wet skinny jeans. Strands of her pixy cut auburn hair frame her grey green eyes and freckled nose. Weather-flushed cheeks splotch her porcelain smooth complexion.

Sandy stutters with an uneasy response, "Of course it's okay, David and I are just friends. Let's settle down, have a drink and warm up. I'll check out the minibar and the menu."

David suggests, "I have some booze in the back of my car leftover from my move. Sandy, while I'm gone you might try room service to see what comes with the suite. Maybe some snacks at least."

As she goes to call, Sandy asks, "May I please have a drink now? A Jack and Diet Coke would be great. I'll pay you back."

David apologizes, "Of course Sandy. Sorry. No problem. I just didn't want to wipe out the minibar. We could be stuck here for a while." He retrieves her drink.

"Thanks. I understand." Sandy changes the subject as she stares into the phone. "Some concierge service this is. Just getting a busy signal."

As if sensing the awkward exchange, Abby says to David, "Look. I can take care of all this. I've got Daddy's Amex and he doesn't care what I do with it. The last time we talked, I was stranded on the interstate. He's totally worried about the storm."

"Wow. You sure about that? This was just about the last room in Atlanta, and it's very expensive. I'd feel a lot better if you talked with him first."

"It's no big deal, trust me. He owns a big-ass recording studio in Nashville. You've more than done your part. The rest is on me, or rather Daddy and his Country music pals."

Sandy takes a sip of her drink. "Well, that's awfully kind but if they won't answer the phone, we just may have to dine on whiskey and nuts."

Abby peels her imbedded iPhone from her jeans pocket. "Okay, if it makes y'all feel better, I'll clear it with him. But I know he won't mind."

"I'll drink to that." David says, opening the mini bar. He empties a Chivas Regal into a crystal tumbler and splashes in two ice cubes. Relaxing in the French Script Wingback, he stares at the vast steel grey and silver horizon. "Ladies, why don't you help yourself to a shower."

"That'd be super. I need to check on the boys and Buddy. If you guys get through to room service, order me a hamburger or something. Anything will taste good about now. And oh, if they have a special on lobster, I'll have that." Laughing, she disappears into the master suite with her drink.

Abby places another call. "I'm right behind you as soon as I can get Daddy."

Sandy lingers as the hot water from the giant sunflower head streams on her head and shoulders. Finally warmed, she retrieves a towel from the heated rack. After a brief blow, she wraps her damp hair and slips into the Luxe doeskin robe and slippers.

Pausing at the suite window, she looks down at the wintry grey and white pallet of street scenes. Dialing her family, she finds her boys are safe at a friend's house. They're instructed to check on the pets. Unable to reach Buddy, she is concerned that he too has been caught in the storm.

Calls complete, she enters the living room and sits on the sectional across from David. Discomforted by the small robe, she pulls down the hem, crosses her legs and modestly seats herself. Crunching on the ice of her emptied drink, she gets briefed by David.

"Looks like we're in for a real mess with more to come right on the heels, sometime late tomorrow. Could be a buildup of eight to ten inches in the metro area. The storm of the century they're claiming."

Catching David's eyes drop to her exposed thigh, Sandy drags a pillow onto her lap.

David turns away and points the controls to the TV. "Let's finish this update and I'll fill you in on Abby's call to her dad."

Sandy takes in the darkened horizon, retreating into a reflective calmness. The boys are fine and her husband is likely holed up somewhere safe. She senses warmth and security with David. Now in an elegant suite overlooking the world, there's a beautiful young girl who wants to pay for it all.

Jack Daniels and the soothing shower help suppress her feelings of guilt and conflict, while circumstances spawn moral relativism.

Bursting from her daydreaming, she yanks again at her rising hem and nervously rambles. "Man, that's a killer shower. Big sunflower head and all. It took some time to take the chill out of my bones. So, what's the deal with Abby's dad?"

"She got through to him. Looks like he's got big time connections with the Marriott folks who own this place. He told her to sit tight and he'd make some calls." As the Westminster door chimes gently bong David approaches. Sandy slides behind a column as David swings open the large carved door.

A suited gentleman greets him, "Mr. Stark? My name is Charles Higginbotham, General Manager. I understand you have as a guest a Miss Abigail Collingsworth?"

"Abby? Uh yes. She and a friend of mine got stranded on the Interstate and I'm letting them crash here only until the storm passes."

"Very well. Her father, Mr. Yancy Collingsworth is much relieved that her safety is assured. We have been instructed to offer our vast array of goods and services to your party. Anything you wish, at no charge. Your comfort and well being will be our priority. Is there anything that we may do for you at the moment, sir?"

"All charges? No shit?"

Sandy spins from behind the column. "We've been having trouble getting through to room service. We'd like to order some food, please."

"Yes, ma'am. We can accommodate. James here, will be your personal valet. He has our restaurant menu with him, a broader selection than room service. The kitchen is backing up with the crush but we can ensure you are serviced expediently."

As Sandy studies the menu, James takes a pen from his pocket and asks David, "Mr. Stark. May I have your autograph? My little brother Kirk is a big fan of yours. Uh... me too."

Having retired three years earlier as an Atlanta Falcon, #68 is still flattered to be remembered. Proudly stiffening his impressive physic, he reaches into his pocket and retrieves a fold of cash. Mr. Higginbotham gives a scornful glance at James.

Sandy places her order, "Seafood, some sushi I guess and some appetizers. A bottle of Chardonnay would be nice. Whatever you suggest. We're all starving, so the sooner the better, please." She looks to David who is signing a $20 bill against the wall. "Anything special for you?"

Handing the autograph to James, he says, "Maybe some beer and Tabasco. And, another robe...a His, please."

The Manager gives a deferential bow and backs away. "Of course. Expect your order within the next thirty minutes. We hope that you enjoy your stay. Have a delightful evening."

Turning to Sandy, David delivers his best highbrow British accent, "Madam. If dinner arrives while I'm showering, would you please leave my robe outside the door?" She laughs as he exits the room.

Moments later, Sandy is on the large sectional when Abby arrives from her shower. Spotting a dish of mixed jelly beans on the counter, Abby fishes out a mango flavor. Rolling the bean around her mouth, she strips off her larger robe and tosses it into Sandy's lap. "Here, Sweetie. It'll fit you much better!"

Impulsively, Sandy turns her head away from the totally nude Abby.

"Give me yours. It seems to be riding up your ass," Abby nonchalantly directs as she fluffs her damp hair.

Embarrassed at the awkward moment, Sandy slowly stands, shields a frontal view and reluctantly removes her robe.

Abby strolls around to get a better look and says, "What a body! You're really hot."

With her eyes to the ground and fumbling to get covered, Sandy hands her "Hers" robe to Abby and stammers, "Uh, thanks. You're not so bad yourself."

Abby cups her breasts and twirls. "Ya think so?"

Unable to avert her eyes, Sandy exclaims, "Abby! Put my robe on. David'll be back any minute."

Calmly slipping her arm into a sleeve, Abby complies, "Okay, okay. It's no big deal. I'm sure it's nothing that he hasn't seen many times before."

Sandy ties her robe and retreats to the sofa. "I don't know anything about that. You wouldn't want him to walk in on you."

"So? Who cares? Let's just chill a bit." Abby goes for her clutch hanging on a chair. "Got some wicked shit here. You cool?" She digs around and produces a colorful Murano glass pipe and a small zipper bag. She stuffs the bowl and takes a light.

"It's been a while. Thanks, but I don't think so." Sandy says half-heartedly.

Abby squares with Sandy on the sofa. Crossing her legs immodestly, she takes a puff and offers, "Here you go. It'll do you good."

After an unavoidable glance into the parted robe, Sandy takes the pipe. "I really shouldn't be doing this." As the draw penetrates, she coughs. After another deep hit, she returns the smoking glass bowl to Abby.

"Abby, just how old are you? You look like you're still in high school, or junior high maybe. I mean you're beautiful, but..."

"So funny! Been hearing that for years. I'm actually twenty-two and a senior at Georgia Tech. I graduate next term and start a job in Palo Alto this summer. Meanwhile, I'm having all the fun I can before shit gets real."

Abby leans in and places her hand on Sandy's exposed knee and looks her in the eyes. "So what's up with that hunky friend of yours? He's sure cute. I bet he's hung."

"Abby! Are you crazy? Sure he's cute, really cute, I guess, but I have no idea about his endowment. We've never dated or anything. I told you that we are..." Reflecting, she thinks of her suppressed feelings about David.

As Sandy's mind wanders, Abby presses, "Well, you have to want to fuck him. Right?"

"Abby!" Her face flushes as she reaches for the pipe.

"Ever thought about sharing? What if we both took him on?"

After taking another deep hit, Sandy holds her breath and strains to ask, "Share? How would we split him up?"

"We could flip a coin. Heads I win, tails you win."

Waiting until the last moment to release the smoke, Sandy manages another response, "Or, heads I win, tails you win."

Springing next to her and perching on her knees, Abby gently strings out her blonde ringlets. With her head beginning to swim, Sandy closes her eyes and exhales. Embracing her face, Abby places her lips to Sandy's and shotguns the cool smoke deep into her lungs. Sandy remains stolid as she tastes the lingering mango on Abby's tongue.

She returns the kiss before pushing Abby away, "You better save that in case you get 'tails'!"

Their squealing is halted as the front door chimes play. Abby stuffs the smoldering pipe under the sofa seat before they cautiously approach the door. Staring through the peephole, Sandy sees James and two other attendants standing at order.

"It's not the NARCS, Abby. They've got our food!" Fighting to appear in control, Sandy gives a chirpy welcome as they wheel in three stainless steel food service carts and a clothes dolly. "Come on in, fellows."

As the attendants fixate on Abby's untied robe, she asks, "You guys have a coin? My friend and I have a bet going." As her eyes meet Sandy's, the women burst out in laughter sending Abby sprinting down the hallway to the bathroom. The funny moment ends abruptly when Sandy sees the thin stream of smoke curling from the seat cushion. A douse of ice cubes does the trick.

The valets feverishly work to complete their delivery. Spread upon the dining room table is a feast of sumptuous offerings. A mixed seafood tower reaches two feet high, surrounded by multiple trays of sushi, canapés, and desserts. French Champagne, chardonnays, and Belgium beer fill out four ice buckets. After uncorking a bottle, the attendants scurry away.

A bottle of Tabasco sits on the bar. Placed on the buffet are two Coach shoulder bags filled with necessities from feminine hygiene and beauty aids, to lotions and prophylactics. Several Hugo Boss boxes are stuffed with cashmere sweaters and jumpsuits ranging in size from XS to L. David's requested bathrobe sits folded beside.

Abby returns wrapped in a towel. As she and Sandy begin to pick from the buffet, David calls from the bathroom, "Ladies, have they delivered my robe yet?"

Chapter 2

Bad Moon Rising

With ice and snow accumulating, the side streets of Marietta have become impassible. Stranded a short distance outside the town square, Buddy Henderson ditches his car in a church's vacant parking lot. Determined to make the seven mile route home on foot, he huffs and wheezes past lines of stalled vehicles on the hilly streets. Attempts to call Sandy are futile. As icy slush soaks his leather-soled shoes, he revises his plan and decides to seek someplace warm.

Making his way towards Old Hwy 41, he recalls a honky-tonk called Buzzy's. The lively spot is a vestige of the past, catering to the working and not so working class. Adjacent to a large trailer park, it has a built-in customer base. As a notorious hangout for lonely hearts and trouble makers, Buzzy's is living on borrowed time as development encroaches.

Struggling up the frozen incline, he sees the reader sign flash: *Billy Ray and the Blues Bros. 2 4 1 Martini Night.* Buddy recalls his early days working dives like this, doing card tricks and hustling pool. Now out of practice and off his game, he reasons to just have a beer, thaw his feet, and trudge homeward. Pushing his way into the frenetic bar, *Bad Moon Rising* blares from the stage.

After folding and stuffing his tie into his coat pocket, he takes a seat at the far end of the bar and orders a Miller Lite. He scans the scene as the crush of patrons fills the room. The ice cold beer goes down smoothly as he taps the empty bottle in time to beat of the band. Pondering another brew, he watches as the bar tender streams martinis into glass after glass. *Hmm,* he thinks. *Two for one is a pretty good deal. Maybe a couple won't hurt. Besides, they're small...about equal to just one regular sized...will help warm me up for the trip home. Sandy would understand. Besides, who's to know?*

A short while later, he is proudly gyrating on the dance floor making all the cool dance moves honed during his college days. Pumping his hands into the air with every beat, he marvels at why such a great band would be playing at Buzzy's. As Billy Rae and the Blues Bros goes into break, Buddy rejoins his newfound friends at a large table. Just one more he declares, signaling to the waitress for another round for everyone.

The click of the door latch and the icy draft does not register with Buddy's unconsciousness. Deep in sleep, he clutches the scratchy wool blanket as a shadow hovers. A millisecond later, his eyes call to the darkness as a figure in blurred motion screeches, "Who the fuck are you?"

Stiffened with fear, Buddy yanks the blanket over his face as the baseball bat smashes his left hand. Avoiding another windup, he rolls over a lifeless form and into the sharp edge of the nightstand, gashing his forehead. On his back and wedged between the bed and fiber paneled walls, Buddy blinks through blood. Having fallen from the stand, a pair of false teeth smiles from his crotch. Engulfed with crushing pain, Buddy knows he is about to die as bat man rounds the corner.

The mass he scaled now sits astride his chest, shielding him from strike two. She screams, "God damn it, Eddie. Put down that thing. You hear me?"

"Now you stay out of this, Rheema Kay. Move aside. I'm a gonna kill that sombitch!" The bat wielder spits a stream of snuff as he winds up for the next strike.

"The hell you are. You cain't come a bustin' in my place like a God damn freak. I let this nice feller come in from the cold an you ain't hurtin' him."

Rheema Kay shifts her weight. Reaching under her backside, she declares. "Well, I do say. Them's my teaf sticking in my butt!"

Replacing her dentures, she stands over her prostrate guest and smiles. "We shore had a good time last night, didn't we, little feller? You're lots o' fun. Good dancer too."

In a desperate need to be somewhere else and not wishing to be brought back into the discussion, Buddy nods his head. As if dueling kettle drums, his injured hand and swollen brain pulse as blood trickles down his cheek.

Her puffy green eyes slash back at Eddie. "And just where the fuck you been all night, you little snake? Been with one a them hoes you hang with. I just know it!"

"No, Mama, No. You done got it all wrong," he cries.

As Eddie and Rheema Kay go at it, Buddy pushes up from the matted shag rug and rights himself. Grabbing a stinky stained comforter, he tucks it under his arm pits to cover his nakedness. *Is this what it's like when Hell freezes over?* He wonders.

As she pokes her finger into Eddie's bony chest, he frantically explains, "Oh no, my darlin'. Hit ain't so. Been using my 4-wheeler and tow chain to pull out cars that been got stuck on the ice. Done froze my ass off helpin' folk...with my heater broke and all."

"You ain't got no ass to freeze off, you scrawny little bastard. If I find out you been fuckin' around on me, I'm a gonna put that bat where the sun don't shine."

Producing a handful of crumpled bills from his jean's pocket, Eddie begs. "Look a here at my tips. Where else can I git this much money?"

As the two banter, Buddy pulls aside a strip curtain and clears fog with his fist on the sliding window. Through the smeared circle he sees steam gurgling from Eddy's exhaust. Wrapped in the grimy quilt, he makes his break to the front door. As he leaps out, the quilt snags on the latch sending him tumbling onto the ice. Bouncing to his feet, he high-steps to the jacked-up truck and leaps into the cab. Cramming it into gear and popping the clutch, the truck springs forward. Struggling to keep control, Buddy lunges forward but not before fishtailing into a garbage can and light pole. Rheema Kay and Eddie appear in the rear view mirror in pursuit.

Out of the park, Buddy shivers convulsively as he fumbles with the malfunctioning heater controls. Near tears, he curses and bangs his good hand on the dash. This does nothing to warm up the truck cabin nor the leatherette seats that have his backside numb and itching.

At ten miles per hour, the 4-wheel cuts through the ice and snow, making its way from one hazard to another. Only the occasional whizzing of spinning tires breaks the ghostly silence. Fearing the slightest miscue, Buddy cautiously steers with his crippled left hand while shifting with his right.

Creeping along, frightening scenarios bounce around his throbbing brain. Attempts to construct a believable story prove futile. Arriving naked in a stolen truck at mid-morning cannot be easily explained.

Details about the night before are sketchy at best. All he knows for sure is that he almost got himself killed over something resembling a sea creature. *Could I have fucked that horrible looking woman?* He asks himself. The pounding head provides a clue as he recalls the rot gut gin. And possibly tequila shots.

As he mashes buttons and turns dials, he angrily asks the unresponsive dash, *Why won't the mother fucking heater come on?*

He thinks about how all this could possibly be explained to Sandy. Way too many loose ends. Take one thing at a time and be calm, he reassures himself.

His cautious deliberation shatters as realization sets in. *The truck...I stole his truck! Holy crap! I'm so screwed. I know what to do...I'll just ditch the thing a block from home with all the other stranded cars. Shit!..can't do that. I'm naked! After I get some clothes...yes, that's what I'll do...ditch the truck. The manatee and her lunatic sidekick don't know my name or where I live. Maybe I can find something to wear at home...if I can sneak in. I think I'm going to be sick.*

Suddenly it dawns on him. With his urgency to flee the swinging bat, he had neglected to retrieve his pants with his wallet and keys. His immediate priorities become clear. He must prevent them from reporting the stolen truck to the police. There is little choice but to return to the trailer park immediately.

Reaching home, he slip slides into his driveway. Nothing is moving in the deserted neighborhood. He remembers a spare key Sandy has hidden. Sneaking out the cab, he steps through the hedges, leaving thorny scratches across his backside. Sinking calf deep in the fresh snow, he makes his way to the back of the house and onto the wooden deck.

Crawling on his knees, he finds Sandy's spare key frozen solid below a dripping down spout. He decides to

35

thaw it with urine, a not so strange activity given the morning. Physics finally overtake shrinkage and the key is freed.

Switching the lock, he enters the back door of the garage. Stashed in the corner are two trash bags of clothing Sandy had readied for a Goodwill pickup. His teeth chatter as he fumbles with his right hand through the assortment.

He curses himself for not heeding her pleas a week earlier, to get rid of some of *his* old clothing. Scarlett signals his presence. Woot, woot, wahoooooooooo. *Will she ever shut up*, he wonders, fearful that she would awaken the family.

He cobbles together a mismatched wardrobe from his family's donated belongings: spandex slacks, women's tennis skirts, gym socks, a reindeer sweater, blouses, panties, a flannel night gown, a pair of athletic shoes, and a pink knitted cap with tie strings. He locates his yellow rain slicker to cover the incongruent garments.

Fully attired, he hops back to the truck and leaves. A neighbor shoveling snow glares as the odd sight rumbles past. Pulling down his bloody pink cap and providing a weak hand gesture, Buddy stares ahead as chugs down the street. Fearing the worse, he retraces his path back to Lot #68B.

As he gets out of the truck, the trailer door swings open. Out steps Rheema Kay. Buddy clasps his hands and falls to his knees. "I'm so sorry, Miss Raymer. Please forgive me."

In a dark blue quilted house coat, stands a mountain of a woman. Her puffy face is mottled with blotches of redness set off by the morning's excitement. Mousy brown hair reaches what used to be her waist. The tip of a pitch fork tattoo shows itself right above her clinched collar. She has not taken time to apply her makeup.

"It's *Rheema* Kay."After taking a gulp from a 1.75L bottle of Popov she calls out, "Eddie, you come look at this!"

"Some outfit you done got for yourself, little feller."

Pushing astride, Eddie raises his bat with both hands, "You stole my truck, you motherfucker! I'm callin' da cops."

"You ain't doing no such thing." Rheema Kay growls as she levels Eddie with a backhand.

Struggling to his feet, he coughs out a sludge of blood and snuff. Swiping his sleeve across his smashed lip, he whimpers, "Ain't no reason for you to do that, Darlin'. You know I wouldn't do nobody no harm."

"Oh yeah? You wanna call the law, eh? You can tell 'em how you done busted in my home and salted him with that bat. They'd be lockin' up both ya. You want that, you little shit?"

Swiveling his loosened tooth, Eddie backs away from Rheema Kay's swing radius. "No, I guess not sweet Mama. Just want my truck back."

"What's your name again, little feller?" she asks.

"Uh, it's...uh...Larry, uh, Larry Jones, Rheema Kay. Mighty beautiful name you have. I don't want any trouble. Just want to go home to my family."

"You's married?" She flashes her chubby pinky. "That ain't what you said last night when you gave me this."

"Oh God," he gasps as he recognizes his Sigma Chi fraternity ring. Lowering his tone, admits, "I had a real fine time. You are so nice. I guess I had too much to drink."

"I'd say so. Both you and all us you done bought drinks for. You was real generous."

"Drinks? Miss Rheema Kay. I'm so sorry. I brought back his truck. May I please have my belongings back?"

Rheema Kay stretches a grin across her broad face. Buddy believes it resembles a giant vagina, but keeps his thoughts to himself.

"Yes siree, we shore did have a time of it. Thought I done lost you in there for a while. You's better than ole Sport and a bucket of Peter Pan." Buddy and Eddie cast puzzled looks toward each other.

Buddy burps under his breath, *Oh my God...I didn't. Sport? Who the hell is ole Sport?*

Checking his watch, Eddie exclaims, "Sport! I gotta go let Sport out!"

With her left hand clutching her crotch, she puckers her lips and says to Buddy, "Anytime you want seconds, you know where to find me."

On his knees, Buddy looks to the ground and says submissively, "That's real kind of you, Miss Rheema Kay."

After gurgling down more vodka, she smacks her lips. "So boys, here's how it's comin' down. Eddie, you're taking Larry here to the mergency room at Ken'saw. You gonna wait for him 'till he gets fixed up and then you gonna take him home. We gonna forget about any of this happening. You got it?"

"But Rheema Kay dear, what bout that dent he done done?" Eddie says.

He leaps backward as she feigns another backhand. "If you open that pie hole one more time, I'm a gonna put a dent in your fender." She turns and points to Eddie's truck. "And don't talk with me about that piece of shit you drive. That dent he done done, done done it good."

As Buddy and Eddie cower to leave, Rheema Kay calls out, "Ain't you forgettin' somethin', James?" Rheema Kay belches a cloud of frosty breath and enters the trailer. Moments later she tosses a black garbage bag to Buddy's feet. He grabs the bag and runs for the truck.

Rheema Kay turns from side to side and flashes open her housecoat to Eddie. "You come on back to Mama. I'll have sump'in hot n juicy waiting for ya. And some Dirgino pizza too!"

Eddie beams, "All right, Darlin'! I'll be back soon." He jumps into the truck and drives out the trailer park. After a brief stop to let out Sport, he and Buddy are off to the ER.

"Madam, I'll need your driver's license and insurance card." the admissions woman asks.

"I'm a guy. I have it in here somewhere." Buddy says.

A little girl standing in line points to him as he rifles through the trash bag. "Mommy, look at that funny woman."

Twiddling her pen, the attendant coolly asks, "Sir, we're waiting."

"Look, my hand's broken and this isn't easy." Having found his wallet, Buddy spills the contents onto the counter and shovels across his license and insurance card.

After being processed, Buddy sees Eddie in the corner patting a seat he has reserved. Two people move away as he approaches.

"I've got to go to the restroom, Eddie."

"You might want to take off that pink hat. People is laughin'."

"I'm afraid to. The blood's coagulated and it's stuck to my head."

"I'm shore sorry 'bout all that, James. Rheema Kay sometimes brings out the bad in me."

"I can see that."

Eddie opens his wallet and pulls out a crumpled photo of Rheema. Holding out to Buddy he says, "We been on an off for years. We met at church. She was a real looker at first and on our first date she took me into the vestibule and...

"Excuse me, Eddie. I have to go."

"Okay, I'm steppin' outside for a smoke."

A man at the lavatory glances into the mirror as Buddy enters the men's room. Drying his hands on his pants, he hastily exits.

Eddie laughs when Buddy returns with his plastic garbage bag of clothing. "So you gonna have to soak your head to get that thing off?"

Buddy tucks the two pink strings into his collar. "I'm glad you think it's so damn funny. Any word on when they can see me?"

"They said it will be some time yet, a couple of hours or so. They's have lots of folks that got fucked up in the storm."

"You think? Is there anything to eat around here, other than from the vending machines? May I borrow your phone? I need to call my wife."

"Sure, here you go. Hey, I got some soup in the truck if it ain't done been sploded." Eddie hands Buddy the phone and exits through the automatic doors.

Pausing a moment, Buddy tries to construct his story. He knows the best defense with Sandy is to get her worrying right away. He places his call.

"Sandy, where are you? Are you all right?"

"Why haven't you called me? she says. "I've dialed you a dozen times with no answer." she demands.

"My phone died. I tried and tried last night but the lines were jammed. I had a problem this morning and have been at the ER all day."

"The ER? Are you okay?"

"Yeah, sort of. I ditched my car and tried to make it home. Only got about half way and stopped at the hospital to

43

warm up. Spent the night on a cot and decided to walk home early this morning. I slipped on the ice and had a little accident."

"What kind of accident?"

"I hurt my hand and I have a cut on my forehead. Been waiting for hours to be seen. The place is crazy." Buddy looks over to Eddie, "I met a nice fellow that's going to take me home after I get fixed up. So how about you?"

"I'm fine. Been sleeping on a cot at the Waverly."

"I thought you were home. I heard Scarlett bark."

Buddy defects his miscue with a question, "You didn't make it home?"

"Of course not. I had to leave our car on the Interstate and hike to the Waverly. Hundreds of people are camped out here in the lobby. The boys are fine, staying over at Jerry's. There's another big system hitting tonight. We're supposed to be getting another seven to nine inches."

"Are those door chimes?"

"Not sure what you heard, but I have to go. They have to vacuum under our cots. Let's talk tomorrow and good luck with your injuries. I love you."

"Those sure sound like door chimes."

"I love you, Honey. Goodbye."

Eddie arrives grinning with two cans of Hungry Man beef stew he has thawed over his idling engine. Buddy goes to the vending machines and returns with a deck of cards, two bags of Sun Chips, and a couple of Cokes. As they scoop the stew with their crunchy spoons, Buddy asks Eddie, "You like card tricks?"

Eddie stays by Buddy's side until his wrist is set and his head stitched. The black sky is streaked with falling snow when they reach Buddy's home. As he backs from the driveway, Eddie hits his horn and yells, "You get well now. And thanks for teachin' me about them card games. Gonna trick ole Rheema Kay to strip for me."

Chapter 3

Pleasant Valley Sunday

Summer sunshine illuminates the stained glass windows of the First Methodist Church of Marietta, GA. Sandy pounds out the classic blessing theme "Praise God From Whom All Blessings Flow" on the prized Brombaugh pipe organ. Looking across the congregation, she spots her husband at the rear of the church.

As Buddy collects the offerings, he lingers in the aisle next to where their twin sons are sitting. Stretching upward with hymnals peeled, they peer onto Becky Whidden's cleavage. Bending slightly backwards, Becky shifts slightly to the right, providing an optimal view. A fellow usher nudges him to complete his task.

Now nestled into the pew, Buddy listens as Pastor Roy tells of Daniel's Diet--the need to eat healthy and take care of your mind and body. Interestingly, the pastor's substantial girth belies Daniel's admonitions.

Following the services, Buddy shuffles towards the front of the chapel inspecting the hair pallets and bald spots of the parishioners along the way. Shalimar and the muskiness of time worn fabrics makes his nose twitch. He is able to hold off sneezing until after congratulating Pastor Roy on his riveting sermon.

Down the stairs and into the summer heat, Miss Wilkes catches Buddy's eye. Making her way through the crowd, she grabs him by the arm with a fierce grip defying her eighty-nine years. He is trapped in the 90 degree sun.

Her steely grey blue eyes burn into his sole. "Buddy Henderson, Coke is just not the same as when I was a child when you could get it for only a nickel."

As sweat streams down the crease of his spine, Buddy interrupts, "Miss Wilkes, I am so sorry, but I'm having problems with a new medication and need to excuse myself." He hastens towards the restroom and out the rear of the sanctuary.

He joins his family in their grey Ford Explorer. As AC kicks in, Sandy orders, "Guys, we've got to get moving. There're lots to do. Boys, you have to get your things together for football camp tomorrow. And Taylor, what time are you girls heading back to Carrolton?"

Taylor is busy texting when mom breaks through the clutter. "Taylor! What time are Becky and Melissa coming this afternoon?"

"Around five. We're stopping by to visit poor Mrs. Cosgrove for a few minutes on the way out."

"Such a nice lady. Saw her last week. That damn cancer has eaten her up. She'll be going to hospice soon. That's so sweet of you girls to stop by but I doubt if she'll even recognize you."

"Yeah, so sad. I still need my wash done and I have few more things to pack up."

Sandy looks into the rearview mirror, "A few more things to pack? You've been hauling your hoard over there for a week. Well, you'd better leave your partying behind because that summer school Scholar's Academy means you have to study for a change."

"I can't *even*." Taylor mumbles as she taps away.

"I don't know about you girls in that apartment. But thank goodness you'll be away from that drug dealer you were hanging with. He was nothing but trouble."

Buddy intervenes, "Yeah. He'll be freezing his little butt off selling dope on the streets up there."

"*Really?* Dad. Sammy is not a drug dealer! You don't know him at all. He's so sweet. If he's moved to Chicago, why do you keep ragging on me? He's gone! And, I'm not going to college to party."

"Your dad and I aren't going to fund your playing around. That won't fly with this new interest you have in West Georgia and wanting to be a nurse. As for Sammy, good riddance!"

Jake goads his fuming sister with a mocking jab, "Oh, Sweet Sammy Sales. How romantic." With her clinched fist tightly gripping her phone, Taylor pounds on his hunched shoulder.

Sandy intervenes, "Jake, stop it! You and your brother are no angels, or Rhodes Scholars for that matter. Sorry, Taylor. My bad. I'm just glad he's out of your life. You can do so much better than that. We're happy you're finally focused on your future."

Nearing home, Sandy instructs, "Boys, we're leaving for camp at 9 a.m. sharp tomorrow, rain or shine."

Buddy says, "Looks more like rain than shine through tomorrow with that hurricane effect and all."

"I want to see your clothes laid out and bring me your laundry. We'll need to run some of your stuff with Taylor's load. The duffels are in the garage. Luke, don't forget to pack the nose drops. Better take along some Tylenol. And Zach, I put the Lotrimin for your jock itch on the dresser. We'll also need..."

"What? No way! Mom! You're not putting their stinky crap in with my things!" Taylor cries.

50

"Yes, way. The dryer's on the fritz and it takes hours to do a single load. Of course, you can carry your dirty stuff back to Carrolton if you wish." Mom gives her the eye in the rear-view mirror.

Both boys giggle as Taylor slings her elbows right and left, "Screw you! You little perves! I can't get out of here quick enough."

Settled in at home with rains in the forecast, Buddy cancels his tee time. After a quick check on the vegetables in his green house, he falls on the couch for an afternoon of the Golf Channel.

Its five fifteen and drizzling when the girls pull into the driveway. Taylor, clutching a handful of twenties, hugs her dad and kisses him on his cheek. Before Mom can stop her, she's off with her friends to visit Mrs. Cosgrove a few blocks away.

In bed that night Buddy and Sandy retire to their bedroom. Sandy sighs as she searches for the remote. "I'm concerned about Taylor over there with Becky and Melissa. It's just hard to believe they've turned into students overnight. Something's up. I just don't know what. Anyway, the girls' classes start tomorrow, so we'll see soon enough. Maybe a spark's been lit."

"At least we'll cut some expenses if she busts out."

"Cut expenses? I saw her working you for money. You've never been able to say no to her. How much did you give the little con artist?"

"A hundred or so. She's only young once and she's a good girl."

"Good girl? You saw what happened to her with that worthless Sammy James. And what about the ones before him? Just how lucky were we to have him move to Chicago before something really bad happened? All she seems to care about is partying and bad boys. She's so damn smart but doesn't give a flip about her future. And, as you surely know, she can con the scales off a snake." Sandy slams the remote onto the blanket. "What a waste."

"She knows how to get to you. You weren't so saintly if I remember."

"Cute. Maybe I was a little wild, but I did grow up...*eventually*." Her self-righteous statement sends her memory flashing back to the snow storm and the events at the Waverly. *Oh yeah, I've really grown up*. She relives those forty eight hours. *Wonder how Abby's job is working out?*

Buddy interrupts her pensiveness, "Oh, she will too. She's still young."

"Huh? Wish I could be so sure." Sandy picks up the remote and scrolls down the guide. "Here's another special on pot. Seems to be a ground swell on medical legalization. There are a lot of people who claim it really helps them."

"Yeah. Helps 'em get high."

"Glad they didn't have phone cameras when we were coming along."

"Those were the days."

"Get the irony with Sammy and what you did?"

"No way can you compare me to that redneck South Philly Stud. I just made some pocket money to get through school. Man, that was some good stuff I grew. If I remember correctly, you seemed to enjoy getting lit up too."

"Yeah. Lucky to get out alive."

"Well, as soon as recreational pot is legal here in Georgia, I can start growing it beside my prized hydroponic tomatoes."

"And when that happens, I'll personally build the ramp for your wheel chair to get into the green house."

"Yeah, probably not going to happen anytime soon. Could have been growing it for years if you'd let me."

"Oh, and get busted for growing pot? Hey, that'd be really cool. Besides, we gave up that crap years ago. Remember our little pact? Stuff damned nearly got us both killed."

"That and a little Jack Daniels." Buddy laughs as he leaves to let out Scarlett. He soon returns with a pile of unopened mail and trade journals.

After futzing with her Facebook page, Sandy opens her calendar. "Maria is coming tomorrow. She and her sister are doing all the carpets and bath rooms so pick up before you leave. And remember, Mother's coming the week of the 23rd."

"Can't wait for that."

"Well, you two just have to get along."

"Don't worry. I'll give her plenty of space. Maybe I'll hike the Appalachians."

Now checking her emails, Sandy reads, "I see we got notice from Mack that he's off on another mission. Probably somewhere on the other side of the world. He hopes to drop by for a short visit before he goes."

"Can't believe he does that crap. He's crazy if you ask me. Must have nine lives."

"He's a special guy and the boys worship him, ever since he took them on that survival trip through the Everglades. I worry a lot but he never tells us anything. No different than when he was a SEAL. Just comes and goes into the night."

Buddy fumbles through his pile of papers, and opens their 2nd quarter statement from Rothstein Investment Advisors. "We've really done well with Michael."

Sandy turns, staring over her reading glasses, "We've got so much riding with him and I'm not so sure about this gold mining thing he's all hot about. Seems too risky."

"He's been working on this for years and it's about to break."

"But we've got most all our money in the same place. Will you at least talk with Robert? He's been after us for years to do a financial review and to diversify."

"Okay, maybe we should. But I'd sure hate to hurt Michael's feelings. I'll give him a call tomorrow for an appointment."

"Thanks, I'd feel much better. Things just seem so uncertain these days. And, I surely wouldn't worry about his feelings. I've got a busy week coming up. How 'bout you?"

"Nothing special. Running some shelf life tests for several new product ideas."

With Wallis settled in at the foot of the bed and Scarlett snoring in her basket, they are asleep by 10:15.

Chapter 4

Rainy Days and Mondays

Scarlett wags her tail in perfect time to the clanging 6 a.m. alarm. A crashing lightning bolt jolts Buddy into action as he and his Golden Retriever make their way downstairs. Thunder rolls and rain pummels as Scarlett creeps outside and finishes her business. With Buddy holding the door, she sloshes through the clay puddles and back into the laundry room.

Sandy hollers from the kitchen, "Don't forget to wipe her feet!"

After retrieving the soaked Marietta Daily Journal, Buddy pours a cup of coffee. Sandy directs him to his healthy breakfast. The bowl of Fiber One cereal and 1% milk topped off with fresh sliced strawberries waits.

As Buddy picks at his bowl, Sandy urges, "Honey, you better get moving. Traffic is going to be terrible. That hurricane has passed through Florida and is working its way up the coast."

A short time later Buddy is off to the McDonalds drive thru. It's 8:20 when he pulls out with two sausage biscuits. Traffic is a mess with all I-75 southbound lanes near standstill. He squeezes his Lincoln MKS between two creeping commuters. Seeing the rows of tail lights trail over the horizon, Buddy settles in for the long trip down town to his job at The Coca-Cola Company.

James Franklin "Buddy" Henderson is one of two children of Mary Beth Henderson of Holly Springs, MS. His adored father, a local C.P.A. died of a heart attack when Buddy was only twelve. The loss was compounded when his distraught older brother Mack left home to become a Navy SEAL. Counseling did little to brighten the disconsolate young boy's spirits.

Living a few doors down was Katie Deason, also fatherless but as a result of a broken home. The delicate, blue eyed brunette was beautiful and vivacious. Experiencing the coming of age, they shared their sorrows and joy. By fifteen they were inseparable. Keeping their trysts a secret was not easy in a small town, but her basement and an old tool shed provided great cover.

A week before her sixteenth birthday, while peddling her bike home after school, Katie was struck from behind by a speeding motor cycle. With her head crushed against a rugged old oak, Buddy never saw Katie's angelic face again. A lifetime of loss had engulfed the young boy.

Out of necessity, Buddy learned to master his environment, shielding himself from hurt and pain. Circling at a much higher intellectual level than most, Buddy Henderson played by his own rules maintaining total control, determined that he knew how to endure life, by his standards. No pain, all gain was his new mantra. No one would ever get close enough to hurt him again.

Preferring an occasional one night stand over a serious relationship, he accepted that few women would put up with his antics. If one risked penetrating his bubble, he would run them off. That was until Sandy came along.

Loving to party, Buddy was well conditioned for the wild life of college by the time he enrolled in the University of Mississippi. His chosen degree in biology was a challenge, choosing fun over commitment. His favorite pastime of hustling became more sophisticated as he focused on the rich trust babies around campus. Whether cards, sports book, or golf, his cunning ability to win became legendary. Despite his campus notoriety, there was always someone willing to take him on.

At last Buddy realized it was time to graduate and get a J.O.B., something requiring minimum effort. Before back-sliding to Poly-Science, Buddy had taken a number of chemistry courses for Pharmacy School. This opened the door for a cushy job at Coca-Cola as Quality Assurance Manager.

After a numbing ninety-minute commute, he sees the *Coca-Cola* script towering brightly against the stormy Atlanta skyline. With no spaces to be found, he circles upward for eight landings before a spot is located on the top parking deck. With his briefcase over his head, Buddy splashes across the lot and into the massive complex.

He stops by the break room for a cup of coffee and a copy of *The Wall Street Journal*. Chatting with co-workers along the way, its 10:05 when he reaches his cubicle nestled deep into the third floor of the Technical Building where he has worked for the past fifteen years. He takes a call.

"Mr. Henderson. Dr. Bates would like to see you."

"Okay. I'm on the way right now." he instinctively responds. As the elevator rises to the 10th floor, he wonders why he is being summoned by his supervisor.

"You may go in." the Admin Assistant instructs.

As Buddy enters the office, the diminutive Dr. Bates is standing with stiffened arms onto his desk. He peers over his glasses, "I called you here to let you know that our rationalization plan is in full implementation mode, requiring that your position be eliminated effective immediately."

"But I thought..."

"That will be all. We're running late here. William McFarland in Human Resources is outside and he will cover the particulars. Best of luck to you, Mr. Henderson. Have a pleasant day."

Moments later in William's office, he surrenders his I.D. tag, parking pass, and phone. After layering the contents of his cubicle into a cardboard filing box, he's escorted to the elevator.

Pressing the down button, William nervously backs away. With a brief nod and diverted eyes, he says; "Good day, Mr. Robertson."

"And, good day you too, Mr. Shit Bag." Buddy says as the door closes.

The Lincoln crawls down the winding parking deck, out the security gate and onto North Avenue. The Coca-Cola Company compound fades in his rear-view mirror.

As he approaches the interstate, his predicament crystallizes as he asks himself, *Who is going to hire a forty-one year old Q.A. specialist?*

Through the slashing rain, Buddy sees the giant neon "V" blinking ahead. Crossing over the interstate, he makes a sharp left into The Varsity.

AC-DC is blaring on Rock97 as he pokes his Lincoln into one of his favorite feeding spots, a local fast food institution for nearly ninety years. He orders his usual, two slaw dogs with chili, an order of onion rings and a medium Coke. Savoring every bite, he delays the inevitable trip home. Settling up, the car hop removes the tray and Buddy steers back into the summer storm.

Arriving home, he makes every attempt to stall the inevitable. On the fourth time around the block, Sandy spots him while retrieving the mail. He finally parks. She approaches to find him sitting motionless behind the wheel. With no greeting, he climbs out and walks past her.

"Honey, what're you doing home so early? You okay?" Sandy asks, as he disappears into the house.

Moments later they sit the kitchen table. Crying, she says, "I can't believe this. That Dr. Bates is an asshole. What are we going to do?"

"We'll figure something out. Hated working at that place anyway."

"More than ever we need to get our money from Rothstein. Have you..."

"I'll do all that tomorrow." Buddy cuts her short as he goes up the stairs.

Later that day, with dinner plans disrupted, Sandy retrieves from the freezer a Zip Loc of her homemade vegetable soup. Nothing is said as she and Buddy stir through their bowls.

She breaks the silence, "Honey, we have to tell the kids. And what about our friends? With social media, it's going to get out. People lose their jobs. It happens."

Leaning over his bowl, Buddy says, "I don't think the kids will be so matter of fact."

"Maybe so. You know Taylor would use this as an excuse if she were to bust out of West Georgia. I think we have some time with the three of them being so busy."

Buddy pushes his empty soup bowl aside. "I'm not the only one. Coke's doing a big layoff at HQ. It's been speculated for months. I'm sure the paper will have something on it tomorrow. Let's see what that says and go from there."

Exhausted, they turn off their phones, take a couple of Tylenol PMs and retire to bed early.

Up before day break, Sandy slips on her running shoes, leashes Scarlett and hits the trails. After two days of constant rain, a thin veil of fog covers the forest masking the sun. Winding over twenty-two miles around Kennesaw Mountain, hiking paths follow the Confederate Army's line of defense breastworks constructed in 1864.

The strenuous run and fresh morning air helps clear her head. The bright sun begins to burn way the fog, striking like a strobe through the hardwoods and pines. Dodging the rocky wash-outs and slick red clay, she makes her way through the route with Scarlett loping at her side.

Debating herself along the way, she tussles with the uncertainties facing the family. Slowing her gate, she rounds the corner. Beginning her cool down, she catches her breath for the last one hundred yards. Suddenly she's startled by a familiar face.

Suspiciously looking around, she calls out, "David! What are you doing here?"

Reaching for her hand, he asks, "Sandy, why haven't you answered my texts?"

She recoils and breathlessly whispers, "Texting? You promised to stay in East Cobb. We agreed not to be near each other." Her eyes case up and down the trail. "What if someone sees us together?"

As she turns to face his soaked chest, the dizzying scent of Versace Eros invades her space.

"I know Sandy, but I just had to..."

Swiping the sweat from her forehead, she backs away. "Damn it, David. It's over. I can't talk. Have a lot going on. I can't see you again. I thought I made it clear. I have to go."

As David inches closer, Sandy spins around and sprints away jerking Scarlett's leash as she trails. Looking back she yells, "It's over. Do you hear me? *It's over!"*

Sandy goes around the house and into the screened porch where she falls into her favorite wicker rocker. Unsnapping her case and retrieving her phone, she pulls up the list of missed calls. She deletes the text from David sent only an hour earlier. "God is that man built." she whispers with her eyes closed still reeling from their encounter.

In the kitchen, she refills Scarlett's water bowl, and opens a can of diet Coke. She jumps as Buddy startles her with the drop the newspaper on the counter, "Here it all is; Coke Lays Off 750. Won't be long before people put two and two together."

"Good." she says. "I'm about to make some calls to friends so the news will be out."

Buddy looks at his watch. "Honey, I have some running around to do and then I'm going to City Club to hit some balls. Be back early afternoon."

"Has Michael gotten back to you?"

"No, but I left a voice mail."

Buddy kisses her on the cheek. "See you in a couple of hours."

After reading Coke's vague press release, Sandy returns to the porch with her drink, a towel and phone. Seeing her mother has left three messages, she knows where to start. Dreading the interchange, she hits speed dial #2.

"Why haven't you returned my calls, Sandra Lee?" Katherine Manning asks.

"I'm so sorry, Mother. It's been wild around here with my business and all. And so much going on with the kids. Buddy's been busy too and has come down with the flu. Maybe it's not a good time for you to visit."

"Buddy busy at work? That's a first. How can he be so busy and have the flu?"

"It's sort of like walking pneumonia. He still gets around but doesn't feel well. Lots of stuff happening at Coke."

"Sandra Lee, you're not telling me something. What's going on?"

"Everything's fine, Mother. We're just busy. Maybe next month when the kids get back to school. When we can spend more time together."

"It's not like you not to return my calls. You sure you're okay?"

"Of course I am." Seeing the caller ID from Candace Miller, she remembers she is to host Bible study that night. "Mother, I'm sorry but I've got to take this call. I'll get back to you later. I love you." She disconnects.

Sandy fears her excuses did not go over well. But at least she would not have to contend with Buddy and her mother going at it until things settled down. The last thing she wants to do is to talk with Candace.

"Hello, Candace. I was about to call you."

"How *are* you Sandy? I know how you must be feeling with all that's going on."

"I'm fine Candace. Not sure what you mean."

"About Buddy. I heard he was in that big layoff at Coke. You must be devastated."

"How did you...? Candace, that's not something I wish to discuss."

"It was in the paper and others are talking. What's he going to do with the job market so tight? I thought..."

"Candace! I was going to call to ask you to get in touch with the Bible study group. It needs to be rescheduled somewhere else."

"Why Sandy, my dear, I thought we could all pray for you. You know, I also heard that Mary Ellen was seeing..."

"I have to go. Please tell the girls I'm sorry. Good bye Candace."

Unnerved by the call, Sandy fumes at Candace having the gall to pry for information to fuel her rumor mongering. After finishing the calls and re-working her calendar, she takes her angst to the kitchen. She decides to prepare a grand meal for Buddy, his favorite, lasagna.

As she squishes the mixture of eggs, flour, and olive oil between her fingers, she gazes into the National Park battlefield that borders their property. Contrasting her plight to the sorrow and loss of thousands of soldiers helps to put things in perspective.

As the dough begins to set, she kneads it into a ball and covers with a wet cloth. Various meats and cheeses are measured and put aside. Homemade tomato sauce simmers in the pan.

So many questions with few answers play roulette with her emotions. Only several days ago she would have posted her pasta creation on Facebook. But now there could be no updates for the foreseeable future. What about Taylor and the boys? How long can they be stalled? Meanwhile, there are obligations.

The run-in with David has her shaken. The effects of their meeting convinces her more than ever that they cannot be trusted alone. All points of contact had been avoided since their salacious winter interlude. Her first step was to resign her position at the Secure America foundation. While David continued to text, she had refused to respond.

Buddy has been at the driving range for over an hour when his cell rings. It's his old friend, Marty Butterfield who lives in Charlotte. Buddy sets his driver against the stand and walks to the side. "Hey, Marty. Long time no talk."

71

"Buddy, did you hear about Rothstein?"

"No, but I have a call into him. What're you talking about?"

Marty sobs, "It's gone. Our money's all gone. Millions up in smoke. That fucking Peru gold mine venture turned out to be a hoax. The S.E.C. is involved. We're all screwed, Buddy."

"Did you just say..." The phone tumbles to his feet as Buddy stares blandly ahead.

"Buddy, can you hear me? Are you still there? Buddy? Buddy?"

The lasagna is bubbling in the oven when the front door shuts. Sandy wipes her hands on her apron and walks to the foyer. "How was golf?" she asks.

When their eyes meet, Sandy sees the same ghostly stare she had encountered only days earlier. She stands dismayed as Buddy floats into Taylor's room, locking the door behind. Suspecting he's still stressed about losing his job, she leaves him alone. He'll bounce right back. He always does Sandy figures.

Several hours later her worst fears are confirmed she reads an email from a friend. She blinks tears as she learns about the collapse of Rothstein Investment Advisors.

Reeling from the recent developments, she flails in her bed with fear and indecision. The Coke situation, she gets. *Those things happen. But Rothstein and their savings--over $300,000? How could we have been so stupid?* Wandering around inconsolably, her emotions whip lash between anger and worry, knowing the word of the Coke firing and the Rothstein debacle would soon be all over town. Circumstances have become dire.

Buddy does not respond to her pleadings. After a day of being in the hot room, Sandy makes her move. Standing outside the bedroom door she pleads, "Buddy, I've got dinner from last night. Your favorite, baked lasagna, Caesar salad, Cuban bread, and a bottle of Chianti. Honey. I love you. Please come out. You must be famished. I surely am."

He murmurs, "I love you too, Sweetheart. Lasagna?"

"Yes. Now come on out. I'm putting the bread in the oven."

73

At last the door cracks open and their eyes meet. Sandy smiles, as Buddy says, "All right, Sweetie. You know when you make la..."

Suddenly they jerk their heads towards the ringing doorbell and banging knocker.

For the past forty-eight hours, Sandy has refused to let anyone in the house posting a NO VISITORS, PLEASE sign. She approaches the door wondering who could be so rude. She freezes at the all too familiar voice resonating from outside. "Answer the damn door, Sandra Lee!"

She holds her hands to her face and closes her eyes, *Oh, God no*. She unlocks the door and whispers across the chain, "Mother, is that you?"

"Of course it's me! Let me in."

Sandy opens the door to find Katherine Manning bracing on a cane. Standing about five feet two, the flowing curls of her Henna dyed red hair reach her shoulders. She's dressed in a jet-black Calvin Klein Blazer with layered top, a satin blouse and skin tight leg pants. Sandy's eyes are drawn to her pink fashion sneakers as her mother waves off a cab.

Turning back to Sandy, she says, "What the hell's going on, Sandra Lee?"

"Uh, Mother. How did you get here?" Sandy backs up.

"On the damn plane! Caught the next flight out with a cheap ticket. I'm tired and my butt hurts."She pushes into the house. "Why's it so dark in here? I need a beer."

Hurrying to the kitchen, Sandy says, "Mother, I wasn't expecting you. I told you it's not a good time."

"It's never a good time for you guys."

Sandy pops open a Coors Light. "Here, Mother."

After taking a swallow, she glares. "This tastes like shit! Is this the same beer from last summer?"

"Might be. You know Buddy and I don't drink much."

"Just where *is* Buddy? You said something about pneumonia?"

"Well, he's been sort of under the weather."

"Sort of under the weather or pneumonia? There's quite a difference you know. What are you not telling me, Sandra Lee?"

"We, uh..."

Katherine's eyes scout around the living room. "What do you mean with that note on the door, no visitors? What the hell's going on here?"

"Buddy's not been feeling so well. He's sleeping in Taylor's bedroom."

"What's he doing in there? It's 5:30 for Christ's sake. Let's get him up and see what all this is about." Approaching the hallway, she shouts, "Buddy! Come out and get me some fresh beer. This stuff is awful."

Springing from his hideout, he meekly replies, "I'm right here, Katherine."

Sandy looks on in amazement as her mother does in five minutes what she's been unable to do the last twenty-three hours.

Katherine stares him down. "You look like you just fell out of a garbage truck. Smell like it too. So, what the fuck's wrong with you?"

With arms languishing, he wobbles his head and evokes a syrupy Southern inflection, "Why Katherine, it's good to see you too. I trust your flight was enjoyable."

Katherine fans her nose as she backs away. "Cut the B.S., Buddy and answer my question. You don't look sick to me."

"God damn it, Katherine! I just got fired, lost most of our savings, and I feel like shit. Other than that, things are just fuckin' great! But thanks for asking."

Sandy sees her world coming apart as the room goes silent. With the kitchen not far away, and the knife block visible, she imagines a murder scene capping off the week.

Katherine's head lifts back at the retort. She resets her posture and crooks out her neck and says, "Big deal. Now go get me my fresh Coors Light and be sure to check the expiration date." As he looks for his keys, Katherine shuffles over to the sofa. "When you come back, we'll talk about it. And pick up a carton of Marlboro Reds while you're at it."

Sandy and Katherine are sitting in the small parlor when Buddy returns. Katherine inspects the cans and says, "You see these mountains? They're not blue yet. Coors Light is supposed to be served ice cold, not like bath water." She removes a can from the 12-pack. "Go put the rest in the

77

freezer to get them going. Sandy, my ass hurts from sitting on that plane. You have some Tylenol?"

Buddy returns from the kitchen and sits down next to Sandy. Katherine rifles through her carry-on, locates a wrapper and tears it open.

"Why Mother, I've never seen you eat candy."

Taking a nibble, she says, "I'll have you know this is not ordinary candy. It's fortified with THC, you see."

"Fortified? What? You're taking dope?"

"Nothing of the sort." she slurps. "It's for my tailbone, when I slipped on the ice." She holds out her hand, "Fruit gummy, anyone?"

Buddy takes a Luscious Lime gummy rabbit and bites off his head.

Snuffing out her butt and exhaling, Katherine turns to Buddy, "So what's the deal with Coke?"

He gives Sandy a 'here we go' look and says to Katherine. "I got caught up in a big layoff."

"Any severance?"

"Yeah, three months."

"Not too bad. So what's this thing about being broke?"

"We've been investing in this gold mine in Peru a friend runs. Well, used to run. It just went tits up and our savings have gone to hell."

Katherine shrugs her shoulders and reaches for her beer. "Doesn't sound like much of a friend to me."

"Mother, our life has been turned upside down this week. We didn't want to get you tangled up in our problems."

"Good God, girl. Shit happens. You just seem to have gotten a truck load of it. No one's sick, right?"

Sandy shakes her head. "Not physically, but we're pretty overwhelmed at the moment." She turns to Buddy. "Honey, I think I'd like one of those beers and a glass."

Katherine hands her a Raging Raspberry turtle. "Have one of these. It'll calm you down."

Sandy thinks about how her stress level has escalated the past twenty minutes and takes the gummy. She opens the package, takes a bite and begins chewing. "You sure this stuff works?" As she smacks and downs the rest of the turtle, Buddy returns with her beer.

"Whoa, gal." he says. You're not supposed to gobble it down all at once."

With her finger to the back of her mouth, Sandy pries the sticky treat from her molars. After inspecting the glob, she sucks it into her mouth and washes it down with a beer. After about fifteen minutes she says, "I don't feel a thing. This stuff can't touch what Buddy used to grow at college. Mother, let me have another one." She recalls the last time she got high with Abby and David months earlier. *This is candy--not the real stuff. Can't do too much harm.*

Buddy says, "Me too. Yeah, this is nothing. Only a little buzz from the beer."

"Look guys. You'd better take this easy if you haven't smoked in a while. I'm telling you 10% THC is plenty to get you high. There's a slow release from edible marijuana. You need to wait at least two hours before the next one."

Sandy holds out her hand and says, "Come on, Mother. We can take it."

"Okay. Suit yourself and don't say I didn't warn you." Katherine says as she tosses each a package of gummies.

Chapter 5

Thursday Morning Comin' Down

Scarlett's rubbery tongue slashes across Buddy's parted lips as her plaintive cries scramble his consciousness. Gagging on her breath, he pushes at her wet nose and squints into the hazy morning light.

Sandy lies next to him, splayed out like a corpse. Buddy has seen her on her better days, easily passing for a college coed. Wondering about the blood smeared on her face, he knows this is not one of those days.

His muddled awareness begins to jell as he recalls the evening before...beer, gummies, dinner, wine, more gummies, bourbon, Haagen-Dazs and sardines. The last treat would likely have been forgotten if not for a chunk lodged in the back of his mouth.

81

More puzzle pieces align. Sometime later, he and Sandy managed to stumble to bed. They briefly became amorous. Severely impaired, the circumstances were not ideal for rekindling their lovemaking skills.

Buddy recalls getting cleaned up for the 'definite maybe' he envisioned. Wasted but determined, he had stumbled into the shower and lathered up. Grabbing Sandy's dulled disposable razor from the soap dish, he took to shaving his two-day stubble.

As he picks at the caked blood on his chin, Sandy begins to moan. Rolling from bed in the direction of the bathroom, she lunges into the closet and grasps her wardrobe. After hurling dinner into her neatly lined-up row of shoes, she slumps forward.

Muffled cries for help weep from the rack of clothes that engulf her. Mustering what strength he can find, Buddy bundles the pyramid of flesh and fabric into his arms. Curiously, the carpet squishes beneath his feet as he drags the lifeless form from the closet. He wonders if he had walked in his sleep as he maneuvers her into the bathroom.

Staunching his wound with a square of toilet paper, he determines the source of the rosy smear on Sandy's face.

Light headed and sweating, he falls to the bed. His collapse is shortened as guttural sounds emanate from the bathroom. Sandy is crouched over the toilet violently dry heaving. "Ohhhhhh. I'm going to kill Mother." she groans.

Buddy sees Scarlett doing that familiar early morning dance, but Sandy has a greater need. Hoisting her under his arms, he lumbers out of the bathroom. After pulling her onto the bed, he wipes her face with a wet wash towel and pulls up the sheets. Softly closing the door, he begs, "Please go back to sleep, Honey. And don't die."

After waddling a few steps into the hallway, he feels a warm squeeze between his toes. With her head low and eyes diverted, Scarlett slinks down the stairs. He follows, thumping along with his right heel. Surveying the wreckage from the night before, he bemoans his circumstances. *No job, bankrupt and getting wasted with my mother-in-law. I might as well be meth head living in a trailer park. This is de ja vu all over again.*

The ice cubes crackle as he pours the warm Diet Coke. Bracing against the counter, the fizz tickles his nose as he chases down two Tylenols. After cleaning Scarlett's poop from between his toes, he finds his pants crumpled in the corner. Balancing himself against the table, he works his sockless right foot down the leg and into his left loafer.

The unexpected ringing of the doorbell sends Scarlett into a barking frenzy. A comical rendition of a bark, a growl, and high pitched woof. Wahoooo, woot, woot, she goes.

The shrill staccato of the door bell and Scarlett's howl startles Buddy as he drags his empty pant leg across the floor. He can make out through the shutters a Cobb County Police vehicle and a red Jeep Cherokee parked at the curb.

Scarlett strangles as she continues to signal the intrusion. Half naked, Sandy rounds the corner digging for her housecoat sleeve. "Who's at the door? God, I'm dying. Buddy, answer the door. No, wait! Put on your pants! No! I'm not dressed. Wait, damn it! Wait!"

Sandy jumps behind Buddy as he opens the door.

"Mr. and Mrs. Henderson?" the first officer asks.

Struggling to appear normal, Buddy responds to the imposing figure. "Yes, officer. Uh, good morning." He recognizes the man standing next to him. "Coach Bryant. What's going on fellows?"

Scarlett charges out to meet her guests.

The officer produces his badge. "My name is Officer Roberts and this is Deputy Garcia."

The visitors stare while Buddy untangles his pants leg as Sandy clings to his waist. With his right hand, he clinches his belt and pants, leaving his left leg and Jockey's exposed. Blotched toilet paper still sticks to his nicked up face. Splattered with lasagna and wine stains, his bulging white v-necked undershirt resembles a Jackson Pollack.

As Scarlett nuzzles between Deputy Garcia's legs, Buddy hops on one foot.

Officer Roberts says, "Sir, would you mind containing your dog? Does he bite?"

"Scarlett is a she and *she* does not bite. As you can see, she does like crotches. *Scarlett! Bad dog!*"

With a watchful eye on the dog, Office Roberts asks, "May we come in Mr. Henderson?"

85

"Of course, Officer. What's going on?" Buddy looks towards the door. "Coach, where are the boys? Y'all weren't due back until this weekend. *Scarlett! Stop! Bad dog!"*

Coach Davis takes off his Georgia Bulldog's ball cap and looks back and forth from Buddy to Sandy. "Buddy, I tried to call all morning but I kept getting thrown into voice mail. What's wrong with your face? Sandy, are you okay? Is that blood?"

Having turned the shade of guacamole, Buddy tries to explain the unexplainable. "Cut myself shaving. We've had some phone troubles lately. Is there a problem?"

As Sandy repositions her exposed breast, Coach Bryant turns away and says, "I would say so. Because I know Officer Roberts, he was kind enough to bring your boys here first to have you and the misses accompany them to the station."

Clutching her bathrobe at the neck, Sandy coughs a response, "The station? What's wrong? Are the boys okay?" Turning to Buddy she whimpers, "What's happening?"

From around the corner Katherine appears in Taylor's pink and black housecoat waving a Marlboro. "What the fuck's going on?"

Officer Robert announces, "Mr. and Mrs. Henderson, your sons have been detained for possession of marijuana."

Deputy Garcia, guarding her crotch like a goalie, fights off Scarlett's nuzzling. While pushing her head away, she spots a candy wrapper at her feet.

At 5:30 that afternoon Buddy, Sandy, and Katherine sit in the family room nursing hangovers. Katherine turns to Sandy. "Don't you ever change the sheets in Taylor's room? And, did you know there's dog shit in the hallway? Don't you have a housekeeper?"

With her elbows on the table and head in hands, Sandy says, "Don't start it, Mother."

"Those Nazi's. I can't believe they did this to us."

Without looking up, Sandy rocks her head and says, "*Did this to us?* Why does trouble seem to follow you around, Mother?"

"Follow me? It was your kids with the pot that brought the cops to the house."

Sandy moans, "And where did the fruit gummies they found come from?"

"Those rednecks. Surprised they could read the label."

"And what about you taking a swing at the officer?"

"That bitch was being rude. And I never touched her."

"Rude? She was trying to take your picture. Thank God you missed."

"She wouldn't let me fix my hair. They could at least have a comb and some makeup available."

"It was a mug shot, Katherine, not a publicity photo."

"All the same to me and screw you, Buddy."

"I already have been after forking up $2500 in bail bonds for my family."

"If we'd been in Colorado, none of this would have happened."

"So Mother, they let teens smoke pot at football camps out there?"

"Maybe not, but most of the teens out there aren't stupid enough to leave a roach in full view of a camp counselor."

For the second time this morning, Buddy steps in it. "I told them not to take their stuff with them. They promised to..."

"You told them what? You knew they were smoking pot and didn't tell me? Well, we can just kiss goodbye any chance of them getting a football scholarship. They'll get kicked off the team."

Buddy takes another swing at the Tar Baby. "Football career? Yeah, right. As for the pot, all the kids do it. I was just trying to get them to be more careful."

"What were you thinking? It's against the law, as we learned so well this morning. Some parents we are. And just think about how much fun Taylor will have with all this after the crap we gave her about running around with Sammy the drug dealer."

Katherine steps in. "Just a minute, guys. There's no good in going after each other. You have kids being kids. It's not the end of the world, for Christ's sake. It's just pot. Get over it!"

Turning to Buddy, Sandy says, "Okay mister drug counselor, you make the call to Taylor before she picks it up on social media."

Buddy leaves to find his phone. A short time later, he returns and Sandy asks, "So what did she have to say?"

"She already knows all about it. A sister of one of the police personnel at the station posted it on Facebook. She thought it was funny as hell. Called us a bunch of hypocrites. I hung up on her." Buddy sighs as he flops on the sofa.

"Laughed? Well, what did she say about you losing your job?"

"I didn't tell her. It just wasn't the right time with her carrying on. The job, the Rothstein mess, and now the pot bust is just too much to swallow. I've got to think this through."

Sandy throws her head back and says, "Great. That's just great. How are we going to explain all this?"

Katherine gets up and goes to the refrigerator and pulls out a beer. After taking several gulps, she burps out the

90

carbonation. "Sandra, just quit your moping and buck up, girl. Hang tailing will get you nowhere. Before we got screwed up last night, I was telling you about the pot business in Colorado. Well, for sure, it's the next big thing. And your boys aren't criminals."

"Oh, yeah? Well, tell that to the judge. It's still against the law! Mother, you always trivialize everything. Just what were they thinking taking pot to football camp?" She directs herself to Buddy. "And, with their father's acceptance!"

"I never condoned anything, I was just trying..."

Sandy looks to the ceiling as the sub woofer resonates from the boy's room. "Those little jack offs. I told them they were grounded." Arising from the sofa, Sandy's voice trails off as she stomps up the stairs.

Katherine sits back down and says to Buddy, "Remember your old days? You two of all people. Just what were you doing at their age? Besides, it's legal in Colorado. When states start to see how much revenue they can make, they all will follow. It's just a matter of time, just like alcohol during prohibition. We better get on the gravy train."

After quieting the music, Sandy returns to find Katherine still on her soap box. "So what are you saying, Mother? You want us to start growing pot in our back yard and selling it in the alleys. News Flash! It's illegal in Georgia. Haven't we just learned that lesson?"

"No, No, No. There are all sorts of ways to make money off of it in Colorado as I seem to remember saying last night. The industry is exploding. They can't keep it supplied. Buddy, you could do this in your sleep."

"Mother! Are you still stoned? You want Buddy to grow pot in Colorado when we live here? Aren't we in enough trouble already? What are we going to do about our problem? The one you helped get us into?" Looking away and wiping her burning eyes, Sandy says, "My God. This can't be happening. What are our friends going to say when they find out we've been busted for pot? The kids and my mother?"

Katherine continues, "So this is a temporary problem. It's everyone's first offence...simple possession, a misdemeanor. You heard what your attorney said. We'll get off with a slap on the wrist, and a small fine and probation. It

92

may be harder on the boys. Definitely some community service, but it's not like the end of the world. We can get through this. Let's focus on the future."

Buddy says. "I don't think it's going to be that easy, Katherine. Let's assume I could get involved somehow, legally, in Colorado no less. How in God's name could something like that be done? We're broke; I'm out of work, and facing drug charges. There are bills to pay and there's college tuition, with little hope of scholarships. I've got to go to work finding work. Must I continue?"

"Well, before the gummies and booze kicked in, here's where I was going last night. You guys kid me about all my friends. Well, they are great friends and super people and we have a wonderful time together. But, most importantly, several of them are in the pot business in Colorado. One's a prominent attorney that knows all the ins and outs. I've been doing research and there's a lot of ways we can make money off this thing. Buddy, you know chemistry and shit, I know how to run a store, and Sandy, you have all types of skills. Besides, anything we don't know, my friends surely do. Holy crap. There are so many ways the family can play this thing. This is a big no brainer."

On the way to the fridge Buddy says, "Wait a minute Katherine, no brainer seems about right. You make us sound like the Trump family. What about the money? Remember, we have none."

Katherine downs the last of her beer and says, "Get me another Coors Light and let's go into the family room. There's another thing I haven't told you."

Chapter 6

And the Poor Get Richer

Katherine settles herself into Buddy's easy chair. After Buddy and Sandy are seated, she begins her story. "You remember old Uncle Billy dying a while back right before I busted my tail bone? Prostate cancer got him at eighty-nine."

"Yeah, he was a weird old duck." Buddy says.

Katherine nods, "Kind of quirky, but we always hit it off. Not many people in the family paid him much mind. He lived in a small apartment in town for years. And then his older sister talked him into moving in with her. She lived alone in her big old home with her parrot."

Sandy says, "Yes, Aunt Marsha! I remember that spooky place and Polly the parrot. What fun we had. Uncle Billy taught me about the finer things of life. Helped me to get away from some of those losers I was hanging with. I was terrified of Aunt Marsha though. And there were always funny noises that no one could explain."

"You know I don't like to talk about that but yeah, Aunt Marsha...sad story. Died of a heart attack in her mid sixties. She was bitter to the end. Married into money but lost her groom to a senseless murder while honeymooning in New York City."

Sandy says, "I remember something about that but not much. But those noises always..."

Katherine interrupts. "They were walking back to their hotel after a play when her husband was robbed and stabbed. She never got over it and never had another relationship. She stayed to herself with that parrot but was very close to Uncle Billy. He was about the only person she had anything to do with. It was always rumored that she inherited a lot of money. Her husband was some big wig in the publishing business. But, aside from maintaining the mansion and an occasional driver for her old Continental, she never showed it off. I remember Aunt Marsha obsessing over books. They would be special delivered to her house on regular basis."

"Yes! I got into all sorts of trouble with her one time."

Katherine leans forward and chuckles, "Oh, I remember that very well. You were only five or six. When I found out what she tried to do to you, I was going to strangle that old bat."

"It's no wonder she hated me. I took one of her packages to play with. Tried using it for a boat in the gold fish pond. She chased me around the back yard with a mop before Uncle Billy could stop her. I never got near her again. After she died, Uncle Billy would read to me out of those books for hours. I was always afraid she was going to pop out of a closet or something."

"Yeah, you floated one of her prized books! She worshipped those damn things and kept them locked away from everyone. Old Marsha stayed mostly to herself, reading all the time. She scared the shit out of you. Hated children and let them know it. Didn't care for me much either. After several instances, Uncle Billy and I decided it was best not to bring you around anymore. She died only a few years later and we started going there most every weekend. After her passing, Uncle Billy read a lot also. Remember him handling those books with gloves? Always thought that was strange. Was only about a six block walk from where we lived. You were over there all the time. Uncle Billy adored you. He and I became closer after the old gal kicked the bucket. It was heart breaking to see him waste away. He barely knew who I was in his latter days under hospice care. Anyway, when..."

Sandy says, "I remember playing all over that huge house. And Polly, of course, what a hoot she was. She had her routine of tricks, crawling all around her tree roost hanging upside down. Knew a lot of words too. Would even sing along with Uncle Billy's opera arias."

Katherine laughs as she reaches for her cigarettes, "And you know what? Polly's still alive!"

"No way!" Sandy says.

"Yup. We didn't know what to do with her when Uncle Billy got sick because she needed daily attention. One of his friends knew the owner of a pet store that agreed to take her. At least she gets a lot of attention in the shop. Kids love her. She talks and sings all the time."

"That poor old bird. I loved Polly. She was beautiful with big yellow head and green feathers. Had the run of the house during the day and was put into her draped cage at night. She was really messy though, kicking those sunflower seed shells everywhere. I remember that she would take a big poop every time someone would say; "Poor old Miss McKnight, poor old Miss McKnight." I have no idea who Miss McKnight was, some old relative, I guess. Funny as hell. Did it every time. I can't believe she's still alive."

Buddy shakes his head. "So we have a nut case, a psycho widow, and a goofy bird that shits on demand. What's next, ghosts in the attic?"

"I'm telling you...there were noises." Sandy says with a hushed tone.

Katherine gives a stern look. "Sandy."

"There's some kind of a bad gene on that side of the family."

"Buddy. He was our dear friend. What do you know? You only met him once. And, if I remember correctly, he didn't care so much for you either."

Slouching back in his chair, Buddy says to Katherine, "Go on."

"He has always been there for me. Uncle Billy never got upset with all the crap I pulled in my younger days. He was very forgiving and bailed my ass out of several situations. He was one of the few people I trusted back then."

Katherine directs herself to Sandy. "You remember years ago, you were still a little girl, when I wanted to go into business for myself to open the flower and gift shop? Well, it was Uncle Billy who loaned me the $10,000 start-up money for my store. That covered the first several months, but it didn't take me long to pay him back. He didn't want to take the money but I insisted. I really had to work my butt off, but it was worth it. I could not have done it without him."

"Mother, you never mentioned anything about this."

Katherine adjusts a pillow to her back and continues. "You just never know about someone. Billy brought me into his confidence. Told me about our mutual gay friends and how they had been working on a plan to sell legal pot. But, it had to be put on the back burner when he got sick. He tried to tell me more in his final days. With him being mainlined drugs at hospice, he would wander in and out of consciousness. Talking about golden books, double yellow gold and pot or golden pot. Something to that effect and making absolutely no sense at all. But this pot thing. He kept circling back to it, telling me that I was going to be rich someday. I just assumed it was the morphine talking."

"So, what did he mean, Katherine?"

"The way I understood it, Uncle Billy was considering selling his home and moving into an assisted living facility. With the extra money, he'd invest in a big marijuana grow house with his friends. His old home is on valuable property. It's like a tree lined oasis in an industrial part of Denver. Uncle Billy stalled when he discovered his home would be bulldozed. So nothing ever became of it. Now they're trying to get me to invest in their $3 million-dollar deal."

"You? Invest?" Buddy asks.

"I'll get to that. So years ago Gabe, Uncle Billy, and his pals saw the big picture about marijuana with the laws changing and all. Nothing ever materialized but Gabe still had his plans."

"I've always liked Gabe." Sandy says.

"So, who's this Gabe guy?"

"Gabe Kaplan, a pot pioneer and activist in Colorado, a visionary but also Uncle Billy's attorney. Mine too. I've known him since he was a teen. His specialty is family law, but he's really gotten a name for himself in the marijuana movement. He owns two dispensaries and leases his pot space from a grow house near Golden."

Buddy says, "It all sounds nuts to me."

"Nuts? Gabe is a big player with this new industry. Being a lawyer he knows all the ins and outs of the laws and politics. Besides, I trust him like a son. With his knowledge and influence, we've got a huge opportunity here."

"Seriously, Katherine. So Uncle Billy and some pals were talking about building a grow house in Denver?"

"Exactly. Aside from financing, one of the hardest parts about getting into the pot business in Colorado is getting the licensing. You just don't up and decide to go start growing and selling the stuff. Gabe with his connections can take care of all that stuff. We were discussing several ideas when I struck out for Marietta several days ago."

"Well, I still don't see how this has anything to do with Sandy and me."

"I'm getting to that. When Gabe called me last week, I was told I had been named executrix to Billy's estate and I had to come in for the reading of the Will. I just assumed I'd have to sign a few papers and the probate court would take it from there. It never occurred to me that I would be left anything...maybe the house at best. You can imagine my surprise when he told me Uncle Billy had much more than I had ever imagined. Furthermore, he had left it..." She reaches over and grabs Sandy by the arm and smiles, "All to you and me, Sandy."

"Me? What are you talking about, Mother?"

"Crazy Uncle Billy left what to whom?" Buddy asks.

"There's the land...and the beautiful old Victorian. But there's more, much more. In his will Uncle Billy disclosed a secret, a really big one hidden in his house. He'd written a riddle addressed to me in old quotes or something like that. Let me get it." Producing a small folded piece of parchment from her purse, Katherine reads:

"The important thing in a book is the meaning it has for you. The important thing in gold is it will prevail over the ashes of currency and the follies of man. In the bird's eye view, in the words of time, search for enlightenment and security. Use them wisely and enjoy life."

Buddy gets up and asks with a grin, "Another beer, anyone? You were saying, Katherine?"

"Keep that stuff away from me!" Sandy says turning to her mother.

Katherine nods. Buddy returns with the beer and takes a seat on the sofa.

After lighting up another Marlboro, Katherine recants the events that had unfolded only a week earlier. "The next morning after our meeting we drove to see Uncle Billy's place. With the key from his safety deposit box, we unlocked the door and entered the musty old house. We sat in the parlor for nearly an hour trying to decipher the cryptic words--books, enlightenment, bird's eye view. And then it hit us. We found a hidden compartment under his big Oriental rug next to where Polly's cage stood. The bird's eye view!

"We slid back the sofa, chairs, and Polly's cage stand. Under the rug we found two pine planks with lift rings. Beneath the planks lay a large carpenter's tool box. We both struggled to pull that heavy ass box onto level flooring. After flipping open the latch, we couldn't believe our eyes."

With Buddy and Sandy leaning in, Katherine drags out her story. "Filled to the top, lay hundreds of filled coin wrappers: penny rolls, nickel rolls, dime rolls, quarter rolls, half dollar rolls, and dollar rolls. We figured Uncle Billy was a coin collector."

At this point in the story, Katherine stands and shouts with the passion of a revival preacher, "They weren't silver. They were *Gold*! Fuckin' *Gold*! That's what he was talking about in his riddle. *Gold*!"

"Mom! Quiet! We can't let the boys here this."

Bracing on her cane, Katherine lowers her voice to a whisper. "There in the tool box, like cordwood, were rolls of U.S. minted gold coins of every type imaginable. Someone must have been buying them from traders and dealers for decades. Every spare cent he had must have been converted to these babies. I'm guessing that old Aunt Marsha may have

105

been in on it too. They could have been hers for all we know."

"Just *how* many, Mother?"

"Over twenty-eight hundred, most in near mint condition. Do you know what one of these highly-graded coins is worth?"

"Not a clue." says Sandy.

"He had 19 St. Gaudens $20 gold pieces. Some of those are worth thousands! There was over a million and a half bucks in that tool box. One point five million dollars! Can you believe that? We still need a formal appraisal. Could be even more."

Buddy declares, "Well, I'll be damned."

And then Katherine reveals, "Sandy, do you know what this means? He divided the estate equally between us two."

Sandy turns to Buddy barely mouthing the words, "Uncle Billy left us one and a half million dollars?"

Katherine reaches for her arm and says, "Yes, he did. But it's more, well over two million, counting the house and belongings. With the money Gabe and his pals can put up, if we still want to go that way, we should have more than enough to invest in their idea. Buddy, you can come out and work somewhere, maybe in a grow house. Then we can..."

"Wait, Mother. I have no idea what you're talking about. That's an awful lot of money but we live in Marietta, Georgia. We have a mortgage and there're bills to pay. We have a child in college with two in cue, if they can stay out of trouble. Buddy can't just take off to Colorado to become a pot grower."

"You just laid out the problem with no solution. I'm talking opportunity here. Of course we can't do this thing willy-nilly. But we've got to do something. We have to have a plan, numbers and budgets and stuff."

"I don't know, Mother. That's a lot to think about."

"Did you hear what I said? You just inherited over a million bucks. Buddy's severance will buy you time to make a move to Denver."

"Make a move to Denver? But, Mother..."

"Okay, let's back up a minute. We have a situation here and I've got some good ideas. Furthermore, we now have the money to stake us. Remind me again about what your plans are to climb out of this tar pit you're in? And Sandy, I know I was not much of a mother and now I can help make it up to you. And, what better way than this? Uncle Billy has given us a chance for a fresh start."

Buddy speaks up. "I guess we could talk about it more. The inheritance news is staggering. And I agree the marijuana business is the next big thing. I just have to sort through a bunch of stuff."

"Phooey!" Katherine blurts. "We'll do what we have to do. We can talk about all this later, but I still have some doubts about Gabe's plans. We might need to slow down this train but regardless; we need his help in getting you a job."

Sandy walks over to the stairs and looks towards the boys' room. Putting her finger to her lips, she softly says, "Thank goodness you said nothing to Taylor. We have to keep this to ourselves until we figure out what to do. No bits and pieces, until we have a plan. Okay?"

Katherine pushes up with her cane and declares, "Let's do Mexican. Go get the boys. It's on me!"

Chapter 7

Nothing Remains Quite the Same

Buddy and Katherine are sitting at the kitchen table when she hits speed dial #3.

"Hello."

"Good morning, Gabe. You up and at 'em?" Katherine rasps in her cigarette voice.

"Huh? Like yeah. It's 5:15, Katherine. What could possibly be so important?"

"Gabe, I've been thinking about this grow house deal. If we do this thing we're going to need a manager. I have the perfect person, my son-in-law. He already knows all about pot growing."

"Jeffrey, where are you going?"

"Are you back with Jeffrey?" Katherine asks.

"We never really did break up."

"You always seem to fight over silly ass things. So what was it this time?"

"Do we have to talk about this now? I'm not feeling so chipper. Maybe later when I get to my office."

"We can talk about it now. It won't take a minute and you need to be getting up anyway. Don't you work on Mondays?"

"Katherine, please."

"I want to get Buddy a job in the grow house like the one you lease from. Maybe as a bud tender. Anything that can get him in the door. To learn the ropes so to speak."

"Slow down a minute. We don't even have our funding put together yet."

"Buddy's a chemist and knows this stuff. He used to run the Pot Grove at the University of Mississippi. And he was a big executive at Coke for years. We need him. Last thing I remember, you were all hot to trot on this thing." As Katherine embellishes, Buddy shakes his head.

"Pot Grove?"

"Yes, the Pot Grove. Where they grow all that stuff in Mississippi at the University in Birmingham or somewhere."

"I think you mean Oxford. And, isn't the Grove where they party and all at football games?"

"Whatever. That's not important. Pay attention. I want to bring him in on our business plans. The stuff you and Uncle Billy had talked about. Buddy would be perfect to run our grow house. In the meantime, he needs to learn, uh, refresh his memory on all this stuff. I want to help him get started right away. Really a refresher course is all he needs. He could be a great bud tender."

Buddy mouths to Katherine; "Are you freaking nuts?"

"Interview? Katherine, we need to talk about this more. Probate will not be settled for a while on Billy's estate. We need to form a corporation, there's licensing, contracts, and..."

"All that stuff can come in time. Right now we need a job in the pot business for Buddy. You can go do all that other lawyer shit later. Can you get Buddy an appointment with your grow house pal? The one you use?"

"Well, maybe. My friend would not be happy to think I was sending in a spy soon to become a competitor. I'd have to level with him. I'm going out there this afternoon to check out some new products and my plot. Not even sure he's hiring but he does owe me a couple of favors. Buddy the bud tender does have kind of a ring to it."

Buddy launches out of his chair. Holding up her palm, Katherine says, "Cute, Gabe. Why don't we just refer to him as Buddy the future Grow House Manager?"

"Okay, so when could he come out if I can get something arranged? Maybe in a week or so?"

"He'll be out there on the next plane. Probably in twenty-four hours. And don't say a word about this being temporary. Let's get the job first and apologize later if we have to."

"That's not right. I need to be straight with him."

"Well, that'd be a first."

"That's so funny, Katherine."

"Just do it Gabe. He's not going to hire a temp."

"Damn it. Okay. I'll call you back as soon as I know something. Good bye."

Sandy returns from her sunrise run in the mountains. After being filled in on the conversation with Gabe, she says to Buddy, "Are you willing to check it out?"

"Yeah, but there's a lot to investigate."

She trots up the stairs. "We have to get moving. Boys! Get up! It's nearly 9:30. You've got work to do."

Banging on their door, she barks day's orders. "You have to clean your room. Throw down your dirty clothes. You've got a ton of yard work. Your dad is meeting with a lawyer this morning. You may still have to go to jail. And just wait 'till your Uncle Mack hears about this." Groans are emitted from behind the door as the twins awaken from the dead.

"Mother, I have to get going on the house. If you can be ready in about an hour, we'll meet Buddy somewhere for lunch, maybe in Acworth, near Greg's office. No one should see us up there. We've got to talk all this through after he meets with the lawyer."

Katherine downs the last of her black coffee. "Okay. I have some more ideas to discuss with you two. Have to do something with this hair. Sandy, I need to borrow your blower."

Buddy arrives at the China Dragon Buffet about half past noon. Katherine and Sandy are seated in a booth in the dark far corner of the restaurant. Before he can sit, Sandy asks, "So how'd it go with Greg?"

Buddy slides into the booth and looks towards the buffet. Turning back to Sandy he says, "He feels he can negotiate a civil citation, a relatively light infraction since we're all first time offenders."

"What about the boys?"

"He wants to get a conditional discharge or diversion, meaning the judge will order the boys to carry out a probationary term and do some community service...to keep it off their records."

"Thank goodness. What about the Rothstein mess? Do we have any hope of recovery?"

"Probably not. It was a business decision gone bad. Chalked it up to greediness on Michael's part. He said we'd might as well kiss that money good bye." Buddy pushes his

114

way out of the booth and stands. "Better get going on the buffet."

Stress eating, the three hastily gobble down plates piled high the sheet pan offerings. Staring towards the buffet, Buddy is stalking more ribs. In unison, the ladies admonish him.

"You've had enough, Buddy."

Katherine piles on. "That's right. We have to lose some of that belly. There's a lot of work to do and you have to be in shape, clean up your act, people to meet and interviews to do."

"You're criticizing me? With you still smoking those stinking cancer sticks all the time. I'll lose weight when you stop smoking!"

"What do I have to do with your problem? I'm not the one out of work and desperate for money. You'd better...."

"Stop it you two! Can we please focus on what needs to be done *now*? I just can't take you going at it with all we have to do. Mom? Buddy*?*"

Buddy and Katherine give complying nods as Sandy takes out her iPad and opens her Outlook Documents file. "OK, let's get started. I'll keep notes."

Buddy begins to check out this hottie in a micro mini across the room. As her stilettos tap and perky boobs bounce, she struts his way with a tray from the buffet. The pretty brunette catches his eye as she takes her seat at a nearby table. Craftily crossing her legs, she flips her hair and smiles at her companion.

Sandy breaks his concentration. "Buddy, Are you with us here?"

"Huh? Uh, yeah. It's cool. Whatever."

Katherine lays out a plan of action. "Okay, guys. Hear me out. I've been thinking about this for a while now and here's how I see it. I can help transition you all to Denver. We've got Uncle Billy's house you can stay in until things get sorted out. I should be hearing something soon from Gabe on the job interview, so we need tickets right away. Sandy, can you handle this end? Buddy, you cool with all this?"

Buddy leers at the hottie making her way to the check-out, swishing her caboose along the way. As he is about to list out of the booth, Sandy raises her voice, "Buddy?"

"Yeah, yeah. But I'm not so happy about being a bud tender."

"It's only temporary until we decide what route we're going to take. Consider it getting paid for going back to school." Sandy says.

"I just don't know. We're just going to up and move to Denver? And moving the kids? That'd be really hard on them. What about Taylor? In her first year at West Georgia, we'd be leaving her behind. She'd be terribly lonely."

Katherine interjects, "Guys, no decision is being made, except to do a job interview. Let's get out there and read the tea leaves, to get more facts to make a decision. We can't turn down something we don't have."

"Tea leaves? Wish I had some now." Buddy groans.

"Damn it, Buddy. I'm not suggesting that you come to Colorado for seasonal work. This is a chance to get in on the ground floor of a brand-new industry. One that's going to be huge."

"Mother's right. We need some options. So, what's our choice? We're in a mess that's only going to get messier the longer we wait. Besides, Denver is a beautiful place, a big city that has lots of opportunities. I loved it when I grew up there. If this doesn't work out, other doors could open for you. You've got a good resume with skills other companies could use. A fresh start might do us good. You and Mom go out there and check it out. Meanwhile, I'll get to work here sorting through all that needs to be done. I have to pay the bills and stuff. And, I wouldn't be worrying too much about Taylor being lonely."

Buddy sighs, "I guess."

Sandy reviews her notes. "There's a lot I can do while you guys are on your way to Denver. Mother, I'll get on the Internet tonight and see if I can find some last minute cheap flights for you two right away. Okay everyone? And Honey, you'll need a resume."

"Resume for a bud tender position?"

"Yes, but you don't know what position you'll be interviewing for. Go for the gold!" Sandy ticks through her check list.

Katherine pulls her VISA card from her purse. "Use my card for the tickets. Sandy, I just remembered I've got a close friend who's an assistant principal at the big high school near Uncle Billy's. She can give you the low down on what you have to do to get the boys registered."

On their way back to the house, Sandy and Katherine are in full execution mode. Gabe rings Katherine's cell to confirm that Buddy is scheduled to meet with the grow house manager late Wednesday afternoon. The trip is on.

Morning traffic is slowed to a crawl as Sandy inches the SUV into the passenger departure lane of Atlanta Hartsfield International Airport. An accident on I-285 has delayed their route for nearly forty-five minutes.

After Sandy pinches in next to the curb, Buddy and Katherine jump out, disappearing into the crowd. Having cleared security, they hustle through the concourse. They enter the plane as the gate closes. Ahead, are two weight challenged women and an infant. Shuffling down the narrow aisle of the Boeing 217, their bags and backsides brush the seated passengers along the way.

The last-minute bookings leave Buddy and Katherine with two middle seats rows apart. First to be seated, Katherine fits herself between two adolescents. With deeply buried ear buds and eyes focused on their Nooks, the kids signal to her a quiet and comfortable flight. After pulling out *Fifty Shades of Freed* and a THC laden fruit gummy, she settles in.

Struggling to the rear of the plane, Buddy waits for the women before him to complete building their nests. Assisted by two flight attendants, they cram the overhead bins and wedge into Row 36, seats A and C. Eyes roll and heads turn as the infant's pitched cries resonate throughout the cabin.

Buddy stares incredulously at his seat selection. It reads; Row 36, Seat B.

Over his shoulder the attendant says with an annoying sense of urgency, "Sir, you must take your seat immediately."

Her associate notifies the passengers over the intercom, "Ladies and Gentlemen. Our flight cannot take off until all passengers are safely seated with their seat belts securely fastened."

Passengers glare at Buddy as he pushes his carryon into the luggage bin. The seat A occupant fights to disengage herself, maneuvering into the aisle. Buddy fits himself into the middle seat.

Stuck in position, he tries to adjust to his confinement. With hands clasped over his paunch, he rests his arms on the spillover from his seating companions. To his right the baby flails away, grunting and wiggling atop her mother's flattened breasts. As he peers through the porthole at an endless line of planes, the seatback in front smashes into his knees. After adjusting the vent above, stale warm air blows downward.

The delaying summer storms pass through the Atlanta area, allowing the planes to begin taxing. After roaring its engines, the plane races down the runway, nosing upwards for the three hour flight to Denver.

Leveling off and securing the landing gear, the pilot proclaims that tail winds should help make up fifteen minutes of their hour and twenty-minute ground delay. Most passengers clap. Buddy does not as he strains to position his attaché atop his chest.

The passenger to his left digs into her purse, producing two grande burritos. After several bites, she stretches across Buddy's stomach and says to her traveling companion, "Keisha, here be yours. Hits real tasty, but kinda spicy for me. Beans and me don't do good."

"Hold on a minute Latisha, 'till I tend to Brianna. Man, she done done a load on me!"

Eyeing the Coca-Cola name on Buddy's attaché, Latisha asks, "You work for CoCola? You know Demarcus McRay? He be my cousin in Chicago. He works for CoCola too."

"No, not really. It's a big company." Buddy sighs and holds his breath as the aroma of baby feces and burrito wafts his way.

"When you guys gonna to put sugar in Fresca? I love Fresca, but hate that after taste."

"I don't work in that department." He exhales.

"You needs to tell 'em anyway."

"Sure. I'll get right on it."

"Keisha, this man works for CoCola."

"He do? Do you get free Cokes, Mista?

"No, you see I..."

"I wanna tell you about an idea me and Demarcus come up wid for one of dem TV commercials."

"Well, actually I don't work for Coke. I borrowed this attaché from a neighbor and forgot to take off the tag. Now if you ladies will excuse me, I'm not feeling so well. I have an infectious virus I got while traveling to West Africa. Talking spreads germs, you know." He strains a series of violent coughs.

That does it for the idle chit chat. Buddy closes his eyes and begins to doze, having empathetic speculation about the motivation of the shoe bomber. He is unaware that Seat A has reached for the overhead call button.

With her wailing muffled by a mouthful of burrito, Latisha rustles from her seat and waddles up the aisle screaming at the top of her voice. "Dis guy done got Ebolie an he gonna kill us all!"

Moments later the flight attendant appears with gloved hands. "Sir! By orders of the captain, you are required to apply this surgical mask for the remainder of our flight to avoid possible passenger contamination."

"Contamination? I'm not contaminated."

"Sir. We will be relocating you to the rear of the plane. Right this way, please." She backs into the aisle as Buddy complies.

Nearby passengers murmur, leaning from their seats to best avoid what has been announced as the plague. Trapped with her child, Keisha buries her face into an air sickness bag.

Having been reseated to the rear of the plane, Buddy tries calming himself. *Surely I can just explain the situation and all will be fine. At least I'm not crammed between those Suma wrestlers.* He rationalizes the predicament as the cattle car makes its way westward.

His disjointed rest is interrupted by the pilot. "Ladies and Gentlemen; If you would check out the starboard side of

124

the cabin, you will see the snow covered peaks of the Rocky Mountains."

The pilot's observations trigger painful memories from January. *Snow! Don't ever want to see that shit again. Why would I want to move to Denver with all that snow? Wonder what the manatee is up to?* Adjusting his surgical mask, he shuts his eyes and lays his head back, dodging in and out of drowsiness.

The captain announces the initial descent into the Denver area. The abrupt bump of the engaging landing gear ends his tormented reminiscing. Upon their arrival, the Center for Disease Control in Hazmat suits greets him as the last person to disembark from the plane.

Chapter 8

So Where Do You See

Yourself In Five Years?

Having cleared security, Buddy and Katherine slink through baggage claim hoping to avoid the crowd amassed near the exit doors.

"Deh he is!" screams Keisha as she points through the huddle of reporters.

"Dat's him!" Latisha confirms charging in pursuit, the throng following.

As Buddy and Katherine flee the terminal, Gabe screeches up in his SL550 Benz. Moments later they are on their forty-two-mile trip to Boulder.

Gabe makes a call but gets voice mail. "Hi Randy, its Gabe. The plane was running a little late so if it's okay, we'll be there around 5:00. Call me back if there's a problem. See you then."

"I'm really sorry guys, but those women were driving me nuts. I didn't think..."

"That's right. You didn't think." Katherine snaps.

Gabe says, "Hopefully that'll be the end of it and it won't be picked up by the news. If I hadn't known the D.I.A.'s Manager of Aviation, this thing could have really blown up."

From the back seat Buddy says, "I really appreciate your help. Can we talk about the job interview?"

Looking into the rear-view mirror, Gabe responds, "Well, I really don't know what he might have. He's doing me a big favor by even seeing us. People are driving him crazy looking for work. I'd be real flexible if I were you."

Katherine looks over to Gabe and says, "And don't say anything about this possible job being temporary. We don't want to give him any excuse for not hiring Buddy."

"But Katherine, I can't mislead him, he's..."

"You're not misleading him. Let's get the job first and apologize later if necessary."

After they exit towards Boulder, Katherine spots a truck stop restaurant at the highway intersection. "Gabe, drop me out here and I'll wait for you guys. I have some calls to make while you do your thing. Need some cigs and beer. You guys take your time. I'll be fine. Go break a leg, Buddy."

After dropping her off, they proceed several miles down a two lane blacktop. They come across a small sign signaling the entrance of Colorado Medicinals, LLC. Surrounded by a ten foot chain link fence topped off with razor wire, the massive facility looks more like a correctional institution than a fancy farm for growing pot. Security cameras catch every move as they pull up to the guard gate. Without prompting, Gabe shows the attendant his driver's license. Checking his computer, he confirms the appointment with Mr. Anderson. After printing off a parking permit and time stamp, the guard instructs Gabe to place it on his dash. The security gate grinds opens as the Benz creeps forward into a Visitor's parking space.

After a few minutes in the small lobby, the two guests hear the door lock buzz. A short bald headed fellow looks through an opening in the security-glass at the reception desk.

Having completed the intros and small talk, they exit to the back yard where thousands of marijuana plants are in varying stages of maturity. Working through the sections, they come to Gabe's harvest that will be in full maturity and ready for bud trimming in about a week. After a brief tour of the grow house, the three return to Randy Anderson's office.

Buddy and Gabe are elated to hear Randy describe a position of Production Associate. The Associate would handle everything--gardening, harvesting, trimming, weighing, labeling and packaging of marijuana and its multiple product forms. A much more comprehensive position than they had thought, the whole gamut is covered from seed to smoke.

The rigors of the flight, missed sleep, and time zone begin to take their toll on Buddy as the late afternoon drags on and the sun begins to set. Randy's office with a Western exposure is located next to the large hydroponics warehouse. A small oscillating fan hums from the credenza.

As Buddy's head begins to bob, Gabe kicks his ankle..

"What the!" Buddy cries out.

"Do you have a question? Randy asks.

"Uh, no, no. I was just excited about all you're doing here."

"I've done all the talking. Do you have any questions Buddy?"

Now alert, Buddy gets into some technical areas that demonstrate his breath and depth of knowledge about chemistry, protocols, quality assurance and process, all necessary requirements for a Production Associate. After about twenty minutes, Randy glances at his watch.

Gabe picks up the signal and says, "So Randy, my man, what do we need to do to make this happen? Looks like we might have a good fit here."

Randy stands and shakes Buddy's hand with a smile, "Please get me that resume by early tomorrow morning. I want to send it to our investor group. I was just about to drop a Help Wanted ad in the paper. Have a noon dead line. I think you're very qualified. Here, take this. It's the job description for the Production Associate. I've been doing all this myself up until now but the demands have gotten too great. I would be your trainer."

As they are about to wrap up, Randy throws a curve. "Guys, as you might know, getting a legal job in Colorado's marijuana industry has been a real pain. The Medical Marijuana Enforcement Division (MMED) has been backed up for quite a while. There are a lot more people applying for jobs than actual jobs. They actually use a lottery system and good luck with that."

Gabe winks at Buddy and turns to Randy and says, "Well, we'll just have to do what we need to do."

Gabe and Buddy thank Randy for his time and agree to touch base the next day. A text to Katherine alerts her of their pending arrival. As they pull up to the truck stop, Katherine is backing out the door with a carton of Marlboros and a 12-Pack of Coors Light.

They agree to discuss their strategy over drinks and dinner at the Village Tavern. Upon entering the restaurant, Katherine stuffs a napkin with an inked message into Buddy's hand; *Just let Gabe talk.. We'll keep him happy until you get the job.*

Returning to Katherine's condo at 12:45, the two are exhausted from the long day. Buddy is ushered up to the guest room where she points out the clean towels, TV remote, and thermostat.

"And drink lots of water. There're several bottles on the dresser. We'll sleep on all this and discuss in the morning."

"Thanks, Katherine and good night."

After hobbling halfway down the stairs, she remembers; "Buddy! Don't forget to send that fellow your resume tonight. And my Wi-Fi password is "flowerpower50. Buddy! Do you hear me?"

"Damn, Katherine. Yes. Good night."

It's still dark Thursday morning when Buddy awakens to the sound of dishes clanking. The smell of cigarettes and coffee drifts up the stairs. He squints at the alarm clock next to the bed. It reads 5:13 a.m.

With a bottle of water, Buddy sits at the small bureau in his under ware. He gets on line. With the job description in his hand, he's able to cut and paste the necessary "buzz words" tailored for the position of Production Associate.

After taking a shower and dressing, he heads down to the kitchen and finds Katherine is emptying the dish washer.

"Good morning, Katherine. Do you always get up so early?"

"I like to get going. Did you get your resume done?"

"Yes, I did. Got a lot of good stuff from the job description he gave me. Looks like a better opportunity than we thought. Don't know what he's willing to pay. We'll have to see. I copied you and Gabe."

Katherine, stoked on cigs and caffeine, takes a seat. "This damn butt bone is killing me after the plane trip and all day yesterday. You surely didn't make anything any easier with your antics. Ebola exposure, for goodness sake. Thank God, there's nothing in the paper about it today. I heated up some cinnamon buns in the toaster oven and there's a coffee mug by the sink."

Pulling apart a bun, Buddy laughs, "I can only imagine if it'd been you sand witched between those three."

"Probably so. Anyway, I've been thinking about what all Gabe was saying about Sandy and me ponying up a million bucks for a 33% position. Furthermore, he wants to be the managing partner and will bring in other investors he knows. You know, I don't play well with others."

"That is a lot of cooks in the kitchen."

"Exactly. Here's an idea I've come up with. It crystallized last night when Gabe started telling us about how he was going to run our business."

"What do you mean *our business*, Katherine?"

"Old Uncle Billy's Victorian. Just what are Sandy and I going to do with that thing? It's beautiful and all but I don't want to live in something that big, particularly with all that maintenance. We either need to sell it or use it somehow to make some money off it."

Into his second sticky bun and smacking, he says, "I'd sell the damn thing. What do you think you could get for it?"

Blowing smoke across the table, she stuffs out the butt in her coffee saucer. "I don't know, maybe three to four hundred thousand. The place needs some fixing up. The home's not in a good area now zoned commercial, so probably the most value's in the land itself. It's got a two bed room apartment built over the carriage house. I'm thinking it can be used for something else."

"For what? We could really use the money right now."

134

"A Bud and Breakfast! What do you think about that? We run a business out of there. A Board and Bud. Don't know what we'd call it but a B & B catering to the pot smoking visitors to Denver! 420 friendly as they say."

"Whoa. You want to do what? I hope you're kidding."

"Listen to me. This house is the bomb." Katherine continues as she pours another coffee.

"Or more like the bong."

"Hey, I like that. It'll be a pot friendly bed and breakfast kicked up a notch or two. An all smoking hotel. Our guests will bring their own stuff, stay in elegant surroundings, have hot cable channels, and a super good brunch and Happy Hour. Shoot. We can even have tours just like they do in Napa. Shuttle to the dispensaries, night spots and restaurants."

"Hold on, Katherine. Heaven knows what it would take to get the house brought up to standards like you're thinking."

"We're going to get a lot for the gold coins. As for the home, just a little refreshing should do. Sandy and I are great cooks and I..."

Cutting her short, Buddy says, "A little refreshing for a 100 year old house? It's going to take a lot more than paint and great ideas. Furthermore, we have to..." He jumps from his chair looking at his watch. "Sandy! I have to call Sandy."

"Sandy can wait a few more minutes. Let me finish. I got some great experience when my best friend's parents ran a B & B. I used to help her on the week-ends when I was in high school. It's just like having guests in your house except they pay for all your trouble."

"Yeah, except these will be strangers all lit up, horny, and raising hell while we play sheriff trying to keep peace and order." He goes to leave, "Katherine, I really need to call Sandy."

"In a minute. Did you ever hear about anyone having fun at a boring B & B? Hell, no. Everyone just wanders around looking at antiques and whispering, wondering about how they can get a drink or smoke a joint. Like they're at a damn wake. No, not fun at all."

"So, let's assume the concept is workable. Who's going to do all this stuff? It's not easy running a hotel, particularly if you have no experience."

136

"Sandy and I have already talked about all that. Sandy and me...with your help."

"I thought I was going to be running a big grow house. And now you're talking about a B & B? I'm not up for changing sheets and emptying ash trays."

Katherine looks at her hand mirror and fluffs her hair. "I'm not talking about that. Nothing would really change for you. That's why getting a good job at the grow house is so necessary. We don't have to get into all this right now. There're other fish to fry and we have to get moving."

"I'm calling Sandy."

"You can call her on the way. I can't wait for you to see this place."

Chapter 9

Wealth on the Shelf

"Sandy, hold on a minute." Buddy looks up from his phone as the two ton land yacht barrels down the highway, "Shit, Katherine do you have to go so fast?"

With both hands clutching the giant wheel, she stares ahead and casually remarks, "You call this fast? This 8.2 liter V-8 can hit 115...and I'm barely going 80."

As the fence posts blur past, Buddy tells Sandy, "Honey, if I live long enough to hear from Dave, I'll call you back."

Katherine reaches into her purse and pulls out her phone. With her left palm guiding the steering wheel, she looks over the screen.

Buddy squirms in his seat as the Eldorado floats over the center line, "Katherine, *please*. You're going to get us killed."

"Good grief, you pussy." She says, scrolling her contacts list. She places the phone to her ear. "Gabe, Morning. Katherine here. You're going to need to cancel that investor meeting this morning. Changed my mind. We'll be there in about fifteen. Will tell you all about it."

It's 9:35 a.m. when Katherine fish tails through the driveway, kicking gravel along the way. Weak kneed, Buddy climbs out of the car as a cloud of dust catches up.

Parked under an aspen, Gabe is talking into his speaker when Katherine raps her cane on his window. He gets out of the car and says, "Katherine, you've really put me in a bind with our partners by walking away from this thing. They're not very happy."

"Walking away from what thing? You're the one that said two days ago that nothing had been put together. You can't walk away from nothing."

"But I thought we had an understanding."

139

"I never committed to a damn thing. It was you that put all this into motion when you read Uncle Billy's will. If your plan is so great, you shouldn't have any trouble raising money. Besides, I have this other opportunity right under my nose."

"Opportunity?"

Pointing to the massive Victorian, she says, "We've got everything we need right here."

The grand 7000 square foot, three and one half story home was constructed during the late Victorian period in 1905. At the time, it was one of the largest residences in Denver having seven bedrooms and a master suite. Situated on 2 1/2 acres, the impressive dwelling was originally built for a local magnate who helped make Denver a supply hub for regional mining operations. No expense was spared to comfortably house his wife and eight children. The clapboard mansion is adorned with details--ornamental trim, patterned shingles, barge boards, brackets and moldings, all made popular during its heyday. Dormers, cupolas, and gingerbread scrolling are set off with magnificent spruce, oak, aspens,

140

box woods, and an English garden. Blended with distinctive Arts and Crafts flair, the dwelling has twelve foot ceilings, nine fire places, oak paneling and heart of pine flooring. Ornate fixtures and lighting are accented with elegant but time worn antique furnishings and fine oriental rugs.

Gabe says, "Katherine, I don't know what you're thinking. You've got some cash value in the gold and this old home. I'd advise you to sell it."

"Hear her out, Gabe. She's got some interesting ideas. We could always revisit your plans after you've produced a Private Placement Memorandum."

Katherine smiles at Gabe and says, "Well, there you go. Let me get a cig and I'll tell you all about it as we tour of our new enterprise."

As she returns to her steaming Caddy, Gabe asks Buddy, "New enterprise? She didn't say anything about this last night. What's she talking about?"

"I had no idea until she sprung it on me this morning. Let her tell you. But yes, there're a lot of questions."

Gabe nods to the house, "Well, after you see this little fixer upper, you won't feel any better. We all know how bull headed she can be when she sets her mind to something."

They walk up the wooden steps and onto the broad, wraparound veranda. Gabe unlocks the nine-foot-high, 2-inch-thick carved oak door that is bordered with beveled glass panes and crowned with a sparkling art glass transom. As they enter the elegant foyer, a stagnant smell hits them in the face.

Katherine takes a draw from her Marlboro and makes her way to the entrance coughing. "Wait until you see this place, Buddy."

"Yeah, just wait." Gabe says, glancing at Buddy with a smirk.

"Buddy, you're going to love it. It's still a mess. Uncle Billy started to hoard a lot of stuff in his later years. It's going a little time to get all this cleaned out but it's no big deal. This place is a gem. A real gem, I tell you. Just needs some TLC and it'll be a show stopper."

As Katherine twirls around, Gabe whispers to Buddy, "There are some strange stories about this place."

"And what the hell does that mean?"

"Katherine refuses to talk about it. But let me just say, you might be getting more than you bargained for."

In the foyer, they see to their right the old parlor Uncle Billy used as a reading room. They step over the rolled-up rug and enter.

"Look, Buddy. That's where the gold hoard was stored, right under where old Polly's cage used to be."

Sunlight filters through the sheers, leveling a soft glow onto the sheet draped furniture. A two-foot stack of Wall Street Journal's are piled next to Uncle Billy's easy chair along with mounds of books, magazines, candy wrappers, and assorted junk. Sunflower seeds are scattered over the tongue and groove flooring, remnants of Polly's antics.

Yanking back the curtains, Katherine exults, " Just look at this place. Isn't it cool as shit? We need to figure out what we want to keep or throw out, everything else to Good Will."

"We'll need some shovels and a wheel barrow." Buddy whispers to Gabe.

143

"More like a dumpster," Gabe says as he walks away. "You guys knock yourselves out. I'm going to unload Uncle Billy's mailbox. I'm sure there're bills in there. I'll be in the parlor sorting through it."

Katherine walks into the dining room and fans her face. "Can we get some air in here?" She grunts as she pushes to raise the three over four paned window glued shut from multiple coats of paint. Buddy joins her to help but the tight window remains frozen.

Buddy gazes up to the ceiling. "Who's upstairs?"

"No one. I didn't hear anything." Katherine says as she moves away.

"I'm sure I heard footsteps." Buddy says.

"You heard nothing of the kind." she says peering under a sheet. "Just look at this place."

The focal point of the elegant dining room is a grand mahogany Queen Anne table for fourteen stretching the length of the 28' X 14' room. Sterling candelabras adorn the setting. At one end is an imposing matching buffet. At the other is a coal burning fireplace set off with hand painted ceramic tiles and crested with a dark green and grey veined

144

Italian marble mantle. Over the fireplace is an imposing oil painting of the original owner, Ezekiel Cauthorn, attired in his black tux with a beaver top hat and cane. Cranberry candle light lusters rest on the mantle's ends making for perfect symmetry.

"Can you imagine what kind of dinner parties they used to throw here 100 years ago? Uncle Billy tried his best to emulate when he would put on the dog for Sandy and me."

"What's down here?" Buddy asks as he twists the knob on the basement door. "It's locked."

"That's nothing. Let's move upstairs." Katherine says walking away.

Now in the master bed room, Buddy is on his knees inspecting the bubbled plaster along the baseboard. As he punches the oxidation fissures, plaster dust powders onto the rotted floor board.

Katherine looks down. "We may need a little plaster work."

In the bath, she is admiring the elaborate tile work when Buddy turns on the faucet. Pipes clang and rumble as orange water splatters the sink. Dollar signs continue to ring

145

up as he points out water stains on the ceiling, cracked plaster, chipped and faded paint, and creaking floors.

Katherine ignores his observations. "We could get a lot more for the master. It's nearly twice the size of the others. Man, I'm smelling money here."

"Well, I'm smelling a money canyon."

"I don't know why you can't see the possibilities here. We just need some creativity." Doing her best Vivian Lee, she butchers a Southern accent, "Why fiddly dee. I can see hunter green velvet swags for the Victorian drapes, just like what Miss Scarlett wore to impress Rhett."

"Oh brother. Went With The Wind revisited." Buddy sighs as he swipes at the rusted water spots on his slacks.

Gabe bursts in heaving for breath clutching a book with both hands. "Katherine, you're not going to believe this! Old Billy has some more surprises for you. Look what I found in the library."

Pulling up a small chair and clearing the debris, Gabe places his find on a game table. He carefully opens a collector's clamshell case with tooled quarter leather and guilt lettering. Nestled inside is a pristine copy of *Grapes of Wrath* in its original book cover.

"That's one of Uncle Billy's old books."

"It surely is! It looks like there are more, a dozen or so. I saw several special ones, Faulkner, Hemingway, Salinger. Christ, there're thousands of dollars worth of classics on just a couple of shelves."

"Christ? Is that in stone or papyrus?" Buddy laughs to himself.

Katherine gasps, "Gabe, you got to be shitting me. Aunt Marsha! Those are crazy Aunt Marsha's books! That's what Uncle Billy was talking about in that riddle in his will. Gold and rare books! I remember him telling me that Aunt Marsha's husband was onc of the financiers of Viking Books and had connections throughout the industry. He and his publishing buddies organized their own "Book of the Month" club. She got a couple of books a month well into the seventies."

Inspecting the Steinbeck, Gabe says, "There must be more. A lot more if she collected books for decades."

147

"Yes! I never thought about how many books she might have. After Aunt Marsha died, Uncle Billy would read to Sandy when she was a young girl. But he would never let anyone touch the books."

"Yeah, Sandy used to talk about him reading to her and all. Claims her love of books comes from that. She'll get a kick out of this."

Holding out the book, Gabe says to Buddy, "Well, let me tell you. She's going to get more than a kick. And you too Katherine. If there are many more of these, this is going to shoot up the estate value considerably. I had a client sell a Hemingway first edition at auction several years back and she got nearly ten thousand for it. I know a rare book appraiser who can help us."

"Ten thousand dollars for a book?" Buddy asks.

"Why yes, and possibly more. Condition and rarity, particularly first editions, that's what it's all about."

Gabe turns the book cover to the title page. "This is not only a first edition but it's actually signed by Steinbeck! This is incredible. The Hemingway wasn't autographed and this is in much better condition, with protector and all. It

148

looks like new. Serious collectors would kill for a book like this."

Banging her cane on the floor, Katherine exclaims, "Guys! Listen to me. Several books a month for over twenty-five years? Think about it. That's hundreds of books, not dozens. They must be in this house somewhere. We've got to find Aunt Marsha's library stash."

Buddy and Gabe look forlornly at each other as Katherine takes control.

"That's what I'm talking about!" She shouts thrusting her cane towards Gabe. Turning back to Buddy, she gives him the 'I told you so' look. "Things just seem to be getting better and better. Looks like we can pay for those plasterers with that baby."

Pulling out a clean linen handkerchief from his rear pocket, Gabe cradles the book and returns it to Uncle Billy's parlor.

By this time, Katherine and Buddy have moved to the next room. Fueled by Gabe's discovery, she ramps up her routine, taking pains to elaborate on her ever growing vision of how the old home could become a Bud and Breakfast. Everything she sees seems to reinforce her reasoning.

"We can make the master suite spectacular. Let's see, it needs brightening up with some fresh colors. God, those drapes are awful. Got to tear up the old plush carpet. It's got that fabulous tongue and groove heart of pine underneath. Just wait until Sandy sees all this. She'll have a field day bringing this place up to the 21st century. We'll just pluck another book off the shelf. Let's keep looking."

"Yeah, and we'll need another Steinbeck just to take care of the bath."

"Well, we'll just have to go find one. Let's check out the third floor. There's a room up there I haven't been in."

Buddy follows Katherine up the winding stairs. They briefly tour three rooms but the fourth is secured with a pad lock. Pulling the old ring of keys from her purse, Katherine tries each one until lock clicks and the door creaks open.

The 14' X 16' room is dark and musty. After grappling for the cord, Katherine lights a single lamp hanging in the middle of the room. Floor to ceiling shelving house Aunt Martha's collection, thousands of books collected over the

150

decades by the old librarian. In the center of the floor is a ten-foot library ladder and small reading table placed under the lamp. A piano stool provides temporary seating for book selection. A hard-bound ledger sits undisturbed since the last recorded book was "checked-out". The blacked-out window panes, pealing and cracking over the years, allow a few splintered rays to back light the fortune in books.

Soon Gabe joins Katherine and Buddy. The three, stand stunned as they study the display of books on almost every subject matter imaginable. Twenty-one branches of knowledge from A. (General Works) to Z. (Library Sciences). Books of each Branch are represented; Science, Philosophy, Religion, History, Language, Literature, etc. are carefully cataloged under the disciple of the Library of Congress, a standard used in academic and university libraries in the U.S. and around the World. Most of the books are in near mint condition with each being protected with Mylar book protectors.

Gabe turns to Katherine who has chosen *To Kill a Mockingbird*. "I can't begin to guess the value of what's in here. But it's worth a lot, a whole lot."

151

"Ha! Looks like old Aunt Marsha and Uncle Billy weren't so crazy after all. They had their own entertainment center here. He never told me about this room. Would just come forth with a new book to read every so often. It never occurred to me to ask."

After pulling the overhead light chain, Katherine ushers Buddy and Gabe into the hallway. Clicking the pad lock shut, she twirls the key ring on her finger and says in matter of fact tone, "Don't think we'll be worrying about how to pay for that Viking Series 7 Range for our new kitchen."

Chapter 10

Paranoia the Destroyer

Staring ahead, Sandy's eyes well up as she sits frozen in her arm chair. Scarlett rolls onto her back with her paws stretched skyward, beckoning a stomach scratch. As Sandy leans over to comply, a tear drop splatters into Scarlett's ear. Flipping to her feet and shaking her head, she draws a much needed laugh.

Buddy's short call with no news has only heightened her anxiety. She wonders and worries as uncertainty smothers her flickering vision of a brighter day. Bewildered with the realization that life will never be the same, she begins to accept that Marietta must be put in the rear-view mirror.

Mired in the current reality of being a mother and wife in crisis, her emotions whip lash from moment to moment. While the excitement of change excites, the fear of the unknown terrifies. She thinks back to her days as a little girl in the old house of Uncle Billy's...about strange happenings she could never explain.

She recalls when she first met Buddy, a day before the July 4th, Atlanta Peachtree Road Race. As she and her date entered McGinty's bar, there sat Buddy perched on a bar stool hustling card tricks.

Sandy remembers being amused by his antics, disarming demeanor and engaging personality. While not particularly handsome, his style commanded the moment. Wearing a blue blazer and khaki slacks, he sported the corporate uniform of the time. His paunchy belly lapped over his belt, straining the starched button down oxford shirt. Catching his prey's eyes, Buddy's shuffling cards were sent flying across the bar and onto the floor.

After studying the enticement, Sandy's date stepped in for his share of the action. Fifteen minutes later and $375 richer, Buddy had taken down another fool. Unable to hold

154

her laughter, Sandy shrugged as her furious date stormed out the bar. Buddy pulled up a stool and introduced himself. With her committed to join 32,000 others for the road race the next day, she made it a short evening. After securing her a cab, Buddy promised to be in front of McGinty's when the race passed the next morning. She assumed to have seen him for the last time.

The next morning, ten thousand bodies deep, she nervously hopped in place waiting for the grueling ordeal to begin. The stifling humidity and broiling sun had Atlanta's misery index rising when the gun shot kicked off the throng at 7 a.m. Cheering and applauding, thousands of spectators created a carnival like atmosphere lining the 6.2 mile stretch through Mid Town. The plodding, sweating, snake like form made its way from Phipps Plaza to Piedmont Park.

Halfway through the race, she vectored to the right as they approached McGinty's. To her surprise, there standing on the curb was a groggy and buzzed Buddy. With his Bloody Mary hoisted, he high fived her as she stumbled past. Squeezed against steaming hot joggers and feeling queasy, she managed a weak smile and hand slap. Now energized,

155

she pressed on, pounding the steaming asphalt mottled with cups, sweat drippings, and vomit.

Crossing the finish line, participants were drenched by fire hydrants spewing upward, helping to mollify the oppressive 91-degree heat. With her hands on hips and soaked, she patiently cooled down while waiting in line for her prized Peachtree Road Race tee shirt.

An hour later, she joined Buddy at the cool confines back at McGinty's, one of the many bars hosting thousands of jacked-up celebrants. The nation's birthday party was in full gear by ten thirty a.m. Scrunched against soured runners, she slammed her third Bud Light. Buddy chomped down his fourth celery stick and motioned toward the rear entrance. A short time later they were stoned, rolling in the cool sheets at her pitch-dark apartment.

Reminiscing about the carefree days of her youth relieved her melancholy. But today, there was little time for day dreaming. She reaches out to Taylor, interested on how her first few days of classes at West Georgia have gone. With no answer, she leaves a voice mail.

Since the boys were rousted at seven a.m., they have been put to work on their long list of chores. Barely moving in the August sun, the two bicker under Mom's watchful eye. Unable to contain a grin, she calls out, "Boys, Uncle Mack will be visiting us tonight. Do you want me to tell him that you don't help around the house?"

Zach hollers back, "What about you guys and Grandma getting stoned."

"I'd be worried about my own problems if I were you. I'm sure Uncle Mack will be really interested in your pot bust."

Returning to her study, Sandy finishes up a few stencil designs for a client's bath. After reviewing her long day, she makes a call that she has been putting off. A short time later she answers her door. The two women give a brief hug.

"I'm so glad you could make it on such short notice, Robyn."

"Me too, Sandy. I had a showing cancelled this morning right before you called. I've been wanting to call, but figured you needed some space."

157

"Oh, Robyn. You're so right. Things have gotten kind of crazy and I needed someone to talk with. We go back a long ways. You're one of the few people I totally trust."

"You've been crying?"

"I guess so, but I'm all right. I told the boys it's an allergy."

"What can I do to help?"

"For starters, you can tell me how much we can get for our house."

"You're selling your house? Where are you going?"

"This is so confidential. You can't tell anyone about what's going on. At least until we get a few things sorted out. We haven't even told our kids because a lot's still in the air. We're thinking about moving to Denver."

"I surely understand confidentiality. So, why Denver?"

"We're expecting to hear about a job offer for Buddy any time now, but I wanted to get a head start on the house. This was all in play long before the Coke layoff."

"Job opportunity? What'll he be doing?"

"Some investors are talking about him working for them out there. Can't say anymore at this time. They're in negotiations as we speak. And, my mother and I have been talking about doing something together for a while."

"Well, I don't think anyone knew you guys were heading down that road. Things really sounded much worse you know, with what people are saying and all. We're surely going to miss you. But hey, adventure is fun."

"I'm having a hard time seeing the forest for all the trees right now. Just so many things to do, like getting a house ready to sell!" Sandy feigns a light-hearted air.

After a brief walk through, the two sit down in the family room. As Sandy hands Robyn an iced tea, the shirtless boys come bolting through the front door. Dodging a blow, Jake spins around the table, knocking over a chair to block his brother's advance.

"You dick head!" cries Luke. "I'm gonna kill you."

Cutting the corner, Jake heads through the kitchen with Luke flailing from behind. As they run out the back, Sandy says, "Those are the guys I worry about, and Taylor."

"They'll be just fine. I was an army brat, you know. Don't let them throw that guilt trip bit on you. Learning to deal with change early in life is good."

"I surely hope so. Buddy and I plan to tell them all at once when he returns tomorrow."

After a lengthy back and forth, Sandy has a good fix on things, though not all positive. While in the same ball park about the selling price, they are way off on significant repairs and spruce-up costs. The home is twenty-two years old and some significant items are coming due. Having to apply four coats of paint to cover Taylor's black walls is the least of their concerns.

Soon after Robyn leaves, Sandy meets with two relocation specialists for estimates on moving their belongings from Marietta to Denver. She believes they are way out of line. Digging through the kitchen drawer, she produces a business card given months earlier by her housekeeper.

It reads: Los Hermanos Locos; Movimiento Asequible Facil; Hector Gomez 678-993-5901. She flips to the backside. The Crazy Brothers; Affordable Moving Made

Easy; Hector Gomez 678-993-5901. It's worth a try she thinks.

"Ola, Maria?"

"Si, senorita Sandy. Como esta?"

"I'm well, thank you. Say, I've got your husband's cousin's card, the mover?"

"Si, si. Hector Gomez. Muy bueno."

"Yes, uh, si. Could you have him give me a call? I'd like to talk about a possible move."

Minutes later Hector is at her door. He convinces Sandy that he is right for the assignment, particularly since they have family in Denver to help on the other end. She is thrilled to be saving thousands versus the other two companies.

A text pings: *eta 9 pm--no dinner, pls. lv @ 3 am. Love M.*

Despite the turmoil, Sandy is looking forward to having a short visit from Buddy's brother, Mack. After their father died when they both in their teens, Mack went off to join the Navy, ultimately becoming a SEAL. Since retiring, he has been traveling the world consulting on

161

"security" matters both within the U.S. government and the private sector.

Its 5:30 and the boys are hounding her for dinner. Not in the mood for cooking, she heats up leftover meatloaf, tosses a salad, and nukes some instant mashed potatoes. Joining the boys with a chardonnay, she picks away at a cluster of grapes.

Deciding to get in a quick run, Sandy abandons her drink. After slipping into her running shoes, shorts, and tank top, she grabs a water bottle and goes to the laundry room. With Scarlett springing at her feet, she fastens the leash to her collar.

Before they can leave, her phone rings. Walking into the back yard she angrily whispers through gritted teeth, "David. I made it clear that we could have no more contact. You can't call me or text me. Don't you understand?"

"Sandy, I am so sorry, but I really need to see you before you leave town."

Sandy pauses. "David, I can't. You know I can't. Why are you making this so difficult? If my family ever found out, I just don't know what I'd do. And, aren't you still married?"

"Nope. Divorce got finalized six weeks ago. She and her boyfriend are off to the races somewhere. She's out of my life so I..."

How could the woman be so stupid? She wonders before regaining her composure. "Well I am! We had a short term thing. A thing I am so ashamed of."

"But, Sandy, it was more than just a "thing". I mean you and Abby were... I just don't know. It's eating me up. I feel like I've had my soul ripped out. You just don't get it do you?"

"Yes, I do get it. That's the problem. It can't work. I've got a family and I'm up to my ass trying to get my life resettled. I can't deal with this right now." From the moment the words leave her mouth, Sandy knows she has left an opening.

"Can you deal with it later?"

She sees a plumbing contractor pull to the curb. "I've got to go. The plumber's here for a problem." With a firm voice, she looks into her phone, "Listen to me. I don't know

163

any other way to say this. Whatever there was between us is over. Do you hear? Over!"

"But Sandy, I..."

"That's it David. No more discussion. Please lose my number as I will no longer acknowledge any texts or calls. I'm sorry. Good luck and good bye."

Thirty minutes later she and Scarlett try again to get their abbreviated run in before darkness settles. Her thoughts juggle as the two make their way up the mountain. David's call and confession has only compounded the degree of complexity she must confront.

Scarlet's tongue dangles as she pants from exhaustion, slowly loping behind Sandy on the path of hardened clay and pine needles. The summer sun is setting behind clouds when they return. Knowing Mack's punctuality, she rushes through her shower to make it down stairs just as the doorbell rings. After a hug and a kiss on the cheek, she says, "Mack, I'm so happy to see you! Let me take your bag."

"Good to see you too, gal." He holds up his small Koskin duffel. "I'm fine, thanks. I travel light you know. I wasn't sure I could swing the visit until the last moment. Hope I'm not barging in on anything."

As her eyes drop down and to the left, she says, "No, no. It's fine."

"So Buddy's in Denver?" Mack asks with a lightened tone.

Her face brightens as she looks back to his face. "Yes. I'll tell you all about that. He sends his regards. Said he'd catch you next time. Come sit down. Can I offer you anything to eat? A beer?"

"No thanks, maybe a water later."

Not wanting to be within earshot of the boys, Sandy ushers Mack into the family room and asks, "So where are you off to now, big guy?"

"You already know the answer to that." He says with a sly grin.

"I was hoping that you'd tell me you were giving a sermon somewhere safe. We worry about you so. You could not possibly stay in as much danger as I can imagine."

"Let's just say I like to take good care of myself. So how's everything? You, Buddy, and the kids?"

Sandy hesitates and looks away. "There's been a lot going on, Mack."

For the next twenty minutes, she unburdens the multitude of crises that have befallen the family, but not a hint of her indiscretions. Mack sits patiently as she goes through every detail of the week's train wreck and the uncertainties that lie ahead. Having almost run out of breath, Sandy stops in mid sentence. "Mack, you haven't said anything. I'm so sorry I threw up all this crap on you."

"Good God, Sandy. I must admit the stars seem out of alignment for you guys. But I'm pretty much a realist. You and Buddy will pull out of all this. And, what can I say about Katherine? In her younger days, she could probably have qualified as a SEAL. So I don't have much concern in that regard. I haven't spent much time around Taylor, but I think she's out of my league." As he pauses, Sandy finishes his thought.

"The boys?"

"They have my attention."

"Oh, Mack. They worship you. Ever since you took them on that survivor trip through the Everglades. So funny.

Buddy and I still laugh about some of those stories. They call you Uncle Rambo."

"I assume they're upstairs?"

"Can't you hear that thumping? I keep telling them they're grounded. I've tried to ban all their electronics. Some good that's done."

"I'll have that water now if you don't mind."

Sandy returns with the water and Mack gives her a comforting squeeze and pat on the back. "Good night." he says. "I'll spend more time on my next visit." He turns to follow the sounds up stairs. The decibel level drops to zero a minute later.

The thought of Uncle Mack counseling the boys brings much needed levity to the long day of uncertainty. Sandy is slurping on a fruit smoothie at the kitchen table when her phone jingles. The call from Buddy comes at last.

Hours later, still restless and awake, she hears the grandfather clock bong three times. Standing at her window she watches as the black Chevy Tahoe backs from the driveway disappearing into the darkness.

Chapter 11

Should Old Acquaintance Be Forgot

"Honey, I'm so sorry I couldn't talk more last night. Katherine wouldn't leave me alone with all that's on her mind. Does she ever tire?"

Sandy laughs, "You're not telling me anything. All this family commotion seems to have her really pumped. You should have seen her in her prime."

"Sure sorry I missed that. So how's Mack?"

"Great as always but never talks much, particularly about what he's up to. He spent most his time with the boys. Was very interested in their pot bust. I don't know what he said to them but they seem subdued today."

"That's hilarious. I think they're terrified of him."

"They are! Saw him leave in the middle of the night. I was still awake mulling over all this good news coming at once, right on the heels of our cratered life in Marietta. I'm stunned about the book discovery. Any idea as to how much it's all going to end up being?"

"Gabe is working with a coin guy and rare book appraiser for estimates and recommendations on how to liquidate. But it looks like the total will be between two and two and a half million dollars, split two ways."

"I don't know what to say. I could never imagine such a thing."

"Who could? Especially the rare book hoard."

"I was recalling when Uncle Billy would read to me. He always wore white gloves. Told me he was afraid of the book worms. And I believed him! He read *Gone With the Wind* in its entirety to me. I hated sitting upright at the table while he carefully turned each page, but I relished every word."

"It's quite a windfall, for sure. So, what do you think about Katherine's B & B idea? You up for making that kind of commitment?"

"Mother went into some of her ideas with me when she was here. I was skeptical at first with the old house and all. But now with the inheritance, it makes more sense. I really believe there's a market for what she wants to do. And what do you think about the grow house job?"

"Looks like it might be pretty cool. Randy seems to be a nice dude. He'd be taking me under his wings. Said the $18 an hour was just to start, to appease his partners."

"That is so good to hear. When does he want you to start?"

"I didn't accept. Wanted to run it by you first but he wants me right away. I told him I needed to come home for a few days. So maybe when I return. I'm spending the afternoon at Colorado Medicinal getting a more detailed orientation. After words, Randy's having me over to his home grilling out with some of the co-workers."

"Honey, that old house scared me as a child. I saw some strange things. And, I could never play in the basement. Uncle Billy kept it locked."

"Naw. You know how kid's imaginations are. Probably nothing at all."

170

"Maybe so but it gave me the willies. Mother refused to acknowledge anything I said. So how 'bout you two? You cool? We can't make this commitment if you'll be at each other's throats all the time."

"Yeah, maybe so. With all to be done, she's not being her normal pain in the ass. She's anxious to get us out here. For once she appears to be concerned about someone other than herself. She carries a lot of guilt about how she delegated your raising."

"But Mother's still Mother and she's not going to change."

"I know. She still nips at me. Really pisses me off."

Sandy laughs, "She's an equal opportunity pisser offer."

"I think she's got some good ideas about the B & B, if she doesn't try turning it into the Taj Mahal. I'm afraid it's going to cost a lot more to remodel than she thinks."

"After what we have to do with our home to get us market ready, I'm sure you're right. I'll be able to help with my frugality. She respects my ideas and our tastes are similar."

After rambling through all the news, there's a pause. Sandy breaks the silence. "Well, Honey, if you accept, this will all be set in motion."

"I know. All of a sudden, a whole lot of things are going our way. I think we'll be fine. In fact, I'm getting excited about all this."

"Yes, it's going to be great. I just feel it. A new beginning for all of us."

"Okay then, I'll accept the position tonight."

Seeing Buddy at the North Concourse curb side, Sandy flashes her lights before working her way between cars. He tosses his carryon into the back, jumps in and gives her a kiss. The traffic to Marietta is inconsequential they immerse themselves in dialog rehearsing their story for their family and friends.

The "secret job" in Denver has been in the works long before the Coke layoffs. There would be no mention of the inheritance to anyone, especially the children. The Rothstein deal hurt but their exposure was small. For some time now, Sandy has wished to be closer to her mother and have been

172

considering a Bed & Breakfast in Katherine's old Victorian. Denver was her childhood home. The whole family loves skiing. Taylor's in college and the boys would finish their senior year in Denver.

"Ha! I just love the part about you always wanting to be close to your mother. And the skiing bit." Buddy jokes.

"Oh, I remember the last time you tried skiing. You broke your collar bone while getting lessons on the kiddy slope."

"That ended that little avocation."

"But mostly this all sounds fairly believable, don't you think?"

"Like shooting the barn with the arrow and drawing a target around it."

Sandy throws up her right palm and Buddy completes the high five.

"Sure you can do all this on your own with me going back to Denver so soon?"

"Yes, of course. You need to get to work and I can handle the boys, particularly since Uncle Mack jerked a knot in their tails."

173

"With us in agreement on our press release, we'd better get to the kids right away."

Sandy reaches for her phone. "Let me try Taylor again. We'll meet her for dinner tonight."

Upon approaching Marietta, Buddy spots a Quik Trip convenience store. "Honey, can you pull over there for a minute? I have to race like a piss horse."

"Your too much. I should probably fill-up while we're here. Great to see the prices going down."

Sandy glides behind a beat up Ford F-150. An open rear window panel reveals a crackled Confederate flag decal. Through the hole juts the head of a black lab. A bent coat hanger radio antenna channels Blake Sheldon crooning *Some Beach Some Where*.

Buddy leaps out, connects the pump and sprints to the Men's room.

Sandy takes a call from Robyn Reese. As they talk, she curiously watches as a large woman rolls from the cab, lights a cigarette and begins pumping gas.

Idling with the A.C. on high, she and Robyn become engrossed in a discussion over the home listing, oblivious to the developing chaos.

Buddy, having finished his jaunt to the toilet, is in line to pay for a Coke Zero and a Little Debbie Honey Bun. Seeing the Georgia Scratcher lottery ad on the counter, he buys a ticket with computer generated numbers. "Feeling lucky." he declares out loud. After paying up, he places the ticket in his pocket and bites open the Honey Bun package.

Sauntering to the rear of the Explorer, he stuffs the last of the gooey morsel into his cheeks, licking the frosting from his fingers. He pops the top of his Coke Zero and takes a big gulp.

"Well, hi dere, lil' feller!" the gruff voice sounds from behind.

With a Virginia Slims dangling from her lips and posing a defiant arabesque, is Rheema Kay Tannyhill. After flicking the ashes, she tosses back her long mousy hair and grins at Buddy.

The super plus Levi's strain to contain while a rose chiffon baby doll tank drapes around the midriff. Her melon-sized breasts float downward with no hint of separation. Bear claw feet flare from the tattered jean bell bottoms, flattening the glittering silver sport slides. The recent Pretty In Pink polka dot mani-pedi accents her Wal-Mart day attire.

With a frozen mouthful of cola and honey bun, Buddy stiffens. A high-pitched voice rings out. "Jesus Christ! If it ain't ole what's his name! Holy shit. Whazzup, dude?"

As Sandy and Robyn continue their conversation, Buddy does half squats pointing to his wife in the car. "Hey, guys, uh, good to see you." Buddy stammers as he looks towards Sandy, who is engrossed with Robyn.

After cramming half his body through the truck window, Sport begins to violently bark. Buddy impulsively pulls the Scratcher ticket from his pocket and hands it to Rheema Kay. "Here, take this and good luck!" Buddy rocks his head sideways towards Sandy.

Rheema Kay drags on her cigarette and studies the ticket. As Sport goes nuclear, Buddy springs up and down. "Please, Rheema Kay."

She glances over to Sandy and smashes the butt onto the pump casing. "That's mighty kind of ya, lil feller. You know where to find me if you ever need some lovin'. You take care now."

Eddie bangs his fist on the truck bed and cackles, "Barely done known who you was without that silly ass pink hat. You done healed up real nice."

After a wink and an underhanded wave, Rheema Kay hoists herself into the cab. Eddie springs in and gives a thumbs up as the sputtering truck pulls away.

Buddy opens the passenger door and returns to his seat. "What was that all about? You know those people?" Sandy asks.

"No, not really. Uh... Had the little guy out a while back to work on the sprinkler system."

"Well, he's going to need more than sprinklers. Did you see her smoking and pumping gas? She could've blown us all to pieces. Strange looking characters."

"Didn't notice." Buddy slinks down as flashbacks of the worst 24 hours of his life rifle through his brain.

Sandy hits speed dial. "Let me try Taylor again. You still have some icing on your chin."

Having missed the sunrise, Taylor snuggles a sand dune as the gentle lapping Gulf waves create nature's perfect sound machine. Fast asleep and crouched in a fetal position, her urine-soaked jorts cuff her ankles. Curious fire ants trail aimlessly across the layer of sparkling sand on her torso. She unconsciously flinches at every injection of venom.

From several feet away, the Teen Witch ring tone blares from deep in her purse:

I'm king and they know it
When I snap my fingers everybody says show it
I'm hot and you're not
But if you want to hang with me I'll give you a shot
Top That. Top That...

Shocked into consciousness, Taylor crawls to the rapping and upends the contents of her purse onto the mound of fire ants. *Top That. Top That* is on its last cycle as she instinctively answers, "Hello?"

"Taylor, did I wake you? It's nearly eleven."

"Huh? I guess so. No. Uh. Mom? Ohhhh." the response trails off.

"Taylor, I can barely hear you. What's going on and why aren't you in class?"

"I'm in the bathroom at school, thick from some bad food."

"Bad food? Do you need to see a doctor?"

"No, no. I'm fine. Got some bad shushi, I think. I have to go. Got to get back to class. Later, Mom."

"Shushi? Wait! Dad and I have to meet with you this afternoon. Can you be at the Cracker Barrel in Bremen at five?"

"You're what? Today? No. That won't work. I'm too busy...schudying and all."

"Schudying? Shushi? Are you sure you're okay? You don't sound okay."

"Yeah, yeah. Mom, that can't happen. We have all kinds of shuff, uh, stuff going on. I'm in the middle of my classes. Okay?"

"What's the big deal, Taylor? We'll all go to dinner. Won't take more than an hour. And you can get back to your schudying. We have serious family matters to discuss."

"Burp. Cracker Barrel? I don't feel much like eating. I'm stu-dy-ing around the clock. I'm jush too busy. Why can't you tell me now?"

As a Harley rumbles in the background, Sandy firms up her position. "Listen to me young lady, this can't be done over the phone. We'll see you this afternoon at five. Goodbye."

Chapter 12

Would You Mind Stepping Out of the Car?

"Shit!" Taylor hisses, seconds before spewing last night's meatball sub onto the contents of her purse. Overcome with nausea, she hurriedly tosses handfuls of sandy glop back into her denim rope bag. As the homeless ants take vengeance, she claws at her midriff and struggles to her feet.

After jerking up her gritty wet cut offs, she grabs her bag and rambles through the dunes and sea oats towards the beach house. Reaching the second landing, she sees Sammy passed out across the sofa. After splashing water in his face and pounding on his back, Taylor steers his weaving form out the house and into the van. Finding the keys in the ignition, she scratches off from the oyster shell driveway.

An hour up the road, Sammy moans against the window, "Where the fuck are we?"

"Heading back to Carrolton. Are you alive?"

"Carrolton? What about the beach? Didn't we just get there?"

"Yeah, I missed the sunrise. Have to meet with my parents about some stupid family crisis."

"You're what? Why am I coming? They can't see me."

"You'll just drop me off and drive the van back to the beach to get the others. Y'all will still have a day and a half. Lucky bastards."

Producing a Zip Loc from beneath the seat, Sammy jokes, "Ha, wait until they find out I have their weed. And the mother fucking cooler too!"

"Great. Roll us one and see if there's another Mikes in there. Boy are they going to be pissed."

"Too bad, so sad." Sammy says as he thumbs some buds into a cigarette paper.

Pulling up Google Maps Taylor declares, "There's a Wal-Mart up the road in Eufaula. We can get something to eat...and itch cream for these God damned ant bites." After a

182

hit from Sammy's joint, she cools her throat with her third Mike's Hard Lemonade.

Sammy pops *Nasty Freestyle* into the player and cranks it up. T-Wayne has them rocking as they cross the Alabama line.

An hour later sheer terror erupts. Pounding the steering wheel, Taylor screeches at the blue light flashing in the rear-view mirror. "God damn it! Fuck, fuck, fuck! Get rid of that shit, Sammy! Now!" Sammy has lunch early and gobbling down the contents of the Zip Loc.

T-Wayne continues as she pulls to a stop.

Homie I be making hits.

I'm the rap Derek Jeter.

Let your bitch ride on me.

Like she was on a feeder.

If the pussy ain't good

Then I probably won't feed her.

As Taylor smashes at the control panel with her palm, a patrolman raps on her window.

Its 98 degrees when the Ford Explorer pulls into the sweltering old town of Eufaula, Alabama. The courthouse clock chimes five p.m. as traffic builds from the county workers making their way home. Buddy and Sandy drive through downtown, taking a left onto E. Barbour Street. After several blocks, they come upon the Municipal Court complex. A few doors down they find the law offices of Jenkins, Topley, and Johnson, one of several large antebellum mansions that house the offices of local attorneys. Acorns crunch under their hot tires as they glide into a shady parking spot next to an ancient hanging water oak. Across the street a bail bondsman's neon flashes; *Open 24 Hours*.

Sandy points to a crimson red GMC Denali with a prestige plate: 1CALLYALL. "That must be his car there."

"Yeah, that's him. We're right on time. Surely hope he's as good as Greg claims."

"This is a real mess. God only knows what we're getting into." Sandy says as she enters the smothering heat.

The wary visitors trudge up the stairs to the second floor of the 1846 Sand Hills Cottage Greek Revival home.

184

Pink knock-out roses and white gardenias frame the stairway. Their pungent aromas linger in the thick, humid air. Sandy and Buddy cross the veranda and enter the formal law office setting and into the frigid ante chamber.

Buddy huffs, dabbing his forehead with a wadded pad of McDonalds' napkins, taking in the icy cold air coursing through the vents. After introductions, the receptionist ushers them into the elegant and reserved waiting room. Sandy studies the Audubon prints that adorn the fourteen foot high walls.

After fifteen minutes, a large figure appears. Near breathless with beads of sweat streaking down his puffy jowls, the man stands well over six feet and pushes 300 pounds. Coatless, his white collared Charvet blue poplin dress shirt chokes at the neck with an overlapping roll of flesh. Saddlebags of sweat circle beneath his trunk like arms. The white French cuffs are clasped together with quarter-sized, gold elephant links. Two-inch black and white herring bone checkered suspenders stretch over his girth, attaching to his pin striped Armani trousers that break over his sparkling Anthony Cleverley dress shoes.

185

A stringy slick comb over is plastered across his mottled and freckled head. The bulbous, thread veined nose hints at football and alcohol abuse. What's left of an unlit eight inch 60 gage El Presidente cigar is chomped between his toothy grin.

His blue eyes skirt all over Sandy's body as he approaches. Removing the stubby cigar from his wet lips, he clasps her outstretched hand and delivers a submissive bow. "Why good afternoon, Mrs. Henderson. J. Calhoun Jenkins at your service. Such a pleasure to meet you. Welcome to Eufaula."

Feeling as though she'd just been undressed, Sandy smiles uneasily and says, "Thank you, Mr. Calhoun. Sorry I can't say it's good to be here." After a short squeeze of his hand, she backs away from the incongruent scents of Old Spice and stale cigar.

"Why yes, yes, of course. I certainly understand. Please feel free to call me J.C. All my friends do." With a gratuitous nod towards Buddy, he drawls, "And you also, Mr. Henderson."

Turning back to Sandy, "My apologies for the tardiness. Was down the street getting briefed on your daughter's situation."

A buxom paralegal leads them into the adjoining conference room and serves up cold bottles of water. Buddy bristles as the attorney unabashedly fawns over Sandy while making the obligatory Southern small talk.

After downing his water, Buddy interrupts, "Greg Ashcroft highly recommended you. Said you were the best defense attorney in south Alabama."

Seated at the end of the fifteen-foot mahogany conference table, J.C. removes the unlit soggy cigar stub and rests it gently in the Waterford ashtray. He pinches a gooey mush of tobacco from his tongue. After a brief inspection, he rolls it between his fingers and flicks the glob to the floor. He takes a swig of water and bellows a laugh, "Best in south Alabama? I'll have you know, I'm the best in the country! Haven't talked with that little scoundrel in a while. Think I'll have some fun with this. You know we played football together at Bama?"

Expressionless, Buddy says, "Roll Tide. Now can we get on with this?"

"Yes, of course." he says looking at his notes. "Folks, your daughter...uh, Taylor, is it? She seems to have gotten herself into somewhat of a situation here."

Sandy asks, "For speeding?"

Casting a serious look, he says, "I'm afraid it's quite more involved. The county clerk informs me she's up against a number of serious charges, several Class C misdemeanors. And, it gets worse. Three Class B felonies. Charges could get added depending upon her priors and circumstances. She's in a holding cell at the moment being processed." He pulls a handkerchief from his pocket and blots his forehead.

"My God! This can't be happening? What did she do? She just told us the speeding bit when she called. We came as fast as we could."

Miffed at his dismissal, Buddy relocates to the other side of the conference table and takes a seat next to Sandy.

Donning his black bone reading glasses, the attorney snaps open his attaché and pulls out his legal pad. After flipping over several pages of notes, he peers over the lenses and says to her breasts, "I'm afraid it's bad...rather bad indeed."

The Henderson's sit stunned as the list of charges are read: Driving while under the influence, speeding 22 M.P.H. over the posted limit, operating a vehicle with a suspended license, under age possession of alcohol, and possession of marijuana greater than an ounce.

And, then it gets serious. Tucked into the empty tire well of the van, the officers had found a compressed tank of anhydrous ammonia, the key ingredient for the manufacture of Crystal Meth. Three plus ounces of pot is stuffed under the passenger seat. Scattered about are several burned-down roaches, sprinkles of buds and a small bong. A container of OxyContin prescribed to a Mrs. Charlotte Cosgrove of Marietta, GA is in the glove box. To top off the find, a loaded .40 Cal. Glock is located between the third-row seats. Upon conviction, all Class B felonies with a potential five to twenty years sentencing. Her bail is set at $20,000.

Sandy's hand quivers as she takes notes of the charges. Looking at the list, she explodes, "Meth? Pot? Narcotics? Stoned and speeding? Possession? A gun for Christ's sake!

Has she lost her mind? And what's she doing with Aunt Charlotte's meds? What in God's name was she doing down here in the first place? She's supposed to be in school. Damn it! I knew she was covering up something when I tried to get our dinner scheduled for tonight."

Buddy asks the attorney, "And, whose car was she driving?"

He turns a page of his legal pad. "Here it is. The van is registered to a Mr. Robert Patrick James of Carrolton, Ga. It seems his brother Samuel was a passenger with her."

Sandy pounds her fist on the table. "That son of a bitch, Sammy James! Just what's he doing down here? He moved to Chicago...or so I thought." As she bolts upright, Buddy grips her arm and guides her back into her chair.

The attorney continues, "He's still in the hospital. Seems as though he ingested a considerable amount of pot before the police got to him. Had to pump his stomach. I understand he's not doing too well at the moment. He'll have most of the same charges. He does not have representation as of yet. The ammonia thing is tricky. It has to be proven to be linked to Meth production. If so, with any priors along those

190

lines, it's very serious. As for the unregistered and loaded firearm, I don't think I need to tell you how bad that looks, particularly with the drugs and all. Don't know about this James fellow. What he's been up to and all. Just can't say, but the more charges proven to be linked to him alone, the better for your daughter. As far as her culpability, the fact that the car is registered in his brother's name is a big deal with all the contents discovered. Nevertheless, in the eyes of the law, she's as guilty as he is. We should probably talk about her bail."

Sandy leaps from her seat. "Bail? Are you kidding me? Just let her little fanny stew in the pen for a while. She's planned all this behind our backs. And those pills. Those girls must have taken them from Melissa's aunt. From her death bed no less! Just wait 'till I get my hands on her."

"Let me tell you, Mr. and Mrs. Henderson. She'll have quite the experience. Our jail is in the midst of an extensive renovation. Let's just say it's not a very hospitable place at the moment."

"What does that mean?" Buddy asks.

"They're having to use their holding cells not only for processing, but short term stays. She'll be thrown in with all sorts of unsavory characters in various stages of sobriety."

Buddy asks, "Will she be in any danger? Wouldn't it make more sense to just bail her out and head back to Marietta tonight, even if it's late?"

"She should be fine, but she won't get much sleep. That I can assure. As for bailing her out, it's up to you."

Sandy crackles and twists her empty water bottle with both hands as she circles the conference table. "I want her to suffer a little bit. Besides, I don't think I could take being with her in a car right now for three hours. It's that damn Sammy, I tell you. He's at the bottom of all this. Stupid. Stupid. I've told her a thousand times."

"So, Mr. Jenkins, how do you see all this coming down? We don't have a whole lot of experience with this kind of stuff. Aside from punishing Taylor in the slammer, is there any reason for us to stay over?" Buddy catches the irony and strikes a quick glance Sandy's way. Falling back into her chair, she bounces her head repeatedly against the rest.

J. Calhoun Jenkins retrieves his gooey cigar from the ashtray and chomps it into the corner of his mouth. Standing, he stuffs his brief case with papers and says, "I suggest you stay 'til tomorrow. It'll give me time to make a few calls. I've got my girl researching these brothers to see if they have rap sheets. Hope to see the prosecutor at the club tonight. Possibly I can get that bail reduced for you. And maybe get the right judge on this. Come by the office tomorrow at eleven and I should know more. It'll take two to three hours to get her bailed out, all the processing stuff, you know. Assuming I am retained, I would like to visit with her around ten in the morning. I would prefer doing this alone."

Looking at Sandy, Buddy sighs, "I guess we have little choice."

"So we should get you on the road by mid afternoon. She'll likely have to return later for her court date and sentencing. I'll have a lot of work to do between now and then to get some of these charges reduced, or possibly dismissed."

"I'm sorry, Mr. Jenkins but could we get some feel as to what we're looking at? Is she going to prison?"

193

"A lot depends upon any priors, her friend's background and so forth. I'll paint the picture real good for her tomorrow. It will mostly depend upon how she cooperates." After a quick glance at his Rolex, he says, "I apologize, but I have an engagement and must be getting along."

Before they can respond, the attorney adds, "You should know that I require a $5000 retainer for cases such as this. It's going to be expensive to manage through the process. She's in a heap of trouble, bless her heart."

"I'll bless her little heart all right." Sandy mocks the Southern put down.

The attorney turns towards the door, signaling the meeting's end. "If I may make a suggestion. There's a nice Quality Inn just a couple of blocks down the street, near some decent restaurants. Downtown has done a real nice clean-up. They have a great complimentary breakfast buffet. The sausage gravy and biscuits are to die for. Have fresh sliced local tomatoes too." He snaps a suspender and guffaws, "Damn, making myself hungry."

He offers Sandy his business card. "Use my name and get a free dessert."

Reading the card, Sandy murmurs, "Priors? No. Her record is pretty clean except for her points. Got her license revoked for three months. She only had another week or two to go."

Buddy is thinking about the biscuits and gravy when he finally processes what he was just told. "Excuse me. Did you just say this is going to cost us twenty-five thousand dollars?"

"Not exactly. Well, not at this moment anyway. The bail seems a bit excessive so I should be able to get that reduced. I'll know more by tomorrow. Of course, you'll get your money back less expenses."

Buddy looks at Sandy and says, "I just don't know where we're going to get that kind of money right now."

J.C. flashes his toothy smile, shakes their hands and says, "No need to worry about the money. My firm and the bail bonds people take credit cards."

"Well, I feel so fucking much better." Buddy growls.

"I understand but there's a lot to consider here, Mr. Henderson." He gives a wry smile and tilts his head upwards and thrusts out his chest. "It mostly rests with the judge, you know. Or rather that I know." He chuckles at his overbearing confidence.

Sandy looks out the window. "I feel like getting in the car and going home. Let her get her own little ass out of this mess."

"I do understand your frustration, ma'am. A lot of dynamics in play that we will not know about until we get into the details of the case. And, since Greg put you in touch, I'll apply a 10% referral discount for my retainer." Glancing again at his watch, J.C. asks, "Do we have an agreement to proceed?"

Buddy and Sandy both nod in the affirmative.

"Mighty fine." the attorney says as he shakes their hands. He picks up his attaché and points to the exit. "So good to have met you both and hope you have a nice stay in our wonderful little town. We'll have the paperwork for our contract ready in the morning. Sally Sue will show you out. Enjoy your evening." 1CALLYALL leaves the building.

A heavy-set black girl squeezes into a space on the bench and says, "I'm Shanice. You don't look like you're from around these parts."

Taylor passively greets with flipped fingers "Taylor. No. Live in Georgia."

"So whatchu here for, girl?"

She shifts a few inches to the side and says her with eyes to the floor. "Nothing much, speeding and some pot."

"Ha. Just wait 'til they're done processing. They'll hang all kinds of shit on your ass."

Taylor makes eye contact and asks, "So how long's that going to take? I've already been in this stinky place for like forever." She notices other detainees listening to their conversation.

Shanice says with a grin, "Better chill, Honey. My baby sister was in here for almost three days. The old jail's a shit hole. Being worked on so they be short lotsa of cells."

"Three days? I can't handle much more of this. My parents are coming sometime soon."

"Things don't move fast down here so don't get your hopes up." As Taylor claws at her pocked stomach, she asks,

"What's wrong with you? You gots the measles or sumpin?"

"No. Fire ants."

"Christ, did you sleep on a bed of them fuckers?"

"Sort, of." Taylor drops her head and says, "Listen Shanice, I'm not feeling too well so if you don't..."

Shanice nudges her with her elbow and nods across the cell. "Look at that bitch! Laughing and carrying on."

Taylor looks up. "Who?"

Shanice points her finger. "Cassie. That skinny white bitch. The one with no tits. She stole my drop. Went over to get it and caught her blowing my boyfriend...right there on the front porch swing."

Taylor sees a flip-off directed her way from across the crowded room."My God. What did you do?" she asks, staring at the taunt.

Shanice stands and returns the gesture with two birds thrust into the air. "Tumped their asses over. Shoulda seen her gag. Bitch almost choked herself."

Taylor's laughter is halted as the target of ridicule pushes to her feet and walks over. Entering her space, Cassie says to Shanice, "You got something to say, cunt?"

"So what if I do? Fuck you, whore."

Cassie gets into her face. "Why'd you torch my ride?"

Shanice pushes Cassie backwards. "Maybe I did and maybe I didn't. And, *if* I done it, was cause you done stole my stash."

Regaining her balance, Cassis defiantly exclaims. "I no such thing, Miss Pyro. You burned up your shit. I ain't had nothing to do with it."

Shanice advances, "You better give it up or I'm gonna rip your scrawny ass apart."

Cassie shoves Shanice between her breasts and laughs, "You fool. Bobby had it on him when I picked him up. Said he was keeping it safe for you. It was him that left it in the car while we uh,...you know."

"You be lying, you skank." Responding to Cassie's shove, Shanice takes a swing and they become entangled ripping at each other's hair. Taylor flails backwards when an elbow crunches into her nose. As the women wrestle on the concrete floor, two deputies rush in and break up the fray.

Hours later Taylor is curled up in the corner of the room when Shanice squats next to her. "Sorry 'bout your face, girl."

Taylor lifts her head from the concrete, exposing the bloody tissues jutting from her swollen nose. "It's you again." She says with a tone of finality.

Looking across the room to her adversary who is scrunched in the corner, Shanice says, "Yeah, they made us promise to behave or they were going to put us together in one of them old cells with no A.C."

"Look, I'm really, really tired and my nose hurts. It's late and I have to get some sleep."

Sitting against the wall, Shanice begins to rant, "Mother fucker. Never trusted that crim. But I done never thought he'd carp my $500 drop."

"Drop?" Taylor realizes she has made a big mistake by engaging.

"Drop...my pick-up place. The jofo musta found out about it. I thought he done looked goofy when I spotted him checkin' me out behind the DQ. Don't likes to admit it, but I think that boofer's tellin' the truth. Good thing it was for mamma. She'll cut me some slack...I hopes."

"The drugs were for your mother?" Taylor asks, not really caring about the answer.

"It's confuzzling. Anyway, I can score some more. Have a good trapper. Some dudes up in West Georgia cook some mean White Lady and Crunk."

"What?"

"Smack. You know...heroin and meth. They done 'bout cornered the market round here. Brothers they say. Call themselves the James Gang. I can get you some. It's pricy, but it's the bomb."

Taylor grabs her by the arm. "James Gang? Wait a minute. West Georgia? It wouldn't be outside Carrolton, would it?" Shanice's eyes widen as she stands and backs away. "Yeah, maybe, not sure. You didn't hear nothin' from me. Forget we done met. Catch my drift?" Shanice moves to the far side of the holding cell squats against the wall.

Taylor's throbbing nose, cold hard floor and intermittent groans portend a fitful night. As she picks at her festering ant bites, she takes in Shanice's revelation and fumes, *Why those mother fuckers.*

An August thunder storm is breaking Saturday afternoon when Sandy and Buddy leave the law offices of J. Calhoun Jenkins. With the legal briefing, complete and paperwork signed, Buddy pays the $4500 "discounted" retainer fee and the newly reduced Bail Bond of "only" $10,000. Calls to Visa and Discover had gotten their maximums increased.

Lightning cracks through the hovering black clouds sending a fiery bolt into a nearby park. Pelted with marble sized droplets of rain, Buddy and Sandy run the two blocks of steaming sidewalks to the Municipal Jail. After passing through the revolving doors and clearing security, they fidget in the cramped and steamy visitor's area.

Lead by a female deputy, Taylor shuffles into the detaining room where her cable ties are snipped. With head lowered, her matted black hair strings down her sullen face. Tissues wicked with dried blood jut from her nostrils. A metallic teardrop bikini halter top can be traced through the crocheted cover-up. Slicing into her seams, her undersized jorts provide little cover. With legs crossed, she slaps the Tory Burch sandal blankly staring at the remnants of her pedicure. After signing off on the personal inventory list, Taylor stuffs her belongings into her clutch and strolls through the buzzing doors.

With the expenses having been settled and Taylor free on bail, the Henderson's turn northward leaving Eufaula behind. Nothing is said as the Explorer winds through the Alabama back country roads. After several hours, they blow by the Hwy 27 exit to Carrolton.

Taylor bellows from the back seat, "Where're you taking me? That's my exit we just passed!"

"You think we're stupid, don't you?" Sandy coldly responds.

"What do you mean?"

"I called the administration yesterday. They told me about you cutting the last three days of classes of your first week no less. We're partitioning to get your tuition back."

"That's not fair! You can't do this to me! This is kid napping!"

Buddy looks over his shoulder. "Why don't you call the police?"

It is nearly seven p.m. when they arrive home. Buddy calls up the stairs, "Boys! Come down. We've got a family discussion."

"You're telling them about me?"

"It's not always about you, Taylor." She follows, "Boys! Get down here now!"

Entering the room, Jake sees Taylor and laughs, "Hi Sis. You look like you spent the night in a gorilla cage. What happened to your nose?"

"Screw you."

"Boys, Taylor, sit down. We've got something to discuss."

"I've got to take a bath, Mom."

"Well, that's one thing we agree on. Please sit at the end of the table, Taylor."

Ordering the children to keep their questions until they have finished, Buddy and Sandy take the next ten minutes to lay out their vision for the family's move to

Denver. Hoping their children will buy the story, they open the floor for discussion.

Taylor is the first to respond. "What am I going to do in Denver? It sucks out there."

Buddy responds, "If you're lucky, you'll be doing what your parole officer says."

"Daddy, you said you weren't going to talk about that."

"I didn't promise anything. The court ruling will affect us all. We're paying a fortune for an attorney but you just may be going to Wetumpka."

"Wetumpka?"

"Yeah, that's where the Julia Tutwiler prison for women is located."

"Mom, Daddy. You can't let them do this to me!"

Sandy unloads, "You're the one that cut classes and made the trip to Panama City Beach. What about Sammy supposedly moving to Chicago? And stealing Mrs. Cosgrove's drugs, for Christ's sake! And the B.S. about wanting to be a nurse? You and your girl friends had this planned all along. Mr. Jenkins filled us in on your little party house at the James brothers."

"He can't do that! It's privileged information. And, it was Becky who borrowed the drugs."

"Privileged information? Borrowed drugs? When you start to pay the legal bills, then you can have some privileges. It looks like your little pal and his brothers will be doing some serious time. Hopefully, Mr. One Call Y'all can hang them for all the crap they found in the car. To have any chance of staying out of jail, you're going to have to sing about their organized crime ring."

Zack points to Taylor. "I knew he didn't go to Chicago! Sweet Sammy Sales got busted again! Ha, ha, ha!"

"You're all a bunch of hypocrites! What about your pot busts?"

"Taylor, you're mixed up with a redneck drug cartel that runs a meth lab. If I have to explain the difference, then you're going to enjoy that first shower at Tutwiler."

Taylor rushes from the room crying. "Daddy! You're so mean!"

Sandy shakes her head and says, "Drama dame can turn those tears on and off like a spigot." She directs herself to the boys who are snickering, "You guys think this is so funny? At the minimum, you'll have a ton of community service in Denver. And in your spare time you'll be flipping burgers to pay back your legal fees and court fines."

As their shoulders slump, she tightens the noose. "And I think Uncle Mack has some plans for you too."

Chapter 13

M-Day Minus Two

Sandy is in the front yard arguing with a short stocky Hispanic man when Buddy approaches with his carryon. "Hector, you've got to get some help over here. We only have a couple more hours of daylight."

"Si, Si, senorita. My cousin come soon. She help mucho."

Buddy puts his arm around her waist. She turns and gives him a kiss. Hector takes a call and strolls away rattling off a string of Spanish.

"Honey, thank goodness you're here."

Buddy scans his yard, "Looks like a plane crash. So what's the problemo with Hector?"

"The problemo of the moment is the packing. The pallet of moving supplies from Amazon arrived two days late so Consuela wasn't available. She had knee surgery scheduled. So Hector and Carlos have been in there handling the crystal and china like a pair of monkeys on crack."

"So much for the $125 we saved on buying that crap in bulk."

"We're way behind on the packing and loading. I seem to be the only one concerned."

"I sure hope we made the right decision going with these guys. The Crazy Brothers Moving Company should have clued us in."

"But they beat the other companies by four grand."

"We don't seem to be off to a good start."

"I guess not. Nothing seems to upset Hector. He just smiles and says, Si, Si. I don't think he understands me half the time. But they do seem anxious to please."

Buddy looks at his watch, "Honey, I have to pick up the Explorer. Is one of the boys around to drive me?"

"Oh yes, I forgot. It's not ready. The mechanic called this morning. Something about the transmission."

"Oh, good God."

A pick-up truck pulls behind the moving van. "That must be the cousin coming to help now. Are those children with her? Tell me this isn't happening."

"Yup. Four of 'em it seems. Maybe you guys can bake some cookies." Buddy laughs as the truck empties.

"Here're some things you can help with, Mr. Smartass. I hope the woman can speak English." She hands Buddy a list as she leaves to find Hector.

The next morning Sandy is brushing her teeth in the dark when she knocks a decanter of Listerine into the sink.

Squinting at the digital clock, Buddy asks, "Why are you up so early?"

She spits and says, "I want to get in a short run before things get crazy. I don't know how we're going to get all this done. And Maria is slow as hell, so I need to help with the packing. At least she's not bringing the kids today. Taylor wasn't very happy about babysitting."

Buddy sits on the side of the bed and stretches. "Ugh, I feel like I got to sleep about a half hour ago."

"Don't forget. You've got to disassemble the BBQ grill and drain the gas from the lawn mower. When you get the Explorer, please stop by the vet and get the pets' records and the Dramamine for Scarlett. And on your way back, if you could swing by Walgreens to pick up our prescriptions. And, there's the..."

"Damn, Honey. It's 5:30." He turns on the bedside lamp. "As for the car, I don't think they're going to have it ready today. I wasn't planning on having the transmission rebuilt."

"Bummer. Just add it to the list. And another thing, when you go to the vet, board Wallis for two days. I can't risk him getting out with all the doors being open. Oh, and remember, we've got that conference call with Fog Horn Leghorn at 2:30."

"Can't wait to hear what that pompous ass has to say. Ever since Taylor spilled the beans on the James boys, not much from him. Only that he claims to be making progress with the Pre-trial diversion program he's trying to get her into."

Sandy looks at the mirror as she twists on a scrunchie. "She's been awfully quiet too. In fact, almost pleasant the last several weeks. She's helped me around here a lot, keeping the boys on task and such. It's strange that she doesn't seem to be stressed out over the mess she's in."

"I guess she figures we can do all the worrying for her. And bill paying."

Sandy gives Buddy a peck on the cheek and runs out the room. "Honey, keep an eye out for a Superior Plumbing van. The guy's coming early to install the hot water heater." She slaps her hip and Scarlett leaps to attention.

Half awake with both arms bracing at the bed side, Buddy sighs into the darkness, "And the hits keep on coming."

Sandy kicks the door as she passes the boy's room. "Boys! We've got a busy day ahead of us! Up, up, up!"

She trips to the kitchen with Scarlett on her heels. After shoveling in the grinds and filling the reservoir, she impatiently awaits the gurgling brew. With a half cup poured, she tosses in a couple of ice cubes. After two hasty swallows of the crackling mix, she grabs a banana and hooks up Scarlett for their last Kennesaw Mountain run.

The August sun is breaking through the pines when they return to find Buddy in the garage. "Sandy" he grumbles. "I don't know how we're getting us and all this stuff in two cars. Do we have to take these damn asparagus ferns?"

"Of course we do. And the peace lilies too. We've had those since we got married. You know what they'd cost out there?"

"I hate to think."

Sandy points to the boxes of miscellaneous items scattered around. "So what about all those paint cans and aerosols? And the cleaning supplies you've got there? And that old bottle of Sambuca we've had for fifteen years?"

"The drivers won't pack it. We'd just have to replace it. There's at least $100 worth of stuff here."

"Well, there you go. And don't forget about Clarence and Elizabeth."

"Not the stupid gold fish."

213

"I promised the boys. They're been their pets since Junior High. I got some heavy gallon Zip Locs for those guys. They'll be fine on the floor board."

She soon has the children seated at the kitchen table. Each is given their personal typed out to do list for the next twelve hours. For the workers, she ices down a cooler of cheap Deer Park spring water on the front porch, no longer feeling obliged to pay more for Coke products. Pizza is scheduled to be delivered at noon. Nestling Scarlett's head with both hands, she rubs her ears and declares, "Bring it on! Right girl?" Scarlett's swinging tail signals agreement.

Lost in the endless stream of tasks, Sandy suddenly realizes the movers are thirty minutes late. She places a call to Hector, but reaches his voice mail. Trying to stay calm, Sandy hammers away at the day's duties.

It's nearly 10:00 when Consuela calls. "Senorita, Sandy. Truck. It has muy poco problema."

"What problem? We have a whole day's work ahead of us. When will they be here?"

"Problema be soon okay. You see. It okay. Soon. Lo siento. Lo siento."

214

"And where is Maria, the packer lady?"

"She no there?"

"No! She no here!" Sandy takes a deep breath and calmly directs, "Forget about her. I'll do the rest myself."

Scarlett cocks her head towards the street. "Got to go, Consuela. I think I hear the truck coming now." Standing on the porch, she sees the moving van crawling up the hill snorting black smoke from the twin vertical stacks.

Scarlett springs out the front door to join the welcome. Pausing to pee, she watches as the unmarked 48' dusty beige van slowly motors to a stop. Sandy reads the identification on the old red Mack CH613 cab: *Los Hermanos Locos* Moving Company; 1390 Chestnut Drive; Dallas, GA 30053; 678-334-0652.

Looking at the graffiti showing through the paint, she says to Scarlett, "That truck doesn't look very clean does it?"

Two men lumber from the cab. The short, sinewy driver greets Sandy with a broad grin, his hand extended. "Buenos dias, senorita Hinson. Mi nombre est Carlos. Poco problema. It okay. We start now. Miguel está conmigo. Hector come después pienso."

215

Sandy shakes his hand. "It's Henderson. Oh, never mind. We're ready, I guess. I thought there was to be four loaders? Where's Hector?"

Carlos hops backwards as Scarlett sniffs away. "Si, Si. We have help. You see. Later. Hector, he later come. You see. Muy bueno." Having moved to the rear of the truck, Miguel flips up the latch and swings open the back door. The loading ramps are secured and positioned onto the street. An impatient neighbor honks at his blocked passage.

Sandy calls from the curb, "Please re-park your truck and I'll take you through the house to go over some things. I'll get my kids to help." She pays no attention to a curious crunch as she walks away.

With the van repositioned, Sandy leads Carlos into the house, walking him from room to room, maneuvering around stacks of boxes and furniture.

With his list whittled down, Buddy joins Sandy in packing the breakables. Taylor and the boys stay busy helping get boxes of items to street side for loading.

Its eleven thirty when Hector arrives making a straight path to the down stairs bath room. Sandy greets him upon his exit, "Hector, where have you been?"

Patting his stomach and shaking his head, he explains, "Muy malas tomalas, senorita. Muy malas."

Not wanting to pursue the issue, Sandy says, "Okay, let's get to work. We're running way behind. And we only have half the china."

Their heads jerk to a tooth jarring sound as their Chippendale dining table smashes into the front door frame. Sandy screams, "*Stop!* Look what you just did!"

Startled by her rage, Carlos and Miguel falter with the other end and punch a fist sized hole in the wall board.

The jittery Miguel shrugs his shoulders. "Eso es lo que hace que sean antigüedades."

Taylor whispers to her mother, "He said, that's what makes them antiques".

Sandy flees into bathroom. Quickly confirming Hector's tamale problem, she reverses her path and pounds up the stairs.

A short time later an order of Dominos pizza arrives. Halting them in their tracks, Carlos, Miguel, and the boys begin to gobble down three pounds of greasy dough, cheese and pepperoni. As they lay back for a siesta, Sandy jousts them into action and begins to pick up the littered lunch. "Okay, guys back to work. We've barely gotten started."

Buddy rushes in from the backyard. "I just heard thunder." Looking at his phone, he says, "A big cell is moving this way!"

"Where did that come from? Our furniture's out front!"

They all levitate as a thunder bolt cracks, followed by a downpour. A half hour later the family is busy blotting their soggy belongings in the steaming sunshine. After helping to spread soaked sheets and towels across their landscape, Sandy retreats to their bedroom.

After a short cry, she takes on another item on her list, the compiling of important documents and valuables. A small suitcase is carefully loaded with what is needed upon arrival in Denver. Sandy locks it shut and stuffs the key in her short's pocket.

From downstairs, Buddy calls up, "Honey, I've got Taylor. Jenkins is supposed to call in five minutes." Sandy hurries to the conference call, leaving the suitcase in the hallway.

James Calhoun Jenkins greets Buddy, Sandy and Taylor. "Good afternoon, y'all. And just how are we on this fine afternoon?"

Buddy answers, "Oh, just ducky. In thirty minutes, we've gone from looking like an Appalachian foreclosure to a Calcutta flea market."

"I beg your pardon?"

"Nothing. So, do we have some good news?" Buddy gets to the point wishing to avoid the $395 per hour small talk he had just initiated.

Taylor leans in to the speaker and smiles, "Hello, Mr. Jenkins."

"Why hello to you. And how have you been, little gal?"

"I've been well, thank you very much, sir. How have you been?"

219

"Just fine and dandy. I've been working real hard to get this mess untangled."

"I know you have, sir. Looks like the Tide's going to have a really good team this year."

"Why yes they are. Our three running backs will be..."

Sandy slashes her eyes to Taylor. "Good afternoon, Mr. Jenkins. Sandy here. So what do you have for us?"

At 9:30 P.M. the moving van is only half loaded. With the realization that productivity has come to a grinding halt, Buddy and Sandy send the movers home for the night.

Trying to position himself on the blow-up mattress, Buddy says, "I told you we should have gotten a hotel room. This thing is killing my back."

Sandy wiggles in next to him and turns on her side. "You're probably right. This saving money thing is about to do us in."

"Maybe we can get them to give us credit for helping with the packing and loading."

Sandy props on her elbow. "That's about as likely as us finishing tomorrow. Have you looked in the trailer? I don't think it's going to hold everything." She rolls to her back. "This all sucks."

"At least we got some sort of good news from One Call Y'all. With the prosecutor going along with the pre-trial diversion program in Denver."

Sandy stares at the ceiling. "Thank goodness she didn't have any priors so this will not go on her record."

"She wasn't too happy about the rehab clinic and the community service."

"No, but she took it better than I thought she would. It all seems strange to me. Didn't you find it interesting about how she responded to that creep? It was almost like he'd already told her. Like it was supposed to come down that way."

"I thought about that too. And I didn't like the way they talked, all chummy and all. Maybe we're just reading too much into it. One thing for sure, her little butt will be on a short leash for the next year."

"I hope so. If she hadn't have squealed on everyone, things would be a lot different."

"That's for sure. It had to be some surprise when they all returned from the beach to find the G.B.I. on their door step. Little Sammy will be out of her life for a very long time."

After a minute of silence, Sandy hears his heavy resonating snore. She leans over and kisses him goodnight.

As Ground Hog day dawns, Sandy is standing in the driveway at 9:10 a.m. when *Los Hermanos Locos* team appears.

Before Hector can get out of the cab, she points to the concrete chunk and pole angling from the red clay. "Look what you did to our mail box yesterday!"

"Si, Si. Lo siento, senorita. We fix. No hey problema."

"Yes, sorry, and no problem. Is that all you can ever say?"

As his eyes cast to the ground, she apologizes, "No offense, Hector. We're all under a lot of stress. Let's get off on the right foot and get going. We're going to have a good day.

"Si, si, senorita Hinson." Hector beams.

222

It's 8:30 p.m. when the van doors slam shut. Hector is strapping the BBQ grill onto the rear with bungee cords when Buddy and Sandy approach.

Buddy restrains Sandy by her back belt loop as she approaches Hector. "We still have a bunch of stuff in the house. What's going to happen with all that?"

"No hey problema." He cheerfully assures the backside of Sandy as she spins away. "We put on other truck later. Que esta bien, senor. We see you in Denver."

Mosquitoes start to swarm as darkness settles in as Hector, Carlos and Miguel pile into the stuffed van. Buddy watches as it sputters and belches down the street.

Chapter 14

Are We There Yet?

Staring at the swirling ceiling fan, Buddy and Sandy lie motionless on the sheetless blow-up mattress. Barely moving her lips, Sandy says, "I'm sorry about the sheets. They're still hanging on the plants along with the towels."

"I don't care. Thank goodness they hadn't been packed when the storm hit." Buddy pushes up from the mattress and walks to the window.

"Aren't we the lucky ones? I don't ever remember being this exhausted. To think we still have a three-day drive ahead of us makes me sick to my stomach."

"Me too. But at least they're on their way."

Sandy sees the silhouette of Buddy putting a bottle to his lips. "What's that you're drinking?"

"Sambuca. Figured this was as good a time as any."

"If I didn't hate liquorish so, I'd join you."

Taking several more gulps, he turns to Sandy. "They're on their way with only 80% of our belongings. How can we expect them to coordinate from that end when they screwed up everything here?"

"We can only hope. Honey, please go quiet the children. They're fighting over who gets the sofa."

"Okay, but my money's on Taylor. She can work the boys like pizza dough."

"Yeah, them and everyone else. At least she's behaving at the moment. Couldn't take tangling with her with all this going on."

After confirming his suspicion regarding the sleeping arrangements, Buddy returns to find Sandy in deep sleep.

Early the next morning Buddy greets Sandy and Scarlett as they return from outside. Sandy rests at on a bar stool and turns through the pages of the Marietta Daily Journal she had picked up from the driveway. "Oh, my God. Did you see this?" She exclaims holding out the front page. "This woman in Marietta just won the Scratcher lottery for $750 thousand dollars."

"Man, that's something." Buddy says with disinterest.

"I'd swear she looks like that big ole gal we ran into at the Quik Trip."

Buddy snatches the paper from her hands.

Wiping the sweat from her face and arms with a wash cloth, Sandy says, "We should have pulled the sheets and towels off the plants last night. The dew has them soaked again. Is there anything that's not wet?"

His head is down with eyes closed as the paper droops from his hanging right hand. "Hello, Buddy?" she says. "Are you okay? We have to get going. What time do we hope to get away?"

He drops the paper to the floor and looks up with a numb expression. "Hope?"

"What's wrong with you?"

After a sigh, he does a negative nod and mumbles, "Ten maybe, I guess."

"How far can we get?"

Buddy looks down at a grinning Rheema Kay Tannyhill holding a 2' by 4' $750,000 check. He kicks the paper with his foot and says, "Has her teeth in."

"Teeth?"

Staring blankly across the room he says into space with no inflection, "I want to make Cape Gerardo by dinner."

"The kids. They'll be crying for food any minute."

Coming to attention, Buddy shakes his head. "I'll run up to McDonalds to get breakfast. When I get back I'll start on the cars so please have everyone get whatever they're taking with them outside on the driveway."

"Good. I'll bribe them with sausage McMuffins."

"I'll need to clear out the garage too. We'll have to store all the leftover furniture and other things in there with the painters and carpet people coming in two days."

"I'd better push everyone back a day or so. Plus the cleaning service. Robyn's not going to be happy about showing the house with all our crap still in the garage. You'd better get going. I'll need that coffee when I wake the zombies."

227

The mid morning sun is sweltering as Buddy loads the driveway full of items that stretch to the street. He curses to himself as streaming sweat tickles his back. *Damn it to Hell. Can't believe I gave away a winning ticket. Have never won a fucking dime.*

Luke comes up. "Dad. They left our bikes. Can we take them with us?" Unsure of when the other truck could come, Buddy agrees to tie them to the luggage rack on top of the Explorer.

Sandy is in the back yard doing a last check. Seeing Buddy's vines bending with fruit, she fills double brown Trader Joe's bags with pinkish green tomatoes. After entering the garage, she pulls open the louvered doors to the hot water heater room. Her eyes are struck by garbage bag of crumpled garments in the corner.

As she sets tomatoes at his side, she asks, "I thought we gave all those clothes to Good Will. And how did that pink cap get so bloody?"

Before he can protest the bag of green tomatoes, Buddy is shocked at Sandy's discovery of his winter night's garments. "Uh, have no idea. Must have been something the boys got into." With Sandy out of sight, he hides the bursting bag of tomatoes behind a bush.

It's nearly noon when Buddy stuffs the last of their goods into the vehicles. Taylor, singing softly to herself, strolls up caressing her pillow with both arms. Removing an ear bud and turning her shoulder, Sandy points to the Explorer and says, "You're in that one, Dear."

"I'm not getting in that car with those clowns. Why can't I ride with you guys?"

"We're loaded to the hilt. Besides, your father and I have some things to discuss." Sandy drags the bag of tomatoes from behind the bush and squeezes them onto the back floor board.

"What're you doing, Mom? There's no room in there! I can't ride with those jerks and all that junk for three days."

Sandy swivels her head and smirks. "Boys," She says. "You decide who drives first and when to switch off down the road. Your sister can't help relieve because her license is still suspended."

Jake jumps into the driver's seat. "I'll drive first."

"Shotgun!" follows, Luke.

"Mom! I don't have a place to sit. There're ferns and shit everywhere. Are those tomatoes?"

"Couldn't leave 'em behind." Balancing a litter box across her pillow, Sandy says, "And here, make a place for this. We'll be picking up Wallis at boarding on the way out."

As Taylor stands frozen, Sandy calmly counsels, "You'd better find yourself a spot. Looks like seats are filling up fast." Sandy pops the trunk on the Lincoln and says, "The suitcase!" She pulls aside the packed items and calls out, "Has anyone seen the small green suitcase?"

Buddy answers, "Nope. It's probably bouncing along the freeway somewhere in Missouri."

"Don't tell me that. It's got the boys' school records and the pet's papers. Plus all our documents, jewelry and cash. We'll need all of that when we get to Denver."

"They'll be there a day ahead of us. We can get it off the transport when it's unloaded."

Sandy goes to the Explorer, opens the door and Scarlett hops onto the seat. After circling a few times, she flops down and snorts.

Getting into the Lincoln, Buddy directs, "We've got to get going, gang. Taylor, if you don't make a decision soon, we'll have to strap you on top with the bikes."

Having completed five minutes of their three day journey, they return to McDonalds for lunch. After two more stops they are finally on their way three hours late.

With the sun having set hours earlier. Buddy sees the next exit ahead on I-55. "There it is. The Drury Suites. God, will I be glad to get out of this car."

"I think our offspring will be too. You get us checked in and I'll try to coordinate the kids and the pets. What're the sleeping arrangements?" Sandy asks.

"It's a suite with two rooms. A private one for you and me and a living area with a pull out. Thought we'd put the boys on that and I'll get a fold up for Taylor. It's pet friendly, so we won't have to sneak in the animals."

Buddy is up early the next morning with plans to be the first in the bathroom. As he clicks on the light, he finds Wallis with position. After turning on the exhaust fan, he leaves

231

with Scarlett. Upon his return, he finds Sandy stripping the pull out.

"Mom! What are you doing? We didn't sleep at all last night?" cries Luke.

"I'm not telling you again. Get up! Anyone staying in bed will have to wait for the bathroom. And the longer you guys hang out, the less food will be at the breakfast bar." Before Sandy can finish her sentence, Taylor has slammed the bathroom door and the boys are dressing.

As they pull onto the freeway, Sandy looks over her shoulder to check on the trailing Explorer. "How far is it to Topeka?" she asks.

"At least seven hours if traffic is okay."

"I'm so glad we put the kids in one car. That constant bickering would have sent me over the edge. Wonder how Hector's doing?"

"They ought to be getting to his cousin's sometime soon. Hard to believe he and Carlos left our house to drive all night. So what's that thing they're going to?"

"It's his fifteen-year-old niece's quinceanera, a Latin tradition for young women going from childhood to young womanhood. It'll be a really big family celebration outside Great Bend. It's off course a bit but they'll still be in Denver a day ahead of us."

The ringing from Buddy's phone wakes Sandy from a deep slumber. At first she does not know where she is. And then she calls into the darkness of the Holiday Inn Express, "Buddy! Get your phone."

He reaches to the night stand and garbles, "Hello?"

"Senor, Buddy. Esto es Hector."

"Hector? It's late. What is it?"

"Tenemous un pequeno problema."

"Are we close?" Sandy asks, peering into the windshield.

"Should be the next crossroads. Hard seeing in this deluge. Crap, it's dark."

Smearing a streak through the fog, she says, "You can wake me now."

233

Buddy adjusts his wipers to high and presses against the steering wheel. "This place is in the middle of nowhere and there're not many road signs. I can't see shit."

Sandy turns to the rear. "Slow down for the kids to catch up." Stiffening in her seat she turns to Buddy, "What are we going to find? Did Hector say anything specific?"

"Some kind of an accident. You know he can't speak English worth a damn. He didn't seem to be his cheery self though. I understood him to say no one was hurt, so I guess that's good."

"Maybe not yet." Sandy turns up the defroster.

As they approach a rural four way stop, a blinking *Road Closed* sign blocks their entry. Buddy gets out into the rain and moves it aside, clearing the way. Several miles down the two-lane blacktop, they find two patrol cars nose to nose, their blue lights sequencing.

As their wipers slash back and forth, Sandy screams into the blurred image before them. "That's our van! It's stuck beneath the overpass!"

234

Sandy manages a weak smile as she sits her overnight bag on the brightly colored patched quilt. She says to the lady standing at her side. "Mrs. Gonzales, I feel so bad bothering you like this with your granddaughter's quinceanera going on. We didn't know you were offering us your room for the night."

"No, no. I insist. I will stay with my sister next door. She snores a little, but it's okay."

"That is so kind. If only we'd been able to find a room. With the bikers in town and all, there was no place within fifty miles."

As their hostess turns back the bed linens and fluffs the pillows, she says, "We are so sorry about the accident. I've warned Hector a thousand times about having an under blunder."

"A What?" Buddy asks.

"Yes. That's when you don't have enough clearance. He and Carlos were relying on their stupid new app instead of reading the road signs. They should know better."

Sandy says, "I'm just glad no one was hurt."

As Mrs. Gonzales folds the quilt, she says, "Me too. Hector is heartbroken and Carlos is trying to forget with Tequila. We will make it right for you."

Sandy gives Buddy quick look of doubt when Mrs. Gonzales clasps her hands and beams a welcoming smile, "You must come to Juanita's celebration."

Sandy peals down her eye lids before the mirror. "I don't think so." She turns to Mrs. Gonzales, "We're terribly tired with the long day and all that's happened."

Mrs. Gonzales wraps her arms around her, "You will be our honored guests. We have lots of good food, much to drink and the Mariachis are starting up. We have many young people to be with your adolescents. And I see your daughter speaks Spanish. They will have a good time."

Sandy says to Buddy, "Honey, what do you think?"

Testing the mattress with both hands, he answers, "How much Tequila does Carlos have?"

The silent dawn breaks to the sound of a clanking bell. Buddy's muffled voice comes from beneath the sheets. "What's that noise?"

Pulling the white linen curtains aside, Sandy laughs as she looks across the cluttered lawn. "It's a nanny goat and her babies chomping on whatever was dropped last night."

"The way we ate, surprised she's still with us."

Sandy dials up the setting on the blowing window unit. "That was really sweet of them to have us crash their party." She hears a knock. Going to the door she says, "Our adlescentes surely seemed to be having a good time when we went to bed."

Sandy opens the door to find Mrs. Gonzales holding a large tray. She sings out with happiness, "Buenos dias, my dear guests. I have some hot coffee and fresh churros for you. A big breakfast will be ready soon."

"Good morning, Mrs. Gonzales. Coffee? Mucho gracious. Please sit it on the bed." Sandy rolls the covers back as Buddy slides to the side.

Mrs. Gonzales backs towards the door. "How was your evening? I hope we weren't too wild. We get carried away at these things."

Sandy says, "Last night was fantastic. We really needed to have a little fun. You haven't seen our children this morning, have you?"

A strange look comes over the woman's face as her dark brown eyes look away. Smiling back at Sandy, she recovers her composure. "Yes, the boys went with Hector to the warehouse. You can go see after breakfast."

"And our daughter?"

Four hours later, the Henderson's begin their six-hundred-mile drive to Denver. Sandy takes her turn at the wheel while Buddy reviews the damaged items on their manifest. "We might come out fairly well on all this."

Sandy adjusts the rearview mirror. "So, how do you figure that, Mr. Houdini?"

"I got full value insurance protection. And, if I might use the word 'lucky', our really nice stuff was left back at our house. The furniture, dishware, and pantry stuff didn't get damaged and most of the things that did get wet from the storm should dry out. Some clothes were messed up but we're going to need new ward robes for Denver anyway."

238

"I hope you're right. I couldn't stand the sight of our life scattered about that warehouse. But I was so happy to find my green suitcase sitting in the middle of the floor. Hector and his cousins must have gone straight from the quinceanera to sort out and dry our things."

"I think they commandeered every coat rack and fan in Barton County. What did you and Mrs. Gonzales decide?"

"She was horrified to discover Hector and Carlos had tried to pack us back home. Said she and her sister would do the repacking. She also told me that she would coordinate all our goods getting to Denver."

"You know, she and her late husband were carriers for Allied for over twenty years. I think she'll keep her nephew in line."

"Keep Hector in line? What about her covering for Taylor? Zack had already given themselves away when he ratted on her being up at 3 a.m. and all. Will she ever learn?"

"I don't even want to think about it." Buddy deadpans.

Sandy puts on her right blinker and decelerates to the roadside. "Are you ready to drive for a while? I need to call the boys' new school."

239

Chapter 15

We'll Leave the Lights On

As they enter the gravel driveway, the halogen lights expose the tall aspens lining the entrance. After several hundred feet, the ghostly glow of the Victorian mansion emerges from the darkness, its spires and gables towering into the sky.

Buddy says, "Spooky looking place at night. We might need to put some exterior lights in our budget."

Pointing upwards, Sandy says, " Look. There's Mother in the spire."

"No. there she is under the gas lamp signaling us towards the rear."

"I'd swear I saw someone moving in the window."

"You're too much." Buddy laughs, as the Lincoln comes to a stop.

Sandy is the first out followed by Scarlett. She gives Katherine a hug. "Mother, thanks so much for coming out so late."

"Welcome to Denver gang. Why are you so late?" Katherine gives Sandy a kiss and walks over to greet Buddy and the kids.

"It's a long story, Mother. We'll catch you up on all the gory details tomorrow. Who's in the house?"

"Nobody. It's a junk heap right now."

"Well, I saw someone in the spire. They were..."

"You saw no such thing, silly. Let's get you settled."

"Maybe so... We're bushed and will want to hit the bed right away. Especially the kids after their night in the country."

As they climb from the SUV, Luke exclaims, "Mom, our car smells like something's rotten."

"That's you, scum bag." Taylor rejoins.

"Right this way, folks." Katherine says as she points the controls to the garage doors. "We're putting everyone in

241

the garage apartment tonight. We'll move Taylor over to my place tomorrow."

At the back of the garage she unlocks the entrance door to a one room suite. Sandy points into the room. "Boys, you'll be staying on the first level half floor. Go get your stuff and go to bed."

Buddy whispers to Sandy, "They'll have their own private entrance?"

" Mother and I have already talked about that."

The boys go to their room and Katherine leads Buddy, Sandy and Taylor up the small stairway to the second-floor apartment. As Buddy and Sandy get a brief tour, Taylor collapses on the sofa, her head against her clutch.

Moments later Sandy finds her asleep and nudges her back. "Taylor! Go down and get Wallis and his litter box."

"Can't he just spend the night in the car? He'll be fine."

Sandy claps her hands together. "You get yourself down there right now. You wouldn't be dragging ass if you hadn't have stayed out all night."

The next morning as Sandy hunts through her suitcase, she hears a horn honk. Peering through the upstairs window, she sees Buddy walking up the driveway with Scarlett on a leash. Coming from the rear is Katherine's red Cadillac kicking up dust.

Luke enters from downstairs. "Sweetie." she says. "Please run down to the SUV and get my black duffle. I need my Nike's."

Moments later he appears with her bag. "Mom, I'm telling you. Something's bad news in our car. And it's gotten worse."

"I'll get Dad to check it out."

On the way out the door Sandy walks past Taylor who is tangled in a sheet face down on the pull out sofa bed.

As Sandy appears from behind the Dipsy Dumpster, Buddy releases Scarlett. She speeds towards Sandy and springs, planting two dirty feet against her chest. She hold her feet out and dances."Honey, would you please see what Luke's carrying on about--the SUV smelling and all?"

Katherine gets from her car. "Good morning. So how did everyone sleep last night?"

243

"Don't remember." Buddy says as he walks to the SUV, "Think we were all down before you got out the driveway. Left the windows open. The fresh mountain air swept through the rooms."

"Better enjoy it now. In a couple of months, you won't be leaving the windows open."

Buddy returns holding out both hands--each with a deflated and dripping Ziploc bag.

"The goldfish!" Sandy shrieks.

"Yup. Looks like old Clarence and Elizabeth bought the farm. They're riper than the 15 pounds of tomatoes you squished 'em with."

"Damn it! Quick. Throw them in the dumpster before the boys can see." Turning quickly to Katherine, Sandy says, "So what's the schedule, Mother? I have to stock up on some groceries but is anything planned today?"

"Not much. Figured you wanted to take it easy after your drive. I assume we'd let the kids sleep in while we get caught up." Katherine points to the Victorian. "Let's go where we can have some privacy."

As they walk up the back steps, Buddy peels a strip of paint from the door frame. "Have you gotten any contractors out here to tell us what we're looking at with this place?"

Katherine swings open the creaking screen door, allowing Buddy and Sandy to enter the mud room. "A few. I've got a list from Gabe but I wanted to talk with Sandy since she'll G.C. everything. I do have a painter who's supposed to be here in about thirty minutes."

Opening the door to the kitchen, Katherine points to the circles and cracks in the plaster ceiling. "Buddy, a plumber friend confirmed what you were saying. The bathrooms are kaput."

Sandy looks up and around. "Wow, this place has really gone downhill since I was last here."

Stepping over an array of trash, Katherine points to the next room, "We can talk in the kitchen. The rest of the house is a mess but much better than before we got the dumpster."

Sandy pulls out a slatted chair and sits down at the sturdy oak table. She glances around and says, "Can we afford all this?"

245

They all turn their heads towards a thump resonating from some distance. "What the hell was that?" Buddy asks.

"I didn't hear anything." Katherine says as she gets an ash tray from the counter and taps out a cigarette.

Sandy looks at Buddy and says, "Well, I surely did."

Pulling a lighter from her pocket, she peers over their heads as if talking to the walls. "Mind if I smoke?"

"What's with the politeness?" Buddy cracks.

"You sure missed that one, Mr. Funny Man. Of course I can smoke! Remember this is going to be a 420 friendly hotel?"

"Okay, guys. We're going to be working a lot together and we can't start off sniping. Back to my question. How're we paying for all this?"

Katherine flicks her lighter and takes a draw. "Buddy, my accountant is ready to meet with you to build a plan. When the contractor estimates come in, we can make some assumptions. Now that we have a good idea on the value of the books and the coins."

"Whenever. I've been thinking. Maybe we ought to leverage the liquid assets in some balanced port folio and finance the remodeling. Rates are good and we'll need the write off, assuming we have some revenue. I don't think we ought to eat up all the capital on expenses. To be safe, we ought to be able to swing all this with no B & B revenue."

Katherine smiles, "My accountant was saying the same thing so you guys ought to get along just fine. As for the remodeling costs, we don't know what we don't know."

"Mother, Buddy really likes this guy he'll be working for at the grow house."

"Yeah. The job looks pretty cool and the people are laid back and friendly. He wants me out there right away so I'll start tomorrow."

"Good. Gabe is still pouting about me working him to get the job. I was talking to one of Randy's investors and they're excited about bringing you on board." Katherine turns to Sandy, "So what's Taylor saying about next week's substance abuse program?"

"That's a good question. She seems fairly resigned to it with little to no comment."

Buddy chuckles, "Personally, I think she's had the shit scared out of her."

247

Sandy raps her nails on the table. "Personally? I don't think *anything* scares her. What about that little stunt she pulled in Great Bend? Just figured the odds of getting caught and did what she wanted."

Katherine says, "What stunt?"

Sandy and Buddy's eyes connect and Sandy says, "We'll tell you all about it in a minute. Let us hear about the clinic you found for Taylor."

Katherine reaches into her purse and produces a small brochure. "Listen to this." *She'll be required to proceed through a highly disciplined routine of approval assessment, medication management, amino acid therapy, nutritional assessment, private and group therapy, and a final dismissal assessment.* There's not much wiggle room there for her individuality. This is the best rehab clinic in Denver."

"Mother, we really appreciate you paying for this. She's got to stay on the straight and narrow for a year."

"I'm happy to help. So how's this all coming down with her?"

"She gets it and knows she has little choice as a first-time offender. She'll be saved from prosecution by diverting her from the criminal justice process."

Buddy adds, "Yeah, old fat ass was able to get this decree before she was formally charged. For her part, she's got the rehab bit, no drinking and drugs and fifty hours of community service. We were lucky to get Gabe on this end, getting compliance reciprocity by the Denver authorities. He'll be coordinating the community service commitments for her and the boys."

"He told me about that and how she will have a probationary officer assigned to her."

"Poor fool." Sandy says nodding her head side to side..

"There's an unknown here, Katherine." Buddy says seriously. "We're still not sure what kind of substance abuse problem Taylor has. We know she loves to get high but we've also seen her walk away from it. Almost like she can turn it on and off with a switch."

"They'll address that at the clinic. She'd better not get caught when she has her little switch in the "on" position." Sandy says.

Buddy pats his belly and drawls, "And don't forget our good pal, Mr. OneCallY'all. He says if she complies with the court order, all charges will be dropped."

"Oh, let's not forget about him." Sandy remarks before saying to Katherine, "I can't get on the same page with her. Hopefully you can, Mother."

"You were rebellious too and had a skull like a rock. But I have to admit, Uncle Billy helped an awful lot with you. Maybe I can do the same with Taylor."

"Something's different, Mother. Nothing seems to faze her. Always plays the system to get what she wants. She got into all that trouble with the James boys and now it looks like she's going to skate with a hand slap. And there's this strange relationship between her and our attorney in Alabama. Can't put my finger on it but she appears to be in total control."

Katherine waves her hand. "Oh my Dear, you worry too much. She's just a really smart girl. A little rebellious but she'll be fine. I look forward to having her with me."

Buddy rocks back in his chair with his hands behind his head. "Be careful what you ask for."

"Mother, I only have a few days to get the boys in school. I'm supposed to meet with your friend Roberta Garcia Tuesday. Thank God we were able to retrieve their records from the warehouse."

"What warehouse?"

"Might as well tell you. We had mucho problema on the way out here."

Buddy says, "Seems like the phrase of the month."

He gets up from the table and opens the back door. "I don't feel like reliving the moment. While you fill her in, I'll call Randy about working tomorrow."

"Good. And see if you can kick start the kids. Don't want them sleeping in all day."

For the next thirty minutes Sandy tells Katherine about their tumultuous move. Katherine is making a feeble attempt at consoling when Buddy returns and says, "Those

251

painter guys are here. And, Taylor has risen from the dead. She's out there talking to one of them."

"She's what?" Sandy stands and goes to the door. "Mother, would you go see to the painters and keep an eye on Taylor. I'll get breakfast started. I saw you had some eggs and bacon and I brought a box of instant grits from the warehouse."

Sandy takes the platter and says to Zack, "Quit picking at the bacon." After piling on scrambled eggs, she pours cheese grits into a serving bowl and sets it on the counter. As the boys load their plates, Sandy calls out, "Breakfast everyone. Serve yourself before the locusts have finished."

Katherine taps her spoon against her cup. "Nothing for me. I'll just have some more coffee." She glances over to her granddaughter who is looking out the window at the painters readying to leave. "So Taylor, what's this I hear about you staying out all night with some Mexicans?"

Taylor swirls around to her brothers who are busy gobbling down their breakfasts. "Did you butt holes squeal on me?" Looking back at Katherine, "Grandmother, they're not Mexicans. They're Hispanics! You sound like Trump."

Leaning over his plate and shoveling in food, Luke mumbles, "Mom tricked me. I told her nothing. Only that you were out as late as we were. It was Hector who told Dad you were shooting Patron with Julio and Paco. And Dad told Mom."

"Daddy! How could you?"

As he constructs a response, Sandy gives a stern look to Taylor. "This has nothing to do with Hispanics and all to do with you drinking and chasing boys. You've got to stay clean, you know. If you get caught with so much as a beer during the next year, you'll be toast. All those charges are pending, you know."

"J.C. promised he'd take care of me."

Sandy grabs Taylor's arm. "So it's J.C. now? You guys are real tight, huh?"

Pulling her arm away, she says, "You don't understand. He's so nice."

"Nice? Like Sammy James the drug dealer was nice?"

As if on cue, Jake and Luke begin their refrain; *"Row, row, row your dope gently down the stream. Sweet, sweet Sammy Sales, he was but a dream."*

"Shut up, Jerks!" Taylor shrieks. "Mom, they sang that crap for hours in the car. You let them get away with *everything*."

Katherine taps louder on her cup. "Who the hell's J.C.?"

"Grandmother, he's a real nice guy that understands me."

"He's our attorney, Mother. A grown man over twice her age."

"And three times her size." Buddy adds.

"At least he cares! I was framed by those assholes that want to screw me over. He's protecting me."

Sandy looks to Taylor. "Framed by assholes that want to screw you over? You were right in the middle of all that mess...you, Becky, and Melissa. And, it was you who threw them under the bus, your so-called friends."

"I don't care what you say. J.C. said I didn't have to worry. He promised."

254

Sandy glares at her daughter. "What is that all about?"

"He likes me. And he likes my tats."

Katherine chokes on her coffee. "He likes your tits?"

"No! *Tats!* Grandmother. He likes my *tattoos*."

Zach holds up his fork like a conductor's baton and begins, *"Row, row, row your dope, gently down..."*

"I don't have to take this shit." Taylor pushes from the table and leaves the apartment.

Buddy looks at Sandy. "Where does she have tattoos?"

Seconds later the door swings back open and Taylor says with a salacious taunt, "And for your information, he likes my tits too!" She slams the door behind her.

Aside from the suppressed giggles from the boys, not a word is said. Katherine breaks the ice. "Are they having a relationship?"

Sandy slings her dish towel against the wall and turns to Buddy. "Did you hear what she just said? I told you something was going on."

Having finished his breakfast, Luke inters the fray. "She's just jacking you around. She ain't doing nothing."

255

"She's not doing anything." Sandy corrects.

Zach bites into another strip of bacon. "Yeah, she's just playin' the old fool, Snapchatting and all. Don't know why he'd be interested in her little titties."

Sandy stands and shouts, "Zach! That's your sister you're talking about. We're paying him thousands to ogle her breasts? This is malpractice. We'll have him disbarred."

Katherine asks. "Snap what?"

Sandy waves her arms. "She's sexting him! Isn't there a law against that or something?"

"Not as long as there're no sexual relations. Gabe had a similar issue a while back with a client that came on to him. It's surely not professional, but they're both adults."

"There you go again, Mother. Everything's no harm, no foul with you. I'll have her packed and ready to go this afternoon." Sandy disappears into the bedroom.

"Keep it light as the clinic won't let her bring much." Katherine says.

Chapter 16

Stirred, Not Shaken

Sandy flops her arm over to find Buddy not in bed. The digital clock reads 1:30 a.m. Hearing a noise in the kitchen, she goes to inspect. Buddy is reaching into a cabinet when she surprises him, "Looking for something to eat?" she asks.

"Oh, hey. Hope I didn't wake you. Want some Chef Boyardee?"

"No thanks. I couldn't sleep either but hunger wasn't the problem." Sandy takes a seat at the dinette. "I don't know what to do about Taylor and all that carrying on with that creepy lawyer of ours."

"I had a hard time containing myself. Katherine has no idea what she's signing up for."

"Thank goodness, she's agreed to put her up. There's no way I could take her in this little apartment. Something would have to give."

Cranking the can opener, Buddy says, "Yeah, me neither but we do have the judge's orders going for us. They've got her by the short hairs so that takes the pressure off. She knows the consequences. That dry out clinic should help show her the light."

"I hope you're right but she's not in there yet. And, it's more than a dry out clinic."

"Surely should be for what Katherine's agreed to pay. She thinks she's going to come out like a little Shirley Temple with a thirty day makeover." Buddy pours the ravioli into a bowl and shoves it into the microwave. "It's all about her attitude, I guess."

"Oh, she's got attitude all right, just not the right kind. We'll see. So what's Randy got planned for you at the grow house?"

"Not sure, but I'll have a full day. For the first time in a while, I'm looking forward to going to work." He tears off a paper towel and gets a spoon from the drawer. "That

258

reminds me. I need to get to those boxes of marijuana protocols I've been saving for years."

"I got a text from Carlita Gonzales earlier. She said they'd be here next week with all our Great Bend fiasco items. Hopefully, they're not too messed up."

Ding goes the timer. Buddy joins her at the table with his steaming bowl. "Who all you seeing this week?" he says with a mouth full of ravioli.

Sandy drags across her legal pad and picks up a pen. "Where do I start?" After writing in a few notes and flipping a page, she says, "Tomorrow will be spent getting the boys registered. Can you believe they start on Wednesday? Mother's friend was a huge help. I have to do some shopping for school clothes too and groceries. Write down anything you'll need."

"Weren't you going to alarm their suite?"

"Oh, that's right. Have to call the security people. Need an estimate on the big house too." Sandy jots down some notes. "I've cut out most of Tuesday and Wednesday to study online for the general contractor duties."

Buddy takes his half empty bowl to the sink, dumps the remainder into the disposal and turns on the water. "I wish you'd rethink that contracting thing. That's a load to take on."

"I know, but we can save 15-20%. They have a lot online, courses, downloads, Youtube and stuff. Just how hard can that be? Besides, I've got Mother to help."

"Pity the fool subs." Buddy says as he opens the fridge and reaches to the back shelf pulling out a Coors Light. He checks the expiration date. "Wait 'till I give Katherine crap about this dated beer."

"Oh, please don't start anything with her."

"It's always me. Anyway, she's got Taylor and that's punishment enough."

Sandy points to a small cockroach scurrying along the baseboard. "That reminds me. I need to call Orkin about the bugs." She clicks her pen several times and says, "Plus, I've got trades people stopping by all week to give me a feel for things. And Gabe wants us to come to his office to go over some of the estate details. He said we can do it late so you can swing by after work. Other than that, not much." She laughs as she checks her watch. "Better get to bed. It's late."

Sandy switches off the lamp and pulls up the covers and asks into the darkness, "You did hear those funny noises over there, didn't you?"

"Sure did."

"Don't you think it's funny that Mother won't acknowledge what we heard?"

"Night, Honey."

Sandy grimaces at the cracking split of the 2" X 6" poplar fascia revealing a powdery series of tunnels. "Termites." declares the man wielding the crow bar. "See those wings? Carpenter ants too, where they swarmed in the spring." He stands the crumbling board against the railing.

"Can't they be sprayed?" she asks leaning in to take a closer look.

"Not exactly." says the Orkin representative. "Gotta tent 'em." He gouges the furrows with a screw driver awakening the colony that has dug in for the winter.

261

"You mean cover the whole house? What will that cost?"

"Oh, not sure. Would have to do some measuring but I'd guess it might run ten grand or so for something this big." He steps between the rows of box woods and looks up at the spiking spires and gables. "This is sure some kind of a place you have here, Mrs. Henderson. There's lots of good areas for them to feed on."

"You make it sound like a buffet."

On his knees and digging with a small spade beneath a footing, he notes, "Would need a special baiting system for them little buggers."

"Little buggers?"

The representative traces along the flooring with a screw driver and punches a hole into a weakened slat. "Of course, you'd need to repair the damage they done. Quite a lot from the looks of things."

"Oh, boy. You're full of good news." Sandy is inspecting the footing with a flashlight when she hears a car door slam. She looks up to see Katherine hurrying up the walkway. "Over here, Mother." she calls.

Without pausing, Katherine curtly answers, "I'll be on the porch."

With the Orkin man dispatched, Sandy finds Katherine in a wicker rocker on the far side of the veranda. She's smoking a cigarette and gazing across the yard. "I can't take it anymore." she says into space as Sandy pulls up a rocker.

"Could we be a bit more specific, Mother. Can't take what anymore?"

"That daughter of yours. I'm on my last nerve."

For a brief moment, Sandy finds humor in her mother's frustration. Tired of Taylor's antics being dismissed over the years, she loves the irony. Taking a seat, she says, "Why Mother, what could the little darling have possibly done to get you so upset?"

"She doesn't pay attention to a damn thing I say."

Listing away to avoid her breaking smile being seen, Sandy begins to rock. "But you've only had her three days."

"Not that much if you subtract the time she's spent out at night."

Sandy's grin disappears. "What do you mean by that?"
263

"She didn't come home again last night."

Sandy's voice raises an octave as she shifts to face Katherine. "Again? Where is she?"

"I'm not really sure but my guess would be with that kid who was over here Sunday with the painting contractor. He's picked her up twice at my condo. He just honks and she's gone."

"Twice? She *just* met him!" Sandy squints her eyes to the back yard. "I remember that boy, the painting contractor's son. I saw them teasing around." She slaps the arm rest. "Damn that boy crazy little brat."

"Dude's really buff. Did you see him shirtless in those painter's overalls?"

"Good God, Mother." Sandy shakes her head and reaches for her phone. "We have to call the police. She can't be running around Denver without us knowing what she's doing."

"Just wait a minute there, Sandra Lee. They'll just tell you she can do just about anything an adult can. I've already talked with Gabe and he said we can't touch her, being eighteen and all."

264

"Well, she needs to be touched, with a two by four."

Katherine gets up from the rocker and stiffens her arms on the handrail. "He reminded me she's supposed to meet with her Pretrial Services Officer Monday." As Sandy begins to key her phone, Katherine says, "I told you it'd do no good to call the police."

"I'm not calling the police. I'm calling little Miss Hot to Trot."

"Whazzup? Mom."

"Taylor. Where are you?"

"I'm at Clayton's."

"Clayton the painter?"

"He just does that to earn some money. He's really a cage fighter."

Sandy holds her phone to her side and sighs. After a pause, she growls, "Taylor, I don't know what you're up to but you're playing those danger games again."

"You worry too much, Mom. It's all good. We'll be by later on today to get some of my stuff."

Sandy disconnects and turns to Katherine. "I'm going to kill her. I'm really going to kill her this time."

265

Katherine reaches down and pops off a loose spindle from the balustrade. As she raps out wood dust against a column, she says, "You know, we might have a few termites."

The discovery of structural issues makes the need for a professional carpenter a top priority. With several recommendations provided by Gabe, Sandy is vetting prospects on the Better Business Bureau's web site when Robyn Reese calls.

"Good afternoon, Sandy. Did I catch you at a good time?"

"Funny, Robyn. Don't remember having one of those in quite a while. So, how're you doing?"

"I'm well, I guess. After you told me about the moving disaster, I hated to bother you."

"Bother me about what? Do we have someone interested in the house?"

"Not exactly, but we do have a little problem."

"Is that all anyone can say these days? What kind of a problem?"

"You sure about this? You've never had a martini." Buddy says as the bar tender places a frosty stemmed cocktail before Sandy.

"Well, I'm having one now." After a cautious sip and a hard swallow, she says, "Yuck!" and pushes it his way. "Here, you drink it."

Buddy reaches for the skewer of olives and strips one between his teeth. "I don't drink vodka. And you ruined it with all that Vermouth. Beer's fine with me." He signals and the waiter appears. "Bring her a lemon drop, please."

Moments later and relaxed with her drink, Sandy thumbs the rim of lemony sugar. "Sorry 'bout dinner. After the bug guy left, things sort of went to hell."

"*After* we find termites, things *sort of* went to hell?"

"Yeah. Robyn called about us having to replace our ceiling. Seems the AC drip pan in the attic got clogged up and overflowed for several days. The wallboard collapsed in our bedroom."

"Our ceiling fell onto our new carpet?"

"Yeah. It's being aired out on the deck but it won't quit raining." She takes a big swallow of her drink. "And another thing. She thinks our asking price is too high. Says we need to drop it twelve to fifteen thousand."

"What? Where'd she come up with that? It was her recommendation."

"You know that beautiful backyard we had backing up to the mountain?"

"What do you mean *had*? That fantastic view gives us a lot premium."

"Gave. They just announced a major subdivision to be cut in. Tricycles will replace the trees. And the surveyor found what we believed was our rear lot line. It was off by eight feet."

"Tricycles? Lot line?"

Sandy pulls the lemon slice from her drink. Her lips pucker as she chews on the sour pulp. "Robyn said they've already begun pushing over the oaks and hickories with big tractors. Makes it hard to talk with prospective buyers with all that crunching and grinding going on."

Buddy murmurs to his reflection in the bar mirror, "Good God."

"And then Taylor and Clayton showed up to get some clothes."

"Who the hell is Clayton?"

"Clayton the cage fighter." Sandy tongues the sugared rim and takes another sip.

Buddy rocks back on his bar stool. "Maybe I will have that martini." He downs the last of his Amstel Light and turns to Sandy. "In five minutes, you've gone from termites to our daughter with a cage fighter. So, who's this Clayton guy?"

Sandy swirls the last of her drink, tosses it down. "That's who she's moved in with."

Buddy pauses and drops his head. "She's already hooked up with somebody?"

"Well, it didn't last very long after what he did to Jeffrey."

"How did Jeffrey get involved? I thought..."

"You don't want to know." Having licked her drink glass clean, she pushes it aside and picks up the bar menu. "Think I'll have the tilapia special with unsweetened iced tea." She slides it to Buddy and flicks her index finger to the bartender.

After ordering a chicken Caesar salad and the tilapia, Buddy holds his empty bottle with both hands and thumbs the sweat. "I'm afraid to ask, but how did this all come about?"

With the lemon drop having soaked in, Sandy loosens up. "You see, Clayton the painter and Taylor hit it off right away so she decided to move in with him. They came over to get some clothes about the same time Gabe and Jeffrey showed up. When Jeffrey began to strut around Clayton, Gabe got all pissed."

"Wait a minute. I thought Clayton was a cage fighter."

"That's when he's not making any money. Stay with me here. So Jeffrey latches onto this stud's arm and whispers something in his ear. Apparently, Clayton doesn't like men."

"How so?"

"Because he cold cocked Gabe."

"I thought it was Jeffrey coming on to him?"

"He wasn't coming on to him."

"But you said..."

"It seems that Jeffrey has gadar deficiency. Got the wrong signals, very wrong signals. He just wanted to fix up Clayton with a friend."

"I'm confused. Jeffrey thought the cage fighter was gay?"

"That's right but he found out to the contrary."

"You've got me on the edge of my seat."

"Clayton took a swing about the same time Gabe tried to come between them. Jeffrey ducked and he caught Gabe right in the chops. Knocked out his two front teeth." Sandy taps her empty glass on the bar and sighs, "I guess some good came out of it all. Taylor decided to stay with Mother."

As the waiter arrives with their dinners, Buddy says, "Please put those under a heat lamp and bring me a Beefeater martini, up and very dry. And the lady'll have another lemon drop."

Chapter 17

Snake Charmer

Sandy props open the large front door and moves aside as two men carefully back through the foyer with an armoire.

The buxom lady in the flowered dress calls out with a slight Spanish accent, "Put that down, Hector. I want some bubble wrap taped around the corners. And tell Paco to come see me with the tool box. There's a big bed on the third floor that has to be taken apart."

"Si, si, Tia Carlita." says the familiar voice.

Sandy approaches from behind. "Mrs. Gonzales, I can't tell you how relieved I am that you're helping with the move."

"Oh, Mrs. Sandy, it's the least I can do after all the trouble we've caused. And, you've given us another chance so we must do our best."

Looking around Sandy says, "You have a lot of help this time. Brought the whole family it seems."

"Yes, my sister Rosa to help with packing. And of course, Hector. Miguel had another job so he could not come." Mrs. Gonzales smiles knowingly. "And it was real easy getting Julio and Paco."

Not wishing to delve into Taylor's night with the brothers, Sandy changes the subject. "Well, it did seem to work out well with you bringing our stuff over here from Great Bend. I assume everything is going into the same storage facility?"

"Yes, plus the remaining load of your Marietta shipment that will be here in a few days. Along with what we brought in yesterday. We'll load all the contents of the mansion first so you can pull out any you need for your apartment."

Sandy turns over pages on her note pad checking household inventory. She looks to Mrs. Gonzales and says,

273

"We don't know what we'll keep until we get our new decor decided. How're you looking on timing?"

"I am so sorry, but we lost two workers this morning."

"Lost? Why?"

"I am not sure but they came screaming down the stairs and out the door. We weren't able to talk with them. But replacements will come tomorrow, Mrs. Sandy."

"That's crazy, Mrs. Gonzales but we have to have it cleaned out with a half dozen workers coming in to tear up the place. Excuse me but I have to help in the kitchen."

When Buddy walks up Sandy is taping a box of dishes. Not wishing to startle her, he gently knocks on the counter and announces himself, "Yoo hoo."

Snapping off the tape with her teeth, she seals the box and stacks it in the corner. She gives him a kiss and says, "Good morning. Thought you'd be gone by now."

"I'm running late. Have a busy day ahead. I was going out the door when Katherine called. She'd tried to reach you first but there was no answer."

Feeling her empty rear jean's pocket, Sandy replies, "Left my cell in the kitchen charging. So what'd she want."

Thirty minutes later Buddy lets Sandy off at the curb of the condo as he goes to park. Sandy rings the call button and she's buzzed up. Katherine is waiting in the hallway when Sandy jumps off the elevator and rushes to hug. "Oh, Mother. Please tell me she left a note or something."

"Kind of. Come inside and I'll show you."

They enter the condo and Katherine hands a paper napkin to Sandy. It reads in black lip stick, "Outta here."

"And just what does that mean?"

"Well, it probably rules out kidnapping."

"That's too bad."

"I thought she'd been acting funny for the past three weeks, ever since she met with her probation officer." Katherine walks to the counter and pours Sandy a coffee as Buddy enters.

After taking a sip from her mug, Sandy asks, "Acting funny?"

"Yeah, normal. If you can use that word with her. She was being all nice and pleasant, even pretending to give a shit about others. I had a strange feeling but nothing more."

275

Sandy shakes her head in disgust before turning to Katherine. "When did you see her last, Mother?"

"Right after dinner. She said good night and went to her room. Nothing unusual there."

"How about her clothes? What did she take with her?"

"Checked that too. Took several of her nicest dresses and some shoes. Best I can figure, a pair of jeans, a couple of cover-ups and a jacket. Just enough to stuff out that shoulder bag of hers. I'd guess a week-end get away somewhere."

"Could one of her boyfriends be involved? What about that painter animal that busted up Gabe's mouth?"

Buddy says, "I wouldn't think so after what Gabe threatened him with. He's damn lucky he didn't go to jail."

Katherine nods, "That relationship went down the crapper when Taylor found out his pay was going to be garnished for a year to pay for Gabe's implants."

"Speaking of money. Where'd she get enough to take off like this?"

Katherine reaches for her purse. "We'd better see if we've got all our credit cards."

As Buddy and Sandy tear into their wallets, Katherine says, "I called Gabe and his paralegal is checking out transportation, busses, trains, and planes." She pokes Buddy in the ribs. "You remember his friend at the Denver airport, don't you Mr. Eboli?"

"Real funny, Katherine." He returns his wallet to his pocket and says, "All mine are here."

"Mine too." confirms Sandy.

"Gabe went on to say what we already know. She's an adult and can do whatever she wants."

"What about her little mess in Alabama?" Buddy asks.

"He talked about that. She's been meeting regularly with her probation officer so she knows the consequences of not staying in line."

Buddy and Sandy's eyes meet and Sandy says, "You don't think?"

Half heartedly Buddy argues, "No way. That's just not possible."

"Oh my God. Of course that's it!" Katherine slaps her hand on the table. "I overheard her on the phone cooing to someone she called Jimmy. I didn't pay it much mind at the time."

"Damn it!" Sandy exclaims. "Her probation officer's name is James Clarkson. Could he possibly be in on this?" Sandy sits down her coffee and talks into space. "I wouldn't be at all surprised if she's soft soaped that poor fellow. Just what could they be up to?"

Katherine answers her phone, "Hi, Gabe. Found out anything?"

It's 8:30 p.m. when Buddy returns home. Sandy is sitting at the kitchen table working on her laptop as he walks to the fridge and pulls out a beer. "You want me to heat up something, Honey?" she asks.

"No, I'm fine. Dave ordered in several pizzas for those us who were working late. We're rushing on these protocols for the licensing requirements. They've got to be done before I leave tomorrow. This crap with Taylor this morning really set me back. What have you booked?"

"The best I could get to Vegas leaves at 3:45."

"I've been thinking about the trip. Gabe didn't give us much information, only that she flew out with this Clarkson guy who had booked a room at the Bellagio."

"At least we know who she's with, especially with his office confirming to Gabe that he'd taken some personal time off."

"This fellow is married with kids and he'd be fired on the spot for such an indiscretion. Just why would someone take such risks?"

Neither Buddy nor Sandy says anything as they both absorb the implications of such an assessment...one that hits so close to home.

Buddy breaks the silence, "Even if I find them, then what?"

"We can't just let our daughter gallivant around Las Vegas with her probation officer." Sandy pauses and says, "I wonder how we can find out what she's up to?" Suddenly she leaps from the table, knocking papers to the floor and yells, "Yes! I've got it!"

Buddy's cab noses forward approaching the grand porte cochere of the Bellagio hotel. As they near, the driver says in a Caribbean accent, "If you hurry Mon, you can catch the fountain show in fifteen minutes. They've got Bieber this month."

"Can't wait for that." Buddy drones handing him a fifty. "Keep the change." Looking at his watch, he sees there's time to check into his room before calling Mack. He pushes into the crowd.

"You know I could get my ass in a sling for doing this."

"Oh bullshit, Mack. You and your black ops guys can get away with anything."

"We're not black ops, Buddy. I've told you we're security consultants."

"I don't have the time to debate the difference. This is about keeping your poor little niece from screwing over some poor bloke."

"You know this wasn't easy to pull off on such short notice. My connection at the Bellagio has just come on board and I had to..."

"No labor pains, please. So what have you got?"

"They're doing dinner at the Mirage and are booked later for the Cirque de Soleil show. Won't be back to the room until near midnight. Maybe later if they hit the tables, so you should have plenty of time. The combo on your room safe is 3894. In there's your doctor's bag."

"Doctor's bag? What kind of silly ass thing is that?"

"That's what we like to call 'em. Play along with me here, Buddy. You'll find a key card for the adjoining room where they are staying. Also in there will be Charlie and the controls."

"What did you say?"

"Charlie the two foot remote control cobra."

"Charlie the cobra? I thought you were kidding about the snake."

"We don't kid, Buddy."

"Taylor is over the top terrified of snakes. It's about the only thing that'll get to her."

"Yeah, it's one of our favorites, particularly with the ladies. Pictures usually work better law enforcement officers like Clarkson."

"I agree. Taylor would probably ask for copies to post on Facebook. So, this thing really works?"

"Like a charmer."

"You guys have a sense of humor?"

"If only you knew. So here's the deal. Charlie was just serviced so he's ready to go. You need to put him under the sheets at the foot of the bed below their feet. When you're ready, just engage the control and you can activate the snake with two buttons: Button 'A' sends him up the middle of the bed towards the sensor on the headboard. Position 'B' sends him scurrying back to your room through your cracked door. They'll be much too busy to notice the exit."

"Jesus, Mack. That's just plain evil."

"We're proud of our work, Buddy. When you're done with Charlie, please put him back in the safe. Someone will come get him."

After carefully positioning Charlie under the sheets, Buddy remakes the bed and sneaks back into his room. With several hours to spare, he decides to go to the casino, get a quick hamburger and play a few hands at black jack. He recalls his old days at the University of Mississippi when he would work the frat houses and casinos in Tunica.

With several hundred dollars to gamble and being a little rusty, he figures to play only a short while. He hits a hot streak. Playing $25 hands, he finds himself up nearly $500 in the first thirty minutes. In his early days playing at his prime, he mastered the art of counting cards. Being out of practice, tonight he does only face cards. In only forty-five minutes, he finds himself ahead of the house by over $1200. With it being nearly eleven, he cashes in his chips and returns to his room. Things are going perfectly, he concludes stuffing the wad of cash into his pocket.

It's eleven fifteen when Buddy pulls up a chair and slightly cracks the door to the adjoining room...plenty of time before Taylor and her partner's expected return.

Moments later he is startled at the sound of the clicking open of a door. The room light flashes through the opening followed by the door closing. *Why aren't they talking,* he wonders as he reaches for the controls. With his ear to the crack, he hears the bed linens rustle. He clicks on

283

the power and sends Charlie slithering towards the headboard. He laughs to himself at the ensuing prospects.

"Yaeeeeeee! Goes the blood curdling scream. "Nyoka giant! Nyoka giant!" Buddy hears a lamp crash to the floor and then silence. It is not the sound he is expecting. Unsure of his next move, he hits the return button and within seconds Charlie makes his way homeward and through the cracked door. He pulls the handle and the lock clicks shut.

What the fuck was that? He mouths under his breath. A short time later, with his ear pressed to the door, he hears muffled and indiscernible voices. After ten minutes of silence, he peers into the dimly lighted room. Finding it empty, he enters. He is puzzled to see the bed covers folded neatly three quarters of the way down. *The turndown service!* He says. *I just scared the shit out of the turndown lady.*

He rushes to retrieve Charlie from his room and returns the robotic snake to the sheets. After neatly folding the spread, he slinks back into his hiding place and waits for the encore.

As his carryon sidles down the conveyor belt, Buddy feels his phone vibrate. After clearing TSA security, he returns the call. "Good morning, Honey. The deed is done."

"I'd say it is. Guess who just wheeled up at Mother's in a cab?"

It's mid afternoon when Buddy returns to find Katherine and Sandy putting a coat of wax on the dining room table. Unnoticed, he sits down his bag and says, "You guys missed one hell of a show in Vegas."

Sandy goes over and gives him a hug. "Welcome home, Siegfried. Or is it Roy? I always get them mixed up. Had enough of the night life?"

"A bit more excitement than I'd planned. That's for sure. So what have you heard from our little adventurer?"

Katherine says, "She had to have caught the first flight back. Hardly a word of explanation. Just some lame excuse about going to visit a sick friend. Nothing about a round trip to Vegas."

"What'd she say about that cryptic note she left?" Buddy asks.

"The chameleon is recalibrating everything now. Upset over a sick friend, friend suddenly got well, and now she's ready for her rehab class. Go figure." As she swirls a layer of carnauba wax onto a table corner, she says, "Typical. Every time she gets her tit in a ringer, she re-writes the script." After placing the bowl in the center of the table, she turns to Buddy, "Do you even know what happened after your snake trick?"

"Not really. Heard screams and slamming doors, a lot of commotion. After I got Charlie safely back home, I shut the door. Couldn't hear much after that. There were a lot of people milling around the hall this morning when I checked out. Just thought it was for some high-profile guest."

Sandy crooks her mouth and raises an eyebrow to Katherine and says, "Just wait until you talk with Mack."

"What do you mean?" Buddy asks.

"I'll let him tell you." Sandy aligns the chairs around the table. "Mother, have you heard anything about when she reports to the clinic?"

"Next week thank God. The 16th I think."

Sandy sighs, "Is it even possible for her to stay out of trouble that long?"

Buddy reaches for a call. "Hi Bro. You guys got a job opening? This shit's kinda fun." He looks to Sandy and Katherine with a big grin of satisfaction.

"I guess you didn't read the Review-Journal this morning." Mack dryly retorts.

"There's a reason I should have?" Buddy's expression quickly turns uneasy as his eyes flash back and forth.

"You can Google it but the headlines go; *Snakes Haunt Bellagio*. Pictures and all."

"Holy shit! Did you say pictures?"

"It seems a housekeeper squealed to a reporter in the lobby. And then it all started."

"What started? What about the pictures?"

"I'll get to that. The Bellagio management was trying to squash the story denying it all. But the housekeeper remained hysterical. Lawrence saw it all unfold."

"Lawrence?"

"He works for me. He'd come to get Charlie and the Doctor's bag but he couldn't get near your room for all the security. The story would have died except she lured the reporter into going to the room to find the snake."

"So? Charlie was back with me by then."

"Not exactly. It seems the housekeeper and the reporter appeared about the same time Charlie made his second appearance just as Taylor and Mr. Clarkson were about to bed down."

"Oh, God. No."

"When they went to knock, the door flung open. Screaming 'Snake!', Taylor flew into the hallway wearing nothing but a large pillow."

"You were going to tell me about pictures?"

"Oh, yeah. After capturing Taylor's backside, the reporter caught Charlie scurrying across the king."

Chapter 18

When You Wish Upon a Stargazer

"What do they want to talk about, Mother?"

"I have no idea. Gabe just said that he and Jeffrey had something big to announce."

"It's not a good time. We've got workers crawling all over the house. Someone always has a question for me."

"It was your idea to G.C. the remodeling."

"I'm not complaining. Still think it was the right thing to do. We're saving a bundle by doing it ourselves."

"And you thought it was going to be a three-month project."

"And you thought it was going to cost half as much."

"Touché. Here's the Starbucks he was talking about in this strip mall. We're ten minutes early." Katherine floats her

Cadillac into the cramped lot. "Why are these spaces so damn small?" She says craning her neck over the steering wheel.

"Mother, they don't make cars this big anymore."

"Of course, they do. Just look at all these trucks." She puts her car in park, leaves the engine running and begins touching up her lipstick. "I've known Gabe since he was a teenager. Long before he came out but I never thought those two would stick together."

"Neither did I, especially after that painter whacked Gabe in the mouth."

"Jeffrey gets in trouble like that, with people misreading his intentions. He thought that goon was signaling he was gay."

"But still Mother, Jeffrey had no business trying to fix him up with a friend."

"I know, but that's Jeffrey. He's just a playful spirit. Never thought Gabe would find someone to meet his standards but anything Jeffrey wants, he gets."

"When did you discover he was gay?"

"Gabe? I'd suspected for a while but when he came to work in my flower shop, it all made sense. After Uncle Billy helped get me started, I sort of foundered for several months. When he suggested I give Gabe a job, it was just me and a couple of part time girl friends. I brought him in as a favor more than anything. A seventeen-year-old kid, working after school for $5 an hour. It wasn't long before I realized he wasn't into girls. It became obvious when our new male clientele gravitated to him, asking that he create their arrangements."

"He did everything from sweeping the clippings to cleaning the dead flowers off grave sites. He was so talented and a quick study. He watched everything I did. Even took some design courses. Within several months, he'd matched my skill level. And you know what? My business picked up almost immediately. I give Uncle Billy and Gabe all the credit for my success."

"But now he's an attorney."

"That's right and a damn good one. He soon realized that being cause driven was his thing--LGBT rights, family law and marijuana legalization. He's like a son to me."

291

Sandy spots Jeffrey as he gets out of Gabe's car. Having a fair complexion and boyish looks, he stands a slender five feet eight inches tall. With frost tipped blonde hair pulled into a pony tail, he could pass for Taylor Swift's twin. The morning attire consists of flip flops, gym pants, and a crop top. "There they are now." she says. "I hope this doesn't take too long. Most of the workers punch out at three-thirty."

After exchanging air kisses, the four find a table in the corner. They each study their Starbuck's creations before engaging in conversation.

Gabe stirs his drink, sips the foam meniscus and gang planks the stick across the top. After squaring the napkin, he centers his cup and says, "Katherine, Jeffrey and I so appreciate you and Sandy meeting with us."

Jeffrey furrows his brow and casts a disturbed stare at Gabe, "Caramel macchiato? I didn't know you liked caramel. And you do know caffeine makes you cranky in the afternoon."

Gabe reaches over, rotates Jeffrey's bottle and says, "And what's that you're nurturing, an Evolution Fresh Ginger Limeade? I hope that wasn't picked in the rain forests."

Jeffrey links his fingers around the label and pulls back his drink. "That's hurtful. I was just concerned."

Katherine breaks in. "Gabe, they did a good job with your new choppers."

"Thanks, but can we not talk about that right now." Gabe caresses Jeffery's arm. "I'm sorry Darling. Maybe the caffeine does have me a little jittery."

As the two smooth over their snit, Katherine sends a glance to Sandy before saying, "Alright, fellows. Now that the planet's been saved, what is it that has you so out of sorts?"

Animated, Gabe turns to Katherine. "I'm just so thrilled to share our good news with our dearest friends." They smile at each other and slide their hands forward, revealing matching rings. Gabe announces, "We're engaged to get married!"

Katherine gushes, "Guys, that's wonderful! I can't think of..."

Gabe continues, "And we want to get married at your place. And have the biggest celebration Denver has ever seen!"

As Katherine drives out of the Starbucks, Sandy says, "You know, Mother. I'm not sure I like the added pressure of having a big wedding at the same time as our grand opening. A lot has to come together in six weeks to make that happen."

"Yes, I agree. But they said they'd be flexible on the date. It's not like they have to book a church and country club."

Sandy digs her nails into the corner of the seat as Katherine weaves in and out of traffic, "Mother, would you please take it easy. The speed limit is forty-five."

"Okay, but you said you needed to get back before the workers left." As horns honk, Katherine glides her Eldorado to the right lane without a turn signal.

"Yes, but in one piece." Sandy closes her eyes and takes a breath as they exit, "Thank you."

Sandy is on the veranda with Buddy and a contractor when Katherine calls. "Good morning, Sandra. Wanted to give you a heads up before our meeting this morning."

"Mother, can I call you back? Buddy's already late for work and we're meeting with the roofer about the slate."

"Jeffrey wants sexually explicit ice sculptures for the wedding."

"You're kidding me. What? A giant penis?"

"A penis *and* a vagina. There're going to be a lot of straight people there you know."

"Sounds crazy to me but I don't want to get between Gabe and Jeffrey."

"Bad visual, girl. Well, they're going to want to talk about it. Just wanted you to be ready."

"I really have to go. See you at eleven, Mother."

Buddy says to the roofer, "Sorry, Will. This is about the big gay wedding I was telling you about."

"I really don't care sir. Just need some direction on the replacement slate...if you want to have it done in a month."

"Buddy, can you believe they're talking about having a penis ice sculpture? And a vagina." Mother's all in a tizzy about it."

"How in the hell do you sculpt a vagina? Maybe do a giant doughnut?"

"You know what that'd look like, don't you." Sandy giggles.

The roofer butts in. "Excuse me. Can we get a decision on the Sea Green? It comes from Vermont and I'm not sure about the lead time."

Sandy takes the tiles and walks into the sunlight. "These are entirely different colors. Ours is so much darker."

"They age, you know. Yours is 100 years older. It'll take a while for them to match."

"Like when I'm 150?" Buddy says.

"Honey, I don't like the contrast but there's not much choice. What do you think?"

Buddy holds his arms upward. "Can you imagine how funny that prick is going to look after a couple of hours melting?"

Buddy and Sandy begin laughing.

"Ma'am?"

With tears streaming, Sandy hands the slate tiles back to the roofer. "I'm sorry. You do what's best. How much are we talking about here?"

The roofer casts a serious look outside a window and computes. "We have about a quarter of the roof needing replacement, where that tree hit several years back. That's about 1000 sq. feet." He turns to Sandy with a matter of fact assessment, "It could run you upwards of $40 grand."

Buddy looks at his watch and walks away muttering, "That's no problema. I'll just change the "2" to a "4" on the spreadsheet. I'm going to work. Maybe we'll be doing some product sampling today."

Sandy goes into the kitchen, pulls four waters from the cooler and places them around the oak table. A small oscillating fan stirs the fetid air. Opening the paned window, she hears the familiar humming of the generator on the back porch. Taking the seat where Buddy had been moments earlier, she sees a happy face grinning through the plaster powder.

As she traces on horns with her finger, Gabe calls from the foyer. "Hellooooo, Sandy. Where are you?" Sandy reaches to the floor and jerks out a spiral of cleaning wipes from their box. "In here, guys." she shouts, as their dust art disappears.

"When will you start with the painting? You've been stripping like forever." Jeffrey asks as he and Gabe appear.

"I wish I knew. They said that the last paint job was over fifteen years ago so an awful lot of prep work was needed. There's all that fancy gingerbread. And scraping and sanding around the scrolling and dental work. The weather's done a number too."

"Have you decided on the colors?" Jeffrey asks.

Sandy points to the swatch book on the counter. "We're matching the original, three of them in fact. We were able to go down eight layers to the first painting around 1905. The main color is white with a lot of accents."

Jeffrey spreads out the colors. "I just love these elegant old ladies. It's so cool watching them come back to life again."

Sandy takes a seat and says, "She's going to be a beauty. But like everything else, it's taking longer and running a lot more than we expected."

Katherine joins the meeting dramatically fanning her nose. "Smells like a shit hole in here."

"And good morning to you, Mother. It only happens when the dishwasher's on."

"Sounds like you've got a clogged U-joint." Gesturing to Gabe she says, "The way things are adding up, I think we're going to have to charge for this shindig of yours."

Gabe looks to Jeffrey and smiles. "If you guys don't charge us, we won't charge you for our branding idea. Jeffrey, tell them what you came up with."

"*Pleiades!* Name your B & B *The Pleiades*." Jeffrey proclaims.

"What the hell does that mean?" Katherine asks.

"*Pleiades* is a star cluster named after mythological characters. It's also known as the Seven Sisters. Pleiadians come from the planet Erra near the star Taygeta and are extra-terrestrials that most resemble humans. They have..."

299

Gabe interrupts, "Maybe we can save the backdrop 'til later, Jeffrey. So how 'bout it, ladies? *Pleiades.* Sort of cool, don't you think. Katherine?"

"It's better than the Cauthorn House which sounds like a lock up for loonies."

Googling the name, Sandy says, "I like it. Does have some panache. I've been so busy with the renovation, haven't had any time to think about it." She reads from her screen, "Yes, here it is. I thought I remembered a Buffet song about the Seven Sisters."

Jeffrey circles his index fingers upward and begins to sing, *"Desdemona's building a rocket ship. Desdemona's going away.* I just love Jimmy."

Gabe says, "That's a perfect lead into what we wanted to run by you, a theme for our wedding that would link to your new hotel. With the *Pleiades* being a star cluster and Jeffrey's favorite flower being the Stargazer lily, we have the perfect match."

Jeffrey stands, clasps his hands and exclaims, "That's right. A celestial nuptial with Stargazers everywhere!"

Katherine says, "We can get a good price through SAMS. Gabe, can you do the arranging?"

"Of course I will. Already have some super ideas." Gabe goes to the sink and pinches his nose. "Wow, Sandy. It does smell terrible over here."

Sandy closes her eyes and strums her fingers. "The plumber will be here tomorrow. You were saying, Gabe?"

He begins to gesture. "Jeffrey and I were talking. Let's say this is the base of the penis. The circumference, say twenty to thirty inches, would be ringed and layered with Stargazers in aqua picks on a Styrofoam collar. We'd have a tub draped in satin and filled with dry ice to handle the run off."

Katherine lights a cigarette and whispers to Sandy, "Here we go."

"That will be so cool. Zig does a great penis but is especially proud of his vagina."

Sandy gives an incredulous look. "What did you just say, Jeffrey?"

"My friend Ziggy Zygote in Las Vegas is famous for his outrageous ice sculptures. He's really mastered the vagina and absolutely loves my Stargazer theme."

Gabe purses his lips and turns to Jeffrey. "That's what we're having difficulty with. Ziggy's signature vagina resembles a red Calla lily, but Jeffrey wants it to look more like a Stargazer."

Jeffrey dismissively flips his wrist. "He's very flexible, Gabe. If you remember, he put a foreskin on Carleton's penis."

Katherine rolls her eyes. "I told you."

Sandy attempts to refocus, "Can we talk about some other things, guys, like how many people are coming and what food you wish to serve?"

Katherine and Sandy are installing shelf lining in the kitchen drawers when Katherine's phone rings. After a moment, her eyes fixate with anger. "Good God Almighty, Gabe. You can't be serious? We're four days from opening and you want to change the food? I'm putting you on speaker so Sandy can hear this shit."

302

"Katherine, I'm so, so sorry but Jeffrey just told me he has a problem with meat. I thought it was part of his diet, getting ready for the wedding. Do you know he's gone from a 30 to a 28 in only three months? I just got him two pair Santorellis from Nordstrom. Personally, I prefer Boss, but they do look so hot and fit so well. And did I tell you we're having our Zegna evening suit fitting tomorrow? We're so excited."

Katherine leans into the speaker. "I'm fucking excited too, Gabe. Look, about the meat problem Jeffrey's suddenly having. We've got more than the prime rib. There's chicken and fish and a ton of plant shit for the crazies."

As the tension escalates, Sandy steps in. "Hello Gabe, Sandy here." Tilting her head to Katherine, she says in a soft and slow tone, "As you required, we've got the delectable free range organic chickens coming in from Fresno, and the special-ordered Patagonian tooth fish is arriving day after tomorrow from Argentina."

"Sea bass, Sandy. I much prefer you refer to it as sea bass. No one would really..."

"Excuse me, Gabe." she says. "But what we call it is not the issue. We've chosen our offerings to please everyone."

"But I don't think you understand. He's recently joined PETA. And told me about an hour ago that we can't sacrifice animals for our nuptial bliss."

Katherine leans to within six inches of the phone. "Fucking sacrifice animals? You're talking about ten grand worth of hair, scales, and feathers on order."

"Please don't shout, Katherine. Weeks ago I gave Jeffrey a copy of the menu we worked out and he never voiced any concerns. I'm always on him to follow up on things. To keep a calendar, to put his dirty laundry in the hamper, and to..."

"Gabe, stop it! I don't give a damn about your O.C.D. vs. the whatever the hell Jeffrey is. What is the opposite of O.C.D.?

"There's no opposite. I guess he never grew out of being a teenager."

"For Christ's sake, Gabe! That was only two years ago. You've been going together for how long?"

304

"That's beside the point, Katherine. We will not have anything to do with a selection that includes animals. I'm really sorry, but that's just the way it's going to be."

"We've got appetizers, the buffet and a carving station, all with wine parings! You've driven me nuts with all these last minute changes. But this takes the cake."

"That's something else we need to talk about."

"Gabe, don't tell me there's a problem with the cake."

"Darling. I'm so upset. Please don't get angry, but yes there is. I have a list here. There're a few things that trigger his allergies."

"Now he's got allergies? You're about to trigger a murder!"

"This is all so upsetting, Katherine. I'm sorry but he cannot have anything with butter, cheese, puddings and custard and sherbert...even icecream which I don't understand. Pistachio has always been his favorite."

"This is no time to play games, Gabe. We've got suppliers lined up for one hundred and fifty guests. And it's the *Pleiades* grand opening. We've got a lot of big wigs coming and..."

"It may be more like two hundred, not sure. We're still getting late R.S.V.Ps. You know how the Millennial's are today. And Jeffrey is so loved. Did I tell you that a bunch of his high school classmates from Tacoma are trying to come? It'll be a big surprise. They hope to charter a bus if they can get enough..."

"Gabe!"

"Please let me finish his 'no can do' list. There's yogurt. And of course milk and cottage cheese. But you wouldn't be serving cottage cheese anyway. It's all workable, isn't it?"

"Katherine? Sandy? Are you there?"

Sandy flinches as Katherine's phone careens into the splash board, chipping off a chunk from an olive picker's head...one of the two hundred hand painted tiles from Barcelona.

Chapter 19

Turn and Face the Strange

In the lobby of Vegan Variations, Sandy moves from the sun streaked couch to a shaded spot next to Katherine. As she fans herself with a magazine, she notices a three-ringed binder on the coffee table.

Katherine is engrossed on Sandy's phone. "Janis, I'm not paying for the fucking tooth fish and free birds." She pauses. "Free range, whatever. Look, I've got three restaurants in the Denver area that will purchase all that shit at my price less 20%. All you have to do is write another P.O."

Sandy leans over and whispers, "Mother, there're children over there."

"Hush!" she says to Sandy. "Not you, Janis, my daughter. Okay, so here's the deal. We'll pay you $3,000 for your trouble. That'll more than cover any costs and a good bit of profit. I am very sorry, dear. Got to cater to the client, you know. Talk with you later."

"So how did that go?" Sandy sheepishly asks as she flips through the binder.

"Damn, it's hot in here." Katherine grumbles as she lights a cigarette.

"It's hot everywhere. Mother, I don't think you're allowed to smoke in here."

"It'll be over before anyone notices."

"So what did Janis have to say?"

"We're good, I think. Because we're old friends or maybe were. There wasn't a contract signed. Plus, Gabe got some of his chef pals to take the meat off our hands. The three grand put some salve on her slit."

Sandy pulls the binder up to her face avoiding eye contact with the glaring mother and curious kids. "*Mother*," she says under her breath.

Katherine takes a fan from her purse. "What's up with the AC people? Those units are just not working right. We do have this little get together in a few days, you know."

"Yes, I know. They're working on it. They say it'll be fine."

"And what about the roof being finished? What if it rains?"

"I wouldn't worry with the drought and all. This place is about to ignite." Sandy flips through the pages.

Katherine reaches over and tugs at Sandy's pant leg. "Why don't you ditch those frumpy Capris? If I had a figure like yours, I'd be sporting some of those hot Wunder Unders."

"Surprised you don't. Mother, are you sure these people can handle this on such short notice?"

"I gave Betty an idea of what we're talking about when I called. She said it could be done but it was going to cost. When we're finished here, I have to get to MaryAnn. She's going to be some kind of pissed. I'll have to buy her off too."

"MaryAnn?"

"Yeah, she's about to finish up the wedding cake we're not going to use. I'm not going to have any friends after this."

Sandy stares off in space. "Join the crowd. I seem to remember having a life once in Marietta."

Katherine scrolls through Sandy's contacts. "You don't have MaryAnn's number? You've got a text from someone named David. Who's he?"

Sandy snatches the phone from Katherine and shoves it in her purse. "It's not anyone. What are you going to do about *your* phone, Mother?"

"It's in a hundred pieces."

"I know that. You can't keep using mine."

"Guess you're right. Let's go by Verizon when we're finished here."

"Oh, great, another thing to do."

"And the printing shop. Thought we needed another 100 cards. On the way home is a florist. Gabe wants a heavier gage wire and more fern for the Stargazers."

"Will it ever end?" Sandy shakes her head as she studies a page. "While you were having your way with Janis,

I was looking through Mrs. Cassidy's Vegan menu offerings. Actually, most of it seems delicious. They even have a Brownie and Sundae station."

"Betty does a great job. The food was never the issue. It's just that Jeffrey jerks Gabe around like a balloon in a windstorm."

Sandy turns and smiles, "Ain't love grand?"

"I've never seen Gabe like this. He's a whirling dervish while Jeffrey's acting like it's a spa day." As a woman enters the lobby, Katherine says, "Here comes Betty now. Keep your fingers crossed and your mouth clean. Betty's very religious ."

Back at the house, Sandy and Katherine sort through the long list of last minute changes.

Katherine flaps her blouse. "It's still hot in here. I don't care what they're saying."

"They're coming back tomorrow with a factory rep. They say it'll be fixed."

"They'd better stop saying and start doing. Two months ago, it would have been very pleasant."

311

"Mother, we had no choice with the construction running behind. Who would have thought we'd be having a drought and a record breaking heat wave?"

"What about the damn painters? Their tarps are draped all over the front, crushing the plants. We need to stage the veranda. Is the paint even going to be dry?"

"I don't think they'll be finished with the front trim. You can't rush painters."

"I told Gabe to get married at the justice of the peace. But *no*, Jeffrey wanted a grand celebration, right slap dab in the middle of a construction site!"

"You know what you said about Jeffrey getting his way, Mother."

"Don't get me going." Katherine checks over the attendee list. "I see we're going to have quite the turn-out from the community--the Mayor, several city council members, even a U.S. Senator. And big players in the marijuana industry, lots of V.I.P.s to get us some great pub."

"I surely hope we get something out of all this since we're only charging Gabe our costs for the reception."

"Well, he's doing a lot of legal stuff for us, so it'll all work out."

"Mother, about the guests. Mrs. Cassidy looked at us like we were crazy when we gave her different figures, three days from the event."

"It was Gabe who said commit to two hundred."

"But one hundred and fifty invitations went out and we only have ninety-eight RSVPs."

"I told him that. He doesn't want to risk being short on anything. I think his pro bono business will take a hit after this soiree."

"Wait until he finds out about the catering. You heard her say she's going to have to bring in extra help to pull this off. And, she's putting the squeeze on all her suppliers so there will be no bargains."

"But he is getting a big break on food costs. Roasted egg plant dip is a lot cheaper than Beluga caviar."

"The guests won't much care with all the pot being consumed. This is probably a better route to take than all the fancy stuff."

"What about the damned "Free From" Vegan friendly cake? Gluten free, dairy free, taste free. Who's ever heard of a naked cake, one with no icing?"

"Bet it won't touch our brownies, Mother."

"I think I'm going to eat them all. And God knows how much he's paying for Mr. Stardust to drive over from Vegas with the ice organs."

"Ziggy Zygote? You won't believe this but I overheard Gabe carrying on with Jeffrey. Something about how much strawberry coulis to freeze into the water to get just the right pinkish tint in the sculptures. Jeffrey was playing around on his computer trying to match with a Stargazer throat."

"Not only that. They were discussing yesterday about straining the stupid strawberry seeds. Meanwhile, Mr. Whatever was going berserk claiming he didn't have time to freeze the ice in the molds."

"Come on, Mother. You're not telling me he's actually got a dick mold?"

"A dick *and* a pussy mold. Must be a big thing in Vegas. But since Jeffrey wanted the Stargazer lily pussy instead of the Calla lily pussy, Ziggy's reluctantly agreed to make one custom for him."

"This is all crazy. Gabe seems to be getting unwrapped. When I talked with him this morning, he was at some fabric shop trying to find silk free satin."

"What the hell is that for?"

"To drape around the drip tubs. Apparently producing the silk overworks the little silk worms. It's another PETA thing."

"Thank God Jeffrey's not wearing a Vera Wang. Next thing you know, he'll have Gabe running around with a net saving the bugs Saturday night."

"Please don't give him any ideas, Mother."

Leaving the building at the same time, Randy Anderson and Buddy meet in the lobby of Colorado Medicinal. Randy opens the door and says, "So tomorrow's the big day?"

"Sure is. I appreciate you letting me go home early."

"I'm on my way out too. Got an hour and a half ride down to Bear Creek. My brother's in town on business and we're going hiking for a day."

"Should be nice down there."

"Better than here for sure. Looks like it's going to be another scorcher." Randy says.

"Afraid so. Something's wrong with our air at the old house and no one can put their finger on it. Sandy's uncle had the units installed only three years ago."

"Holy crap, I can't imagine."

"Please don't. Sounds like you're going to have more fun than I. Sandy needs my help and some grass for the brownies."

"You're not giving her the Stargazer?"

"Good God, no. That's for you, me the editor of *High Times Magazine*. He wants to feature it in their next edition so that'll get the word out."

"That's super. I think it's a sure fire competitor for the next Denver Cannabis Cup. I'm even a little fearful of that shit. 36% THC is the strongest we've ever recorded."

"Just a hit'll do it. Maybe that can be our slogan."

"You did one hell of a job with those Afghani Kush strains. That Indica-dominant cross is going to be a big seller."

"Thanks, and what a great coming out party. As for Sandy and Katherine's little bakery, they selected a 10% Banana Kush to infuse the coconut oil."

"Coconut oil?"

"Yeah, that's what the Vegans use to bake with. Makes incredible brownies they say."

"Sounds delicious. Were you able to get any more tents?"

"Not from the rental companies. It's a big week-end with the Gay Rocky Mountain Regional Rodeo in town. Had to buy three from Wal-Mart." Buddy checks his watch. "Going to get them now so let me run."

"Look, we'll be getting back late tomorrow afternoon. Would you mind if I brought along my brother to the reception?"

"Sure, no problem. See you tomorrow, Randy. Travel safely."

"Thanks and good luck with your AC and brownies."

Sandy places a folding chair in the shade under a large aspen. "Over here everyone. Let's find a spot away from the painters. I know you're hot so I'll try to keep this short. Everything's typed up but wanted to walk it through and answer any questions."

"First thing in the morning, we're placing the luminaries along the driveway leading to the front steps. The lighting folks are installing flood lights around the house as we speak. *The Pleiades* will be shining bright.

The special events people will be here very early with the big tent, tables and chairs for the table settings. Boys, you'll need help Dad set up the extra tents."

Try to stay out of the way of our worker bees. The painters and roofers will be hustling to get their jobs done.

The catering company will come mid morning to get their bars and stations set up. Gabe and several of his friends will be along early afternoon with the flowers and decorations. The beer, beverages and ice will be delivered around two.

Mother and I will be in the kitchen the rest of the today working on our Vegan Friendly Brownie and Sundae creations.

And no one is to enter the Sir Walter Raleigh smoking room. Dad will have some special guests and they are not to be disturbed."

"I bet they're in there getting stoned." Taylor sighs.

"Not so. They're talking business. This will be a pot friendly hotel so we expect to see people smoking all over the place." She gives Taylor a stern look and says, "*Adults*, that is."

"Mother and I will have all rooms in the house decorated, lighted, and standing tall. With no overnight guests, we can show off our accommodations. The wedding and reception is serving as our grand opening so we want the *Pleiades* checked out. There will be brochures and business cardall around. If anyone asks about reservations, send them to me."

"If you need to use the bathroom, use one of the portable johns. Gabe and Jeffrey will have the master to shower and dress for an hour but will honeymoon at the Four Seasons. Other than that, stay out of the rooms."

Sandy spots Taylor who has wandered over to chat with a carpenter. "Taylor! May we have your attention back over here?"

Fanning her face with a piece of cardboard, she sashays towards the meeting.

Sandy coldly says, "Thanks for rejoining us, Taylor. You will be working with Mrs. Cassidy to replenish the buffet items, keep the bars restocked with ice and glasses. Anything she says. She wants you ready to go by one."

Positioned with a view of the worker, Taylor turns to her mother, "She's a tyrant, Mom. We met with her yesterday and she's treating us like slaves."

"You will be her slave for the day. You're getting paid well, so no complaints."

"Got it, Mother." Taylor disengages and begins tapping on her phone.

Zach hollers back, "How much is she getting paid?"

"None of your business, you little twerp. You're outside help!"

"Enough Taylor. Boys, as we discussed, after lighting the luminaries you'll get on the tents, chairs, and tables. Do anything Mrs. Cassidy or your father orders. You and the other guys should be dressed, white shirts and ties, ready to park cars by four."

In unison, Zach and Luke cry, "Ties? It's too hot to wear ties."

"Yes, ties. This is a formal wedding." She turns to Katherine. "Mother, I need your help with the last minute punch list for all the rooms. Oh, those WoodWick teakwood air fresheners came in yesterday. Need to place one in every room." With a nod to Taylor, "And Taylor, you'll have to have the little room bouquets done before two."

Taylor mumbles with her usual disconcerting tone, "The master already informed me."

Sandy turns a page. "Let's see. Oh, the ice caterer from Las Vegas is expected around two-thirty. There will be a martini luge in the living room and out here we'll have a creation on each side of the entrance."

"Creation? Well, there's a euphemism for you." Katherine cracks.

Sandy laughs. "Funny, Mother. you sound like Buddy." She sees his car approaching. "And here he comes now." She continues to read through her notes detailing activities.

"For the wedding itself, no one needs to do anything for that. Another company is handling the stringed lighting, seating, stage platform, flowered archway, bouquets and so forth. They'll also be setting up a large dance floor following the vows. Gabe has all that arranged."

"With the wedding being at five, we expect guests starting around 4:15. The lighted walkway will channel everyone to the front entrance where they will be ushered through the house to the wedding and reception area out back."

"The wedding will end about 5:30 followed by the photo shoot. The cocktail reception will begin at 5:45. So boys, there will be a second wave of parking and don't forget about lighting the luminaries during the wedding."

"Buffet dinner will be served at 7:00 followed by dessert, cake cutting, and toasts in the living room. The harpist is scheduled to perform from 7:30 until 8:30. The

Brownie and Sundae station will be in the parlor. The band comes on at 8:30 and plays until midnight at poolside."

"Are there any questions?"

Taylor streaks her hair with her fingernails. "When are they going to fix the air conditioner?"

"They're back here first thing tomorrow. That's all I know. Anything else?"

As he walks onto the steps, Buddy raises his hand. "Is there a place I can take a nap for thirty-six hours?"

Sandy folds her notebook and fans her face, "Anyplace you want day after tomorrow. Right now we need to get started on the brownies. I'll see you and Mother in the kitchen."

Moments later Buddy slings his attaché onto the counter. "Okay, ladies I brought the 10% THC banana Kush you wanted for the infusion. I have an ounce for sixty servings. That should give everyone a nice buzz."

As Buddy snaps open the attaché, his cell rings. "Just a minute, this is Security at the grow house." He walks into the hallway with a concerned look. Seconds later he bursts back into the kitchen. "I have to go. A fire's broken out at the warehouse. I'll call when I know something."

Katherine clicks the portable fan on high and ties her apron. "Bummer. Bet the firemen will rush to *that* call. At least he left us the pot."

Chapter 20

That Damned Old Rodeo

As the warm morning sun cuts through the oaks and aspens, Buddy steers the wheel barrow down the winding driveway. Every eight feet he places a silver luminary bag while Luke weights it with a scoop of sand. Jake follows with a candle for each of the seventy lanterns.

From behind, Sandy pulls a small roller cooler. "Keep hydrated everyone. It's going to be a long hot day." She looks up to the western gable as two men tether from a spire. "I'd hate to be one of the roofers. They have to be baking."

Buddy stops and opens a bottle. "Have you been in the house this morning? Any change since they refilled the Puron?"

"It's just 79 with the three units going all night. They called to say they're on the way now." Sandy's foreboding is obvious as she shakes her head. "I can't think about not having any air."

Buddy grabs the handles and continues along the drive. "Heavens no. The special event people have the right idea. They got here at 7:00 with a team of six and they're almost finished."

Sandy begins shuffling the placements. "Be sure to stagger the bags and two feet back from the drive. Gabe wants to save these for a friend's wedding next month so we don't want them squished. And, don't forget to light these things during the wedding. I'll be too busy to remind you."

She calls down the drive to Buddy, "Have you heard anything about the weather? They were saying something this morning about possible storms in isolated areas."

He looks back and says, "Hot is all I know. But it hasn't rained in weeks. We'll be fine."

"I told Betty last night to order another five hundred pounds of ice. Can't have too much of that. She wasn't sure it would be available on such short notice."

326

Katherine's Cadillac turns onto the property and slows to a stop. Taylor is asleep in the back seat. She rolls down her window and says, "Looking good, gang. Buddy, glad to hear the fire at the grow house wasn't too bad."

"We were real lucky. The sprinklers kept it down until the fire trucks arrived. Wrecked my night though. Didn't want to bother Randy at the lake. And by the way, he's bringing his bachelor brother to the reception. He's about your age and a pretty cool dude according to Randy."

"I don't know. We'll see." As the AC service van comes from behind, Katherine pulls away. "Sandy, I'll get started on cleaning the kitchen before Betty and her crew arrive." With a raised voice she says over the back seat, "Maybe Taylor will come to life soon."

"I'll get Sleeping Beauty going right after I see what's happening with the air." Sandy follows the service van up the drive.

Having lined the driveway with lanterns, Buddy points the wheel barrow towards the house. "Come on boys. Let's get started on the tents."

At noon Sandy goes out back and finds Buddy and the boys under a tree. Dripping in sweat with aluminum poles across his lap, he's reading directions when Sandy asks, "You've only got one tent up?" He does not answer. "Honey, you have to go back to Wal-Mart. Get every fan they've got."

Katherine and Sandy are in the dining room pushing on a stuck window when Gabe comes stomping through the front door. Fanning his reddened face with both hands, he exclaims, "Gracious, it's hot. You need to turn on the air!"

Sucking on her scraped palm, Katherine looks up. "You have a good grasp of the obvious, Sherlock. The AC has gone tits up."

As he starts to snivel, she says, "Good God, Gabe. It sucks but it's not worth crying over."

"It's not the air conditioner, Katherine. It's Jeffrey. We broke up."

"So what's new? This is no time for your damned drama."

Sandy pushes forward, blots his tears with a napkin and places her arm across his shoulder. "It's alright, Gabe."

328

She gives a back off look to Katherine and says, "I'm sure it's just a misunderstanding."

"No it's not! First it was the food, and then it was the cake, and then the coulis. Do you know we got a perfect match for the Stargazer and when he discovered the strawberries were not organic he..."

As Gabe slumps downward, Katherine grabs both shoulders and shakes him. "Gabe, snap out of it! We have a wedding in less than five hours."

Another series of sobs begins before Gabe chokes out, "The horses. The poor horses."

Katherine and Sandy repeat, "Horses?"

"Yes, I was surprising him at the rehearsal dinner last night with a horse drawn carriage. He threw a hissy fit and flew off saying that he had been disrespected. How was I to know PETA had a thing against that?"

Sandy softly says, "You two just need to take a deep breath, hug and make up."

Wringing his hands Gabe cries, "But I don't know where he is. I haven't seen him since last night."

"How could you break up if you haven't seen him?" Katherine asks.

"That's just how it goes. We both know when it's coming."

Katherine squints her eyes and says through clinched teeth, "You listen to me, Gabe. You're just going to have to delay your little break-up. There's no time for that shit."

Sandy looks out the bay window. "Doesn't he drive a cobalt blue Prius?"

Gabe beams at her side. "Oh, yes! That's him! And that's Billy behind him with the Stargazers." He rushes out the door. Minutes later they return to the foyer holding hands.

Katherine comes around the corner. "Well, that was quick. You fellows rehearsing for an unreality show?"

"That's not at all funny, Katherine. I've been sick with worry, but thankfully he's fine. Just look at this fantastic outfit." Gabe feigns a swoon as Jeffrey twirls in his pink glitter cowboy hat, skinny jeans and spurred boots. "We both apologized and that's good enough for me." He stands back in deference. "So where have you been my little Buckaroo, riding the back forty?"

Jeffrey demurs, "I was so angry about the abused horses, I went out with some PETA friends. I had a little too much to drink and slept over."

Gabe raises his eye brows and asks with a softened but strained inflection, "You slept over where, my Dear?"

"It's nothing, really. So this morning they took me out to protest the Regional Rodeo. It's terrible what those poor creatures are put through to entertain us. Do you know they..."

"Wait a minute. You went to a Gay Rodeo to protest animal abuse?" Katherine says exasperatingly as she walks away. "It's five o'clock somewhere."

Jeffrey clasps his hands. "Why yes. And you know what? When we got there they were about to have a big brawl. Bodies were glistening in the hot sun as they pushed against each other. Gary Masters was there shirtless in overalls. I haven't seen him since he got that cute trainer. You just would not believe how that man is ripped. And

331

Jackie was there with Celeste. She's put on some weight since her..."

Gabe taps his watch and says with a forceful tone, "Jeffrey, we have a wedding to attend to. Remember?"

"Guess who else I ran into? Roddy the Rocket Man, one of the best bronco busters on the circuit. The last time I saw him was at that Ft. Worth party when he was wearing those outlandish assless chaps."

"Oh I recall that little scene."

"You were so jealous."

Gabe does a demi-pointe. "That's *enough*, Jeffrey!"

"Don't be so mean. I want you to know we stopped the about to be fight. He cooled the cowboys and I calmed down my PETA friends. And guess what? Roddy agreed to have the goat dressing taken out of the rodeo."

Katherine returns with a Coors Light and asks, "What the fuck do you dress a goat with?"

"Tighty whities. It's really stressful on the goat." Jeffrey explains.

Katherine downs her beer and crushes the can. "I can only imagine."

Jeffrey kisses Gabe on his blotched cheek and declares, "Anyway, we're all friends now so I invited everyone to our party. Isn't that cool?"

Katherine pulls another beer from the fridge and sits at the dining room table. After lighting a Marlboro, she gestures to the Free From cake. "At least there's no icing to melt on that ugly ass cake. Have you ever seen anything so hideous?"

Sandy sits a stack of dessert plates on the buffet. "It'll be fine, Mother. Besides, our brownie and sundae station will be getting all the attention. I briefed Betty's daughter Rhonda on the rules. No more than one square per person, adults only. She's a very religious girl and has a stellar reputation."

"Those are the types to worry about."

"And what about Taylor? With her probation ending yesterday, I am terrified of what's on her mind. I surely don't like the timing of this shindig. I'm afraid she'll see it as her coming out party."

"I guess you need to worry about 'em all. But I must say, ever since that dust up with the snake at the Bellagio, Taylor's really towed the line."

"Right. Let's see, Mother. She seduced her probation officer and almost cost him his job and marriage. It's a miracle he wasn't caught with her at the casino. Somehow they managed to keep that little adventure under wraps. The only reason she's behaved is because he was smart enough to break it off and get her reassigned to a new officer. One that's been no nonsense."

"I'd say. Some kind of a bad ass. He's watched her like a hawk. Even did surprise checks on her every week or two. He'd just pop up at my apartment, do a breathalyzer and take urine. She found someone she couldn't work. He was an ugly mother fucker though."

"He's one of the very few people I've ever seen that she couldn't get to."

"Or care to... As I was saying, she's done all her community service, remained sober and somehow managed to stay in junior college. She goes to class, studies and has avoided trouble. That's all I care about. She was such a pain for the first couple of weeks. So this is all good."

"I wish I could share your optimism. I feel like she's been in a cocoon for twelve months, ready to spring upon some unsuspecting fool. Like that Alien thing that grew in Sigourney."

"You're always finding something to worry about, Sandra Lee. Speaking of such, what's she up to?"

"Mrs. Cassidy has her assembling the favors. I'm sure she's tackling that task with glee."

Katherine looks up at the portrait of Ezekiel Cauthorn. "Would love to see you in that fancy beaver hat today, Mr. Big Shot. I haven't been this damn hot since I was in Marietta." She thumps pollen from a lily in the display before her. "This place smells like a funeral home."

Sandy blots her face with a damp dish towel and drapes it around her neck. Nodding into the hallway, she says, "I know. Stargazers drive Buddy nuts. Make him sneeze like crazy. So how're our little love birds holding up?"

"Gabe is pin balling around while Jeffrey lounges on the veranda sipping a Suja Green Supreme."

"I'm not going to even ask what that is, but I've got the scene. Mother, please tell me Jeffrey was kidding about inviting the rodeo people."

"I hope to hell he was. But who knows, maybe he'll have the unemployed goats too."

Looking at the thermostat, Sandy says, "We're going to die tonight. It's 84 in here and it's even worse up stairs."

Katherine stuffs her cigarette butt in the empty beer can and shakes it around. "I saw some of the fight outside. So what was the deal with the AC?"

"Something about the evaporator coil being defective. It wouldn't hold the Puron. The manufacturer didn't want to take the blame or fulfill the warranty."

"So the service guy decked him?"

"Right after he drove his company car into our only good unit. The police hauled them both away."

"Aren't they the lucky ones? At least the jail's air conditioned. Where's Buddy?"

"He and the boys got the last tent up as the sun baked down. They're over at the apartment taking showers now. Some good that'll do. Mother, this is turning into a circus right before our eyes."

Katherine looks to the front of the house. "Who keeps on ringing that damn doorbell? Everything's open."

"Whoever it is, they have Gabe carrying on." As Sandy walks towards the front, she says, "I don't think he's holding up very well, Mother."

"No, he's not. Wonder what's got him going now."

In the broad center hall Gabe and a small man are arguing. Jeffrey is perched on a loveseat fanning himself with his cowboy hat.

Katherine spots the Ryder refrigerator truck at the entrance. "I see our little ice artist has arrived from Vegas."

She and Sandy stop in their tracks when they reach the front door. Sandy points and giggles, "Mother, that doesn't look like a penis at all."

"Exactly!" declares Gabe. "That's what I told Ziggy. We're paying for a perfect penis and he brings us this?"

Jeffrey quips, "A perfect penis? Now that's something to think about."

Katherine slides a vertical stroke on the five-foot phallic. "Looks like a half-ass cream sickle to me." Glancing to her left she adds, "And what's with the big glob of raspberry sherbet? That's supposed to be a pussy?"

"Glob? You didn't say that!" Ziggy shrieks.

Jeffrey goes over and peers inside the oblique figure. "Why it does match the Stargazer throat, don't you think Gabe Darling? But I do have to agree with Katherine. It doesn't very much resemble a vagina."

"And just when was the last time you saw a vagina?"

"You rascal. I do have two sisters, you know. There was this time when Carla decided to..."

Ziggy stomps his feet. "I said I had to have three days to freeze the molds! You two kept dicking around over that silly coulis coloring. They didn't have time to set."

Jeffrey swipes the ice phallic and licks his fingers. "Ziggy, you must admit, they do have a realistic tone. I think the coulis turned out real well. It's very tasty but I still think we should have strained the seeds."

Ziggy throws up his hands and storms to the truck. "I have to turn in the rental and catch my plane. The luge is in the living room. Have a nice fucking wedding."

Swirling his hand around the vulva, Jeffrey turns to Gabe. "I'm so upset. It doesn't look at all like the Stargazer he promised."

Sandy's eyes widen as she sees the disappointment sweep over Gabe's face. "Mother, I hear Betty calling. She wants us in the kitchen."

Katherine dries her hands on her apron. Looking at Gabe she says, "You guys created works of art alright. Quite the conversation pieces." She leans down and picks up the folded silk free satin and slings it to Jeffrey. "At least be happy about all those little worms you sent into retirement."

Betty Cassidy says to Katherine, "I don't know how you expect us to work in this place." My truck's arriving any minute with the hot buffet items and the kitchen's already boiling."

Taylor whines from the kitchen table, "And the chocolate truffles are melting."

Tossing her hair in the breeze of the fan, Sandy says, "And to think we were going to cook-off the meat."

Betty looks to her in disgust. "That doesn't make me feel any better. I'll still have to turn on the stove to heat up the broccoli Delmonico, mushroom phylo, and..."

Katherine opens a counter drawer and pulls out a kitchen towel. "Betty, we don't have any damned choice. Here, try dipping this into the boys' designer ice puddles."

Sandy takes the towel and wets it in the sink. "Mother's just kidding, Betty. We're trying to do the best we can. Here, wrap this around your neck."

Betty takes the towel and points. "Well, at least get these brownies out. I need the space. And Katherine, I'd appreciate it if you wouldn't curse."

Before a retort Sandy says. "Mother, where can we hide the brownies until the reception starts?"

Katherine grabs a tray. "The china is cleared out of the buffet. Let's put them in there."

Sandy is on her knees with a sheet pan of the THC infused brownies when Gabe walks into the dining room holding two

340

coat bags. "Jeffrey doesn't want to wear our evening suits. He says it's too hot and I've paid a fortune for these Zegna's."

Sandy pushes the brownies deep into the buffet and stands. "You know, Gabe. He might have a point. You guys will be miserable in those outfits. It's 92 degrees and rising. Maybe we ought to notify our guests to come causal. As cool as possible."

Gabe sits the suits across the chair and wipes his forehead. "Oh no. This cannot be happening. We wanted this to be so elegant."

"It will be Gabe. Who else will have a venue like this, loaded with Stargazers, and ice creations and a great band? And a harpist too. It'll be wonderful and so memorable."

Katherine offers no consolation. "You shouldn't have waited until our renovation was finished. The delay's turned this into Hell's Kitchen."

Gabe begins to sob, "Everything was booked when we tried to find another venue. Besides, Jeffrey was so intent on having it here. It was to be his dream wedding."

"And it will be Gabe." Sandy says glaring at her mother.

341

"You're all nuts." Katherine stands and walks out of the room. "Taylor and I have to get going."

Gabe stares blankly at his feet and asks, "So how would we get to everyone?"

After a violent sneeze, Buddy joins in, "Gabe, you can post on Facebook and do a GroupMe notice. Have invitees notify other invitees. The word will be out in no time."

Gabe jumps from his chair. "Good idea. I'll get Jeffrey to do it while I run over to my place to get us a change of clothes. It's almost 3:00 so we have to move fast."

The man standing in the doorway moves aside as Gabe blows by. He steps forward with his sweat stained cap in hand and says to Sandy, "Mrs. Henderson, one of my men has heat prostration and I have to take him to the emergency room."

"That's awful, Will. I hope it's not serious. Did you get finished?" Buddy asks before another sneeze.

"I'm sorry. We did the best we could do but there's another square left."

"Another square? That's nothing."

"Yeah, another hundred square feet. About a ten by ten section. We've got it covered with at tarp and tied to a chimney. Don't think it'll rain. But just in case. If Johnny's okay, we'll be back Monday to wrap it up. I'm sorry but I have to go."

Sandy says, "If it's all you can do. Good luck with Johnny. See you Monday." Her expression changes as she glares at Buddy and shakes her head. "I'm not at all happy about having a big blue patch on our gable."

Avoiding the subject, Buddy eyes a large corrugated box with dampened edges. "That must be the martini luge. I'll get it set up in the corner."

Seeing the eight liters of Grey Goose Vodka and Bombay Sapphire gin squared on the buffet, Sandy thinks, *Note to self. Keep the kids away from the brownies and Buddy away from the luge.* She calls to Buddy, "While you're working on that, I'm going to the apartment to get cleaned up and dressed. I have no idea what I'm going to wear."

Chapter 21

Feed Your Head

Sandy is blow drying her hair when Buddy walks in. "People should be arriving any minute now." He says.

"Okay, I'm about ready. With all we have to do, I'll only have a few minutes to poke my head out back to catch the vows. Did you see that strange text Jeffrey sent out?"

"About the revised dress code?"

"Yes. Look at this." Sandy pulls up the text and hands her phone to Buddy. *come cool & cas 4 prty & pls. tell bffs.* "Sounds sort of vague, doesn't it?"

"I guess. Who all did that go to?"

"It didn't say but that doesn't concern me so much. It's the "tell best friends forever" bit. What if it gets passed around to friends of friends?"

"We can't worry about that now." Buddy gives Sandy a kiss on the cheek. "You look great, Honey. Love that sun dress on you. It matches my guayabera."

Sandy laughs. "Thanks. I hope we don't steal the show."

"Not even close. I'm going to check on the parking. Anything to stay away from those stinking flowers."

Sandy brushes out her hair. "I'm right behind you."

Before entering the house, Sandy stops in the shade of a tent and pulls a Fiji water from the ice tub. As she twists the cap and takes a swallow, she's drawn to the melodic sounds of the five-piece string quartet readying for their performance.

Across the way, dozens of lounge chairs and recliners circle the lighted pool spotted with floating votives. Jets churn and bubble 90-degree water in the adjoining hot tub. Sandy muses about who will be the first to take a plunge.

To her right is a massive main tent covering twenty-five tables for eight. Each is adorned with a white cloth accented with favors, dazzlers, and a striking Stargazer centerpiece. She laughs recalling how Gabe and Jeffrey fussed over every detail.

A fifty-foot double sided buffet is lined with hot and cold food stations soon to be filled. Flanked at the ends are two smaller tents that house open bars. A fourth tent covers a circular setting of appetizers and horderves to be offered for the cocktail reception.

Adjacent are twenty rows of ten wooden folding chairs. A cedar shaving aisle splits through the center leading to a 25' X 25' stage. A satin kneeling bench rests beneath a Stargazer and greenery cloaked arch way. While an attendant places a fan on every seat, another fills a wicker basket with Stargazer petals. Long strings of white paper globes attached to the limbs of the hardwoods softly glow in the late afternoon sun.

To her left towers the *Pleiades*, the stunning late Victorian Queen Anne style mansion. Aside from the unfinished slate roofing and the sticky front porch balustrades, the painstaking restoration to her 1905 splendor is complete.

The elegant and inviting setting is a testament to her endurance--a tortuous but exhilarating journey since their upheaval in Marietta. Beaming with the pride of accomplishment, she feels this grand and glorious evening will signal the start of their new life.

A call across the way cuts short her reflections. "Sandy, I need you in the kitchen."

Standing on the back veranda, an anxious Betty Cassidy says to her as she approaches, "I still haven't seen Taylor since I sent her to find more glasses. I've got two other girls running late and things are piling up."

Sandy glances around the yard. "I'm sure she'll show up. Let me check on Gabe and Jeffrey first and I'll come give you a hand."

She lightly raps on their door. "How're you guys doing?" She is relieved to find the couple in a joyous mood.

With his arms in the air, Gabe's unbuttoned shirt flaps as the box fan blows from the window. "I'm melting like the penis." he laughs, as he clicks the dial to high.

Jeffrey tweaks his collar and smiles in front of the full length pier mirror, "Don't you just love our matching Colima

347

Beach Wedding shirts? Gabe was going to surprise me with them on our honeymoon to Kauai."

Gabe leaves the fan and gives Sandy a hug, "Sweetie, Jeffrey and I so appreciate what all you and Katherine have done to make this special. We're so excited."

Jeffrey does a group hug. "Aside from the AC being out, everything's turning out perfect. I think our guests will be thrilled by the new cool and cas dress code."

Sandy says, "I was going to ask you something, Gabe." She looks at her watch. "It's 4:30. Where's Arthur?"

"I don't know. He told me at the rehearsal he'd be here by 4:15. He's known as Mr. Punctuality at the office. Always ten minutes early to everything."

"Well, you're licensed. Maybe you can just marry yourselves."

Gabe squeezes Jeffrey's hand, "I will if I have to!"

Sandy turns to go, "Guys, I've got to help in the kitchen. I love you both. Break a leg."

She passes Katherine in the hall. "Mother, have you seen Taylor since you got back? Betty's looking for her."

Katherine, fanning herself with a brochure, says. "No I haven't. Looked all over the place so I'm about to leave her." She looks out the front. "Say, don't you think it's strange that no one's here yet? I mean the wedding's in thirty minutes. Shouldn't some people be arriving? The driveway's empty."

"That is weird." Sandy says as she opens the front door and kicks down the door stopper. "Might as well keep the door open to help circulate the air." She and Katherine walk onto the wrap around veranda. At the bend in the driveway, they see Buddy hobbling towards the house with a line of people sluggishly trailing behind.

Drenched in sweat and panting, he pounds up the front steps. "A large bus is blocking the driveway!" he huffs.

Gabe and Jeffrey approach and Gabe points. "That's a motorcycle cop coming across the yard!"

"He's running over the luminaries!" Jeffrey cries out.

They all rush down the steps as the Harley rumbles to a halt with blue lights flashing.

"Are you the owners of the house?" the officer asks.

Buddy, Sandy, and Katherine all answer, "Yes, sir."

"You've got a CoachWays bus from Tacoma stuck in a ditch at the entrance, forcing traffic to back up onto 34th Street."

Jeffrey springs forward. "Tacoma?"

Katherine turns to Gabe, "I thought you were pulling my leg." Gabe shrugs his shoulders and says, "I wanted to surprise Jeffrey."

Jeffrey throws his arms around Gabe. "They came! I can't believe it. Where are they all staying?"

Gabe smiles and says, "The Holiday Inn Express. Have had it booked for months."

The officer blots his face with a handkerchief and addresses Buddy, "Excuse me, sir but we've got to free the jam right away."

Buddy eyes the streaming procession of guests and says, "Please have them park in the lot we've reserved across the street until we can get the bus moved."

"Right. Want me to call a wrecker?"

Sandy says, "Yes, please do, officer." She looks to Buddy. "That's over a hundred yards they'll have to walk in this heat."

"Look!" Jeffrey exclaims, "That's Jimmy there and Carleton, and..."

"And Arthur, our officiate running down hot in a black suit." Gabe solemnly observes.

Sandy bolts up the stairs grabbing every wash cloth and towel she can find. She dumps them into a wicker basket by the front entrance and douses with a pitcher of ice water. As Luke trudges in she pulls him aside and points to the cold wet towels. "You've got a new job until the parking resumes. When these run out get a box of the spiral dry wipes in the garage."

After spray painting a bed linen, Buddy and Zach string it across their ten-foot stone entrance columns. Guests grouse as they duck under the splotched banner that reads; *Driveway blocked. Parking Across Street.*

One by one the wedding guests trickle in, the first forty-four being Jeffrey's surprise attendees from Tacoma. Gabe is patient as Jeffrey greets each with a hug. With the delayed arrivals, the wedding starts thirty-five minutes late.

The wrecker hooks up to the bus at 5:15, freeing the passageway. As Buddy and Luke untie the banner and reposition the luminaries, the first of the reception guests begin to pull into the entrance way. The four parking boys rush to the circular drive as cars begin to line up.

Sandy comes into the kitchen to find Betty and Katherine hard at work. Temperatures continue to rise as trays of sheet pan items roast in the Viking ovens. Later Sandy looks into the back yard as the wedding progresses and sadly acknowledges, "We're going to miss the vows."

"I guess so. Looks like Gabe was right about the hundred and fifty guests for the wedding. A busload of friends just showing up. Can you believe that?"

Betty places a pan of bubbling stuffed zucchini on the island. "Yeah, we should have plenty of food and we're just about caught up. Half my help was stuck in the traffic jam out front." She props open the back door and asks Sandy, "Can we get another fan in here? I'm drenched."

Buddy gasps from the doorway, "Something's wrong! Cars are stalled and the boys are running their asses off. They can't keep up."

"That's ridiculous," Katherine says. "We've got another thirty-eight RSVPs for the reception. That could

352

mean only fifteen or twenty more cars. They hear a police siren burping in bursts. "It's that Deputy Dog again. Now what does he want?"

As they reach the front of the house, the officer is talking to dispatch. Unsnapping his helmet, he approaches Buddy with a fearsome scowl. "Sir, we have another situation. Your guests are blocking the street again."

Buddy looks across the yard. "Officer, I don't understand. We cleared the bus and most of our guests are already here."

"I don't know about that sir. But the lot across the street is filled. You must free your driveway immediately. Traffic is stalled for blocks. I might add, that the Mayor is sitting about twenty cars back."

At nine-thirty Katherine, Sandy and Buddy huddle on the far corner of the veranda amidst tarps, rags and paint cans. "Mother, let me have one of your cigarettes."

Buddy holds his hand out. "Me too."

353

Katherine lights two in her mouth and passes to Buddy and Sandy. "What in the fuck are we going to do? They're still coming." She lights a cigarette for herself and braces her legs against the balustrade.

Sandy says into the darkness, "Our landscaping is destroyed and the house is filled with wasted people."

Katherine un-sticks her shoes. "Damn it. The shit's still wet!" Waving her hand towards the sea of vehicles before them, she says, "It's all those nut cases Jeffrey invited."

Sandy says in a monotonous tone as smoke floats from her mouth, "And you thought he was kidding about his PETA pals and the rodeo."

"And everyone else within a hundred miles. Everybody's best fucking friend." Katherine says as she takes off her shoes.

Buddy slowly rocks back and forth, staring at the few luminaries left standing. "Our front yard looks like the road to Mecca."

Sandy nods towards a couple splashing water on each other from a bird bath. "Or more like Woodstock." Her attention is drawn to a skinny guy canter levering on the edge the steps. "Stop! You're peeing on our house!" she screams.

His wobbly face casts a glazed-over look right before listing over the rail and flipping into the flower bed.

"Nailed the landing." Buddy says.

Sandy throws her head back. "This is an all-day plane crash."

Katherine pulls a painter's rag from a bucket and daubs it with paint thinner. As she wipes her shoe she says, "Sandy, Did you ever find Taylor?"

Sandy takes a deep drag and exhales to the bead boarded ceiling. "She came floating by a while ago. I think she was baked. First day after her probation. Big surprise there."

Buddy says, "I saw her earlier by the pool passing out horderves."

Sandy sits upright. "Horderves? We didn't pass out horderves."

"Who knows? Maybe Betty gave her some stuff."

Sandy eyes the rumbling western sky. "Is that thunder?"

Katherine looks up. "Sure as shit was. Lightning flashes too off in the distance."

"That's a long way off. Nothing's happened around here in quite a while." Buddy says.

Sandy walks across the veranda. "Well, things are sure happening around here now." Returning to the rocker, she points backward. "Guys, we've got some people acting goofy. Like they're very stoned or something."

Finished cleaning her shoes, Katherine says, "I'd say. Did you see what they did to that stupid looking cake? They devoured it like a pack of pit bulls. Gone in five minutes. And we never got to toast the newlyweds. The champagne was already gone. Jeffrey left crying with Gabe close behind."

Buddy laughs, "That was right before the harpist went topless."

"Yeah, what's with that? She's nearly sixty for God's sake. And, where did she get that Stetson she was wearing?"

Tossing the paint rag aside, Katherine says, "From the cowboy the Mayor was slow dancing with. Saw it all."

Wait a minute. "The Mayor's gay?" Sandy asks.

"Not sure, but he was very wasted. When he cut in on his wife and the cowboy, she was pissed. So she took the hat from her dancing partner and plopped it sideways on the harpist. When the harpist lifted her arms to adjust the hat, that's the Mayor's wife yanked down her halter. Popped her boobs right out. Kept on playing though. She didn't miss a stroke."

Buddy shakes his head, "Never heard the *November Rain* interlude played on a harp. Slash would have been proud." He looks into the dining room window. "I see the martini luge is getting a work out. Good God, there's a dude chugging a bottle of Bombay."

"Don't get any ideas." Sandy half heartedly warns.

"Ha. The Stargazer is keeping me from it. Can't be buzzed when I try that." Buddy stands, takes the last draw of his cigarette and flicks it into the dark. "Katherine, you interested in meeting Randy Anderson's brother? If so, we need to get going."

Katherine shrugs her shoulders. "Sure, why not?"

"Good, you two can talk while I take Dave and the *High Times* writer into the smoking room to sample the Stargazer."

"You guys take it easy. Can't have you shooting the moon on us. We need help with this conflagration of misfits."

"Don't worry about that, Honey. Going to only take a hit or two. We know this is crazy strong stuff. Let's get going Katherine."

Sandy gets up from her rocker. "I need to go tell Betty that the Brownie and Sundae station is off. That's the last thing we need. I just don't know how everyone got so wrecked." She eyes the boisterous group at the luge. "First, I have some booze to hide before things get further out of hand."

Katherine says, "The parlor's stuffed. You couldn't set up the brownie station in that room anyway." Grabbing Buddy's shirt tail, she says, "Lead the way. I'm right behind you." They enter the crowded foyer and push through the steamy crowd of bodies.

Following from behind, Sandy works her way into the dining room. Reaching the martini luge, she discretely removes the last two bottles of Grey Goose. Unnoticed, she maneuvers to the far end and squats before the buffet. After putting away the bottles, she feels along the empty shelf. *The brownies! Where're the brownies?* She wonders.

Buddy comes up from behind and pulls her to her feet. With his hands on her shoulders and staring into her eyes, he says, "I went into my attaché. I still have the Banana Kush, but the Stargazer's gone!"

"That can't be right! Mother got the Kush from your bag. We made the brownies with it." Sandy bites her lip and sinks her nails into his arm. They turn their heads and scan the room.

Buddy leans down. Attempting to talk over the boisterous throng, he speaks loudly into her ear, "Honey, I had two bags of pot. You made the brownies with the Stargazer!"

Before Sandy can react, a crack of thunder sends a sonic blast throughout the house. Guests flee from the windows as another lightning bolt shudders the ground seconds later, sending everyone tumbling for safety. Wind gusts slash waves of rain onto the veranda.

Sandy hugs Buddy as successive claps rattle the windows and shake the walls. The overhead chandelier flickers and sparks. Panicky screams follow as the room goes black.

Sandy points outside during another thunderous flash, "Buddy! That's hail bouncing off the railings!"

His eyes blink at the percussion. "Jesus. They look like cue balls."

Chapter 22

Wrecked

As day breaks, the unexpected overnight storms have cleared, leaving the Denver skies robin egg blue. A nearby mourning dove makes its plaintive cry, giving Sandy a gentle wake up call. She instinctively pulls the covers over her head blocking the bright rays that cut through her apartment window.

Between the twilight of sleep and awakening, her sub conscience shuffles. *What day is it and what do I have planned? There're things to do for the wedding. The wedding!* As her senses jell, she elbows Buddy's backside. "Honey, wake up! We've got to go to the house!" Wallis springs to the floor prompting Scarlett into her morning stretching and scratching routine.

With her first concern being the boys, Sandy hustles downstairs to their suite. She cracks open their door and is relieved to find them burrowed beneath the covers. After flipping the light switch, she yanks up the shades and delivers a sing songy greeting, "Good morning, boys. Rise and shine." With a bed linen in each hand, she drags their coverings onto the floor. Her effective technique always received the same growling disdain, *"Mom!"*

After feeding the pets, she gets the coffee brewing and reaches for the fruit bowl. She's looking through the blinds and chewing on an apple when Buddy appears.

He gives her a kiss on the cheek and takes a seat at the counter. "Some grand opening, huh?"

"I'm checking to see if the house is still standing. That hail was terrifying. At least what I can see looks okay."

Buddy gets two mugs from the cabinet and goes to the final hissing of the coffee maker. He pours her a cup. "Yeah, that storm kind of put a kibosh on things." He retrieves a bran muffin from the refrigerator and pops it in the microwave.

Craning her neck over the sink for a better view, she says, "Maybe it was a God send. With no electricity and the food being wiped out, the mass of humanity swarmed elsewhere. It was pitch black dark when we left at 10:30." She takes a swallow of coffee and turns to Buddy. "Do you know what happened to Mother and Taylor? I didn't see either one of them after the storm hit."

"Sort of. I introduced Katherine to Randy's brother. She was chatting him up when Randy and I went in to smoke, what we thought to be the Stargazer, with Johnny from *High Times*. Never saw her again."

"God only knows where Taylor went, particularly if she was stupid enough to eat any of those brownies she was handing out. It's highly unlikely she and Mother went home together. So how did you handle the pot mix-up with the magazine guy?"

"He was miffed at first but I left him with the Banana Kush. Hopefully that mellowed him out. After I went to find you, I never saw him again either. So much for the Stargazer publicity."

"We might get some publicity all right. There were some pretty wasted honchos last night. Hopefully they all got home safely."

"Believe me. Whoever ate one of those brownies will leave a trail. And not a very long one."

"I still can't believe Mother cooked up the Stargazer. I knew something was wrong straight away."

"Like when the harpist kept tweaking her tits in the strings?"

"Buddy, that was Miss Emily Yarborough, a lovely lady. She's a renowned musician in the Colorado Symphony. I don't think playing topless is part of her routine."

"Bet her gigs will increase now."

"Seriously, she was one of the first ones to space out. I saw she was getting goofy a little before eight. So Taylor must have given her a brownie around 7:30. Our poor home. And Gabe and Jeffrey with their wedding being ruined."

"Don't know about the home but they seemed to be having a time of it. They can have a fight, break up and make up faster than any two people I've ever seen. I saw them right after Miss Emily's sonata, dancing it up around
364

the pool. Jeffrey had the band playing that Buffet song about Desdemona."

"Seven Sisters?"

"Yeah, that's it. He was leading a conga line. Looked like several generations of The Village People. They were trying to hop and kick in unison when Jeffrey missed the turn and they all peeled off into the deep end."

Sandy puts her face in her hands and sighs, "Oh, noooooo."

"Honey, do we know how many brownies were given out? One's a killer and two's enough to put an elephant down. I should never have brought over that shit."

"No, but there were sixty in the batch. Taylor must have found them hidden away in the back of the buffet."

Luke walks in zipping his jeans. He grabs a banana from the fruit bowl.

Sandy snaps her fingers, "That's it! I remember Mrs. Cassidy saying the last time she saw her was when she went for more glasses in the buffet."

Barely audible with a mouth full of banana, Luke says, "That cooker lady was seriously crunked-up last night."

365

Sandy gives a puzzled look. "You mean Mrs. Cassidy the caterer?"

"Yeah, that's her. I saw one of Jeffrey's cowboy friends sling her around his neck like a calf. Tossed her in the front seat of his F-250 and took off into the night."

"Betty Cassidy? That can't be true. She's married to an associate pastor at the Methodist church."

"I don't care who she's married to but she sure went off with that cowboy." He flips the banana peel into the trash and casually asks, "So what's for breakfast?"

Sandy closes her eyes and grimly murmurs, "We haven't even gotten out of our kitchen and we discover a kidnapping." She makes a sullen gesture to the fridge. "I made a batch of regular brownies. Go get Zach. We need your help cleaning up after the party."

Luke laughs, "Really, Mom? You and Grandmother lit up half of Denver last night and you want us to eat one of your brownies?"

"Fine, leave 'em." Sandy looks up to Buddy as she laces her shoes. "I'd really like to get a run in this morning but we can't put this off any longer. I'm afraid to go over there."

"Me too." he sighs. "Let me throw on some clothes and we'll face the music."

As Buddy hits the garage open button, Scarlett slinks under the rising door and streaks towards a patch of grass.

After a few steps, Sandy stops. "The tents have collapsed!"

Buddy picks up a half empty Heineken bottle warming in the sun and pours the skunky remains to the ground. Glaring at the flattened tents, he says, "That explains why everyone came crashing into the house when the storm hit".

They come upon a ten-foot broken tree limb sliced across a tent cover. Buddy drags it aside, revealing one of the two drink bars. Clawing out an unopened bottle of Jack Daniels, he says, "Barely touched. They were hit like Pompeii."

He walks over to the deep end of the pool with a soggy paper lantern strung to his foot. Taking an aluminum cleaning pole from the rack, he sticks it to the bottom. Seconds later a dripping bra is fished out and slung to the side. He calls over to Sandy, "There's a closet full of clothes down here. And a whole lot of other stuff I can't make out."

"Any bodies?"

"I don't think so, but it's a big pile."

"Well, I have you beat. There's a naked woman asleep over here on a chaise lounge. Find something to cover her before the boys see her."

Buddy drops the pole and joins Sandy. He gives his assessment of the moribund figure. "First of all, that's no lady. It's Lisa Benson, the Mayor's wife. Secondly, we used all our towels sopping up the melting strawberry coulis. And lastly, I don't think the boys would be interested."

With her hands on her hips, Sandy laughs, "Of course. I didn't recognize her with the bandana. She's the one who pulled down Miss Yarborough's top."

"I wonder where the Mayor ended up?" Buddy says as he looks towards the house.

Sandy walks a few feet away and begins to tug at a tent corner weighted down with rain water and debris. With

Buddy helping, they curl back a section revealing a table and eight chairs. "A ha! A table cloth!" Sandy declares, as she drags it towards Mrs. Benson.

Noticing Luke gawking at the naked form, Buddy orders, "Go get that pole and fish out all those clothes clogging the drain. And hang them on the pool chairs, the ones not underwater."

With his arms languishing, Luke whines, "Dad."

Buddy gives him the look.

After draping the woman, Sandy gazes around the cluttered grounds. "Honey, the event people should be arriving any moment to get their stuff. At least Mrs. Benson will be covered when she wakes."

"Don't want to miss that." Buddy laughs.

Zack calls from the cabana. "Mom, Dad, there's someone in the box woods."

Buddy answers, "Are they awake?"

Zach is leaning over as his father appears. "Not sure. Her face is covered with a cowboy hat. But she's moving some."

369

Buddy kneels down to the female who has begun to awaken. "Are you okay?" he asks.

Rolling over she groans, "Where am I? These bushes hurt."

Buddy looks away from her puffy eyes. "Mrs. Harris?"

"My clothes?" The woman asks as she palms the cowboy hat across her bare breasts. Propping on an elbow and squinting, she whispers, "Where are my clothes?"

Buddy nervously fidgets. "Maybe you can find them over there by the pool. Uh, on second thought, maybe you ought to stay right here." He turns to Zach who is distancing himself from the scene. "Go get another table cloth under the tent and bring it over here."

Sandy is at the edge of the pool dragging out a chair and tangled garments when Buddy comes up. Looking towards the cabana, he says, "Zach found Senator Harris's wife zonked out in the bushes, naked as a baby jay bird."

Holding out a dripping pair of pink polka dot boxers with two fingers, she answers, "Bet these aren't hers." She slings the shorts into the building pile of wet clothes and

370

says, "Honey, I'm not feeling too well. We've got two naked dignitary's wives and a caterer missing...along with my mother and our daughter. And, we haven't even gone into the house."

"Shouldn't we find a way to get these cow girls clothed?"

They both turn to Luke as he unhooks a pair of trousers onto the soggy mass of garments.

Sandy says, "You're right. I'll get the dryers going."

"Good idea. They'll all be coming to life soon. We're going to have our own Walking Dead episode."

"Maybe we should set up a triage. That's it!" Sandy retrieves her phone from her short's pocket and begins to text; *Shopping List...Wal-mart: 2 Cs. Red Bull, 40 lb. ice, 20 beach towels, 20 hand towels, 200 ct. Xtra st. Advil. DD: 6 doz. doughnuts, 2 Gal. Box O Joe.* She calls out, "Zach, read my text and come get my Visa. *Now*, and hurry!" Turning to Luke she points to the wet stack of garments. "Get a basket and wring out those clothes. I'll meet you in the laundry room."

Untangling the lantern from his foot, Buddy says, "I think I'll walk the grounds for more casualties."

Looking back at the house, Sandy says, "I'm worried about Taylor."

Buddy turns towards the Victorian mansion sparkling in the morning sun. "She's probably crashed in there somewhere." His eyes dart upwards to the top of the giant sycamore bordering the eastern side.

"Our roof! That's our roof tarp!" Sandy exclaims. "Please go check out the house to see if our roof leaked. And see if Taylor's in there. I don't think I can take it right now." Out of the corner of her eye a figure approaches. She turns to see Mrs. Harris wrapped in a table cloth and stumbling her way. Buddy takes off to inspect the house.

Sandy is wringing out a blouse when Luke lumbers over with an arm load of clothes. "Sort them out on the table, men's and women's."

"How do I tell?" Luke asks as he drops the incongruous assortment.

Throwing the blouse into a basket, she says, "Here's another load. Take it to our apartment. The dryer should be about finished. And bring some more hangers."

Buddy nudges her shoulder. She turns to see him holding two Bloody Mary's. "Thought you may need one of these." he says.

"You just don't know." Sandy reaches for her drink and sits down in a pool chair.

"Saw Mrs. Harris leaving in her table cloth."

She squeezes a lime wedge. "Yeah. She got me to call Uber. Didn't wish to wait for her clothes."

"And Mrs. Benson?"

"Still sleeping it off. I'll let the event people get her up." After a few swallows, Sandy asks, "So, break it to me gently. Did you find Taylor?"

With a weak smile and cocked brow, he takes a deep breath and says through an exhale, "Got some sort of good news and some maybe not so good news."

"Can't wait for this." Sandy plunges a celery stick up and down into her Bloody Mary.

"Found Taylor and she's okay, I guess."

"What does that mean?"

"Remember that carpenter's helper she was flirting with?"

Sandy takes a gulp and chomps on the celery. "Can we start with the good news?"

"The leak in the dining room didn't come from the roof. So that's good, I reckon."

"A leak! And where did it come from?"

"That gets us back to Taylor and the carpenter kid. Found them asleep in a guestroom tub with the water running."

Sandy drops her chin to her chest. "Please tell me you're trying to be cute."

Buddy purses his lips and gives a negative nod.

Sandy slings the ice cubes from her drink across the pool deck. "Good God Almighty! What do you mean she's in the tub with the carpenter's helper? The last time I saw her she was distributing dope to our guests."

"At least she still had some of her clothes on." Buddy says with a weak shrug.

"Oh, I'll sleep better now." Sandy says as her eyes drill into him. "What else did you find, for heaven's sake?"

"You'd better come take a look."

Sandy droops her shoulders. "I guess you're right." As Buddy turns and walks towards the collapsed tents, she asks, "Where're you going?"

"To make a couple more Bloody Mary's."

"Make mine a double." Sandy says as she saunters towards the house.

Chapter 23

No Vacancy

Sandy is sitting behind her Queen Anne desk cater-cornered at the rear of the parlor. She is entering data into her accounting software Quick Books Pro when she hears the delicate tinkling of the door chimes. A tall dapper man in his mid sixties enters with a roller carrier, a shoulder satchel, and hanging bag.

"Good afternoon. Welcome to the *Pleiades*. My name is Sandy."

"Hello." he says, handing over his driver's license and American Express card. "I have reservations."

"Very good, sir." Sandy opens her guest book. "Yes, I see Mr. Longworth. We have you down for three nights in our Master Suite. Is that correct?"

"Yes, it is." he says, as he signs the register. "So how long have you been open?"

"Oh, several weeks now. We got set back this summer with a big storm that moved through the area."

"Yes, I saw that. Your place is beautiful. My companion and I are looking forward to our stay."

"You Saw?"

Katherine appears. "Mother! Wasn't expecting you this afternoon." Sandy turns to her guest, "Excuse me sir, you were saying?"

Katherine sidles up with a two-wheeled travel bag. The guest bows and kisses her extended hand. He turns and smiles, "I think you might know my friend here."

Flipping her hair with a girlish glint in her eye, Katherine says, "Hi Sandra Lee, I take it you and Jo Jo have met?"

Sandy stammers, "Uh, Jo Jo? Yes. Joseph Longworth, of course. But Mother, you didn't say you were..."

"Never mind. So here we are." Katherine smiles and asks, "Got the master ready?"

"Why of course. You ought to know, you dressed it out yesterday." She nervously looks at the computer screen and back to the couple. "So you'll be staying here with Mr. Longworth?"

"It's Jo Jo, Sandra Lee. And yes, I will. He's in town on business and we've got several art functions to attend."

Katherine and Joseph embrace. He gives her a kiss and says, "We've got a fabulous week-end planned, Darling." He looks up to the chandelier and laughs, "Hopefully, the electricity stays on."

Katherine winks at Sandy and coos to her companion, "Didn't cause us any problems last time." She grabs the roller bag. "Come on Jo Jo, I'll show you to our room."

After flicking through the TV channels, Sandy puts down the remote and says to Buddy, "I have never been as stunned in my life when I saw Mother come in with that man...Jo Jo she calls him."

He finishes brushing his teeth and says to the mirror, "Got to give the old gal credit. She moves pretty fast."

"I'd say. She hasn't told me a thing about this guy. She split with him when the storm hit and she didn't show up until the next afternoon, with no explanation. Acting like... like her granddaughter!"

Buddy pulls back the sheet and stops to think. "You know, I didn't say anything but Randy sort of hinted that something might be going on with those two. He let it slip that Katherine took his brother to the airport the next day. He clammed up when I pressed."

"What do we know about him, other than he says he's an art dealer?"

Buddy gets in bed and kisses Sandy, "Good night, Honey. Of all the things you have to worry about, your mother shouldn't be one of them. Him maybe, but not her."

"I just don't like her shacking up with this stranger right under our nose."

"Is he paying the house rate?"

"Yes."

"Then, good night, Babe."

Katherine scoops up a serving of sausage and egg casserole, sundried tomatoes and mozzarella. As the gooey mixture strings across her plate, Joseph playfully catches the cheese with his finger and lifts it to her mouth. She sticks out her tongue a laps it in, giggling as she plops a serving on his plate.

Sandy is fixated on the interchange, when a guest walks up with her plate. "Do you have any more of those luscious white chocolate strawberries?" she asks.

"I'm so sorry but our supply seems to have been depleted."

The woman laughs and says, "These wake and bake guests can wipe you out at a moment's notice." She looks Sandy in the eye. "You don't remember me, do you?"

"I'm sorry. Your face does seem familiar. Megan must have checked you in."

She pauses. "Megan? Interesting girl. I'm counsel woman, Jenny Baxter. My husband and I were at Gabe's wedding."

"Of course, Mrs. Baxter. I apologize for the crazy evening."

380

She places her hand on Sandy's shoulder and smiles, "Call me Jenny and there's no need to apologize, Honey. My husband and I haven't had sot much fun in years."

"Oh? That's so good to hear. How late did you stay?"

"Not very. Frank is a physician and was on call that night. The reception was barely underway when he got an emergency. As we were leaving, a pretty young girl passed by with a big plate of brownies. I wrapped a couple in a napkin and threw them in my purse."

"You had two? There was a terrible mix up and that..."

"I know all about it but they were really small, like someone had cut them into little one inch cubes."

Sandy gazes into space. "That explains why so many people got stoned. Taylor must have cut them up before passing them out." Looking back to Jenny she asks, "Did you get home okay?"

"Oh yeah. We swung by the hospital about the time the storm hit. On the way home our street was blocked by a fallen tree. As we waited for it to clear, we ate the brownies. Twenty minutes later, we abandoned our car and skipped and sang our way home in the drizzling rain. Straight-laced

Frank had never been stoned before. Let's just say we had the best sex of our lives that night. And so we're back here to celebrate our anniversary."

"What a terrific story. I appreciate you giving us another chance."

Looking for a place to sit she says, "No problem, dear. From what I've heard, our story's quite benign compared to others."

Not wishing to rehash the havoc, Sandy clears a spot and pulls out a chair. Her phone rings. "It was so nice to meet you Jenny. And I hope we can help you recapture that wonderful evening. If you'd excuse me, I have to take this call."

Sandy walks into the keeping room. "Hello Gabe. Thanks for getting back to me."

"Sure, gal. So how's business?"

"Almost too good. We're booked for several weeks. That's one reason I called. Megan's not cutting it and I need some help right away. Do know anyone who'll actually work?"

"Please, be patient with her, Sandy. I can't tell the Governor that we fired his daughter on her third day at work...after how he's helping us."

"This girl is nuts."

"You know what his firm has been doing behind the scenes with all the fallout from our wedding?"

"I understand but I have a business to run."

"Sandy?"

"Okay. I'll try to work with her. Can you at least see if Dad can place some grey matter into her air head?"

"Thanks. I'll talk with him. She's just a kid who needs some direction."

"I'm going to give her some direction all right."

"Why don't you just assign her to Katherine?"

"Mother's in another world at the moment."

"Her new boyfriend? Ha! Heard about him from Buddy."

"Gabe, Mother seems to have gone overboard with a guy that no one knows about."

"He's Randy's brother so he can't be too nefarious. Besides, isn't that her business? After all, she is an adult."

"You'd never know it. That's the other thing. Can you check him out? He says he's an art dealer but I'm not so sure. He complimented me on my fake Modigliani."

"Aren't all Modigliani's fake?"

"That's my point. Please see what kind of tracks this dude's got. Should be really simple. Right?"

"Okay, sure. Won't hurt, I guess."

"Thanks, Gabe. I have to go. Smell something burning in the kitchen and it ain't pot."

Staring her down, Sandy grows impatient as the call continues. Finally, she interrupts, "Megan, may we talk?"

Megan gives a disgusted look and turns away. Loud enough for Sandy to hear she says "Let me call you back. I'm being pestered again." She drops the cell into her apron pocket and goes to the Sub Zero. After retrieving a Starbuck's cappuccino, she pops the top and begins to glug.

With her hands on her hips, Sandy snaps, "Megan, this isn't working out."

"So what's not working out?" Megan casually asks as she studies the ingredients on the bottle.

384

"You, me...*the job*. You don't seem to think about what you're doing."

"What's there to think about?"

Sandy softens her voice to an angry whisper. "Like this morning for instance, when you delivered our entire inventory of chocolate coated strawberries to a guest's room."

"What's the big deal? He gave me a twenty for 'em."

Sandy clinches her pants leg, takes a breath and says, "We *don't have* room service, Megan."

"That's for food. Strawberries are fruit."

Fall is beginning to curl the leaves as Sandy and Scarlet jog through the tree lined neighborhood. While different from the meandering hills of Kennesaw Mountain, the tranquil early morning setting fascinates her as she watches the city awake. The high altitude has taken some adjustment, but the cool fresh air offsets the humid assault of the South she had endured for years. Having completed her first anniversary in Denver, she is encouraged by a deep sense of accomplishment with the excruciating transition. With the

385

Pleiades in business, she feels that any challenge, no matter how formidable, can be overcome. Nevertheless, her utopian visions are always subordinated to the current reality of running a business.

Recovering from her run, Sandy is enjoying an iced tea on the veranda when a black Escalade with smoked windows slows to a stop at the entrance.

She watches curiously as the chauffeur opens the back door. Out steps a man followed by two scantly attired young women. Scarlett bolts towards the fresh set of crotches. Doing her customary profiling, Sandy begins to speculate about the prospects of a F.B.I. raid as the garish man approaches sucking on a joint. She stands and says, "Good afternoon, sir. Welcome to the *Pleiades*. How may I assist you?"

The short, heavy set man with double sleeve tattoos appears to be in his late forties. Sporting an orangish tan, his streaked blonde hair is pulled into a bun. Three knotted gold chains loop down his slick chest. Stretched to its limit, the flowered silk camp shirt hovers around his baggy khaki cargo shorts. Trunk sized calves lead to his Birkenstock

386

sandals strapped to his swollen feet. He flips his roach into the flower bed, removes his Oakley's and says in a strong New England accent, "Bianchi is the name. I'd like your best room for the next three or four days."

Sandy opens the front door and is taken back by the strong scent of Old Spice and marijuana. "Come in please and I'll check our availability, but I'm afraid we're booked at the moment."

"Why that shouldn't be a problem, Missy." he guffaws, signaling his party to follow. The two women and the driver hustle their baggage into the foyer. His companions giggle as Scarlett smashes her brown wet nose into their bottoms. He rips open a Velcro side pocket, produces a wad of cash and hands the driver a fifty. "One of the girls will be in contact."

Sandy says, "Sir, you may wish for him to stay a moment until I check some dates."

He disconcertingly responds as the limo pulls away, "Let's see what you got, Missy."

At her desk, Sandy logs onto her system. She keeps her eyes on the screen and says, "Sir, it looks like our first room availability won't be until week after next and the master suite a week later."

Sandy is in the kitchen talking in a hushed voice on her cell, "Mother. We might be having a change of plans about your stay."

"The hell you say."

"There's this gentleman, uh, man out front from Ft. Lauderdale. He wants your room for the next several days. Can you and Joseph find another place? I called the Ritz-Carleton and they have availability."

"Well, he can't have it. We're all settled in."

"I don't think you understand, Mother. He gave me ten Ben Franklins, on top of the regular room rate."

"So what time's early check-in at the Ritz?"

Sandy hurries into the parlor to find the man seated on the sofa with his two friends. Ignoring her, they are amused at something playing on his phone. "Excuse me sir." she says. Pushing closer, she imagines their interest as either a cat video or a porn site. Raising her voice, she announces, "Sir, we might be in luck. There seems to be a guest that wishes to check out early, freeing up the Master Suite."

Without looking up, he says, "Told you it wouldn't be a problem, Missy."

Sandy bites her cheek and answers in a measured voice, "If you don't mind, it will take me about thirty minutes to have your room ready. My guest is away and we'll need to remove their belongings and prepare for your stay."

Squeezed between his fawning companions, he taps his diamond bezel Rolex President. "Okay, make it snappy. We need to get some rest, don't we girls?" They gush with gratuitous laughter as Scarlett nuzzles every seam.

Sandy retreats up the steps. She pauses at the landing to take a call. "Hi Gabe. That was quick. What did you find?"

"It's real easy these days. So here's the scoop on Mr. Longworth."

Chapter 24

Behind Closed Doors

Unable to see her feet, Sandy has her arms tucked around the stuffed bed sheet as she carefully maneuvers down the winding staircase. Finding Buddy at the bottom, she cries, "Oh thank goodness you're home early."

"I have to meet the gutter guy."

"Oh, I forgot about that. I'm in a panic readying Mother's room for another guest that just popped in."

"You're kicking Katherine and Jo Jo out of the Master?"

"It's a long story. Would you please bring down their bags to the back porch?" A lamp shade wobbles as Sandy brushes by with her load of linen.

Backing out of her way Buddy asks, "Why are you doing all this? Where's Megan?

"I sent her insolent ass home."

"My, my, aren't we the little tyrant today?"

"Please get Mother's bags. And while you're at it, we need three water bottles and the fruit basket refilled. And replace the soap and shampoo from the hall closet. The vacuum is in there too. You need to do a quick run through. I've cleaned the bathroom and changed the sheets."

Buddy takes a few steps up the stairs and leans over the rail. "What are you going to do about replacing Megan?"

"I didn't exactly fire her...sent her on her way to think about things...if she's capable."

"So now you're in a fix."

"I've called Carlita and she's got her cousin coming to help for a day few days." Pushing into the laundry room, she hollers back, "Please hurry with the room. Mother's on her way here now to pick up her stuff. I'll keep an eye out for the gutter guy."

Katherine is fumbling through her bag when Sandy proclaims, "Mother, Joseph is a porn king."

"He's no such thing! He just makes sex toys. You want to know what a porn king looks like? Just check out that creep and his little crack heads in our parlor."

"Mother, hush! They'll hear you." Sandy cranes her neck to see into the hall. "Besides, you're not dating *him*."

"And just what business is it of yours about who I date?" Continuing to dig into her bag, she asks, "Where's my Wet Kitty dress?"

"Please tell me you're kidding."

"The hell I am. Jo Jo had it custom tailored for me. We've got to go back to the room."

"Mother, your friend is in the porn business and he lied to you about being an art dealer."

"He never lied to me. After we got to know each other, he told me he used the art dealer bit as a cover. I mean, you can't tell someone right off the bat that you make dildos."

"*After* you got to know each other? You picked him up at the reception and disappeared for twenty-four hours."

392

She flips her wrist. "Shit, Sandra Lee. Everyone disappeared when the storm hit."

As Katherine tosses out the contents of her bag, Sandy blinks, "Stilettos?"

Clicking the heels, she smiles, "Kind of sexy, don't you think?"

"No I don't. You got a whip in there too?"

"It's called a flogger. And no. Jo Jo has it."

"I thought I was kidding."

Katherine turns to Sandy, "I seem to be missing some of his samples. Did you look under the bed? I'm going back to my room."

"What samples? No, wait. I don't want to know about all your sleazy stuff."

"It's not sleazy! I'll have you know he's the owner and CEO of EazyPleezy Industries. He's in town making sales calls."

"Sales calls? On what, porn shops? And you think that's cool?"

"They made that little Rabbit you keep in your purse, Miss Goody Two Shoes."

393

"Why have you been in my purse, Mother?"

"You know, they now make ones that glow in the dark. JoJo has several samples. I have one for you if I can find my goodie bag."

"Mother! Why were you in my purse?"

Katherine darts her eyes left to right. "I was looking for a light."

"You know I don't smoke."

"Whatever." Katherine begins to repack her bag. "He told me all about what he did for a living when he brought out the rainbow lambskin. We need to go back to the room."

"The rainbow what?"

"The rainbow lambskin leather flogger you were asking about. You can't believe the margin on those things. They sell on Amazon for $35 and he gets them made in Taiwan for only $4.25. And, that little Rabbit you use..."

"Mother, have you lost your mind?"

"Not at all. He's handsome and very rich." Buddy appears unnoticed as Katherine spans her hands apart. "And, he's got one hell of a schlong too."

Buddy grimaces as he holds out a wooden coat hanger draped with her Wet Kitty. "Way too much information," he says, distancing her dress as if it were a rattlesnake.

Katherine exclaims. "There it is!"

Flipping it her way, he grunts, "Here you go."

Katherine displays the dominatrix outfit. "Pretty classy, huh?"

"Let's give it up for Katherine." Buddy laughs and presents a bulging plastic bag. "I think this might be yours also."

"Give me that!" Katherine snatches the samples.

"This is disgusting." Sandy says, as she turns and bumps into a young woman standing in the doorway. "I'm so sorry. You must be Isabella."

Buddy backs away and says under his breath, "Awkward."

The demur girl drops her eyes to the floor and quietly responds, "Yes, ma'am."

Outside, Buddy looks on as the gutter man shears away soil from the side of the house with a spade. "It ain't the gutters, Mr. Henderson. It's the build-up over the years all around the house. Water's draining into your walls and not away as it should. That's why you have the wood rot in your sub floor."

"Build-up?"

"Yeah, dirt, debris, tree roots, a hundred years of crap. Done got it up near a foot over the original grade."

"What does all that mean? Can't it just be cleared away from the house?"

"Nope. Don't work that way. Gotta do a French drain."

"What's that entail? Anything named after the French can't be cheap."

"You're funny, sir, but I think the man's name was French."

"I feel so much better. What're we looking at here?"

"You'd need to bring in a backhoe. Take it down a couple of feet, put in gravel and a drain pipe. Usually runs about $25 a foot." He walks off the western side of the house and returns, "I'd have to measure, but I'd be guessing about six to seven grand to do it right. Could be more but I doubt less."

"Seven thousand dollars for a drain?"

"Afraid so. But then you'd have the landscaping to deal with. When you dig up them tree roots, you'll kill them trees." He looks up at a century old English Oak. "I don't know but you got a half dozen or so. Some really big boys. They planted 'em too close to the house back then."

"We're going to lose all our trees?"

"Sure will have a bunch of good fire wood."

Sandy nervously looks at the wall clock wondering where the day has gone. She says to the young Hispanic girl sitting across from her, "I apologize Isabella for that scene in the kitchen. We try to run a clean operation here."

The girl blushes and drops her head. "I understand. I'm not here to judge."

"So you're at South University?"

"Yes, I'm taking classes while going through concernment."

"Concernment?

"Yes, I'm considering becoming a nun."

Sandy gulps as she recalls the scene she had witnessed in the kitchen. "So, how soon could you start?"

"I guess Monday, Mrs. Henderson. I'm on break from school for a week so that would work."

Sandy leans in. "How about now?"

Isabella's face brightens with a big smile. "Yes, yes. Senorita Henderson. But my brother is waiting outside for only a short time. So I will need a ride home tonight."

"Honey, I'll drive you myself." Sandy's phone begins to vibrate on the table. "Excuse me, this is a guest."

"How may I help you Mr. Bianchi?" Sandy listens for a few seconds. "Just a moment sir." She spins her cell and forces a smile. "Isabella, go send your brother on his way. When you come back, we'll get on the laundry." Isabella passes Buddy as she leaves the room.

Sandy digs her nails into her palms before asking, "So what is it that you need, Mr. Bianchi?" She gouges the ball point pen into her note pad as she delivers a chilly response, "That sounds like a threat, sir. Yes, I know, but we really can't do that sort of thing."

Sandy pauses as her guest continues. "We'll see what we can do sir. Yes, I understand, sir."

Buddy walks in to find her sitting at the table spinning her cell and cursing. "Squatty body and the bimbos?" he asks.

With the pen clinched in her fist, she traces dark blue circles around the pen holes. "You need to go to Wal-Mart."

"What for? Traffic's a mess right now and I've got other stuff to do."

"We need a king mattress cover and four Fleet enemas."

"Screw him. We're not on call for his kinky shit."

She continues to gouge with her pen. "I tried to tell him that. He said they could do without the enemas, but the mattress cover would be a necessity." Sandy tears off her punctured doodling page. As if making a paper airplane, she begins to crease it with her fingernail.

"Just tell him go to hell."

"The asshole began to detail their sexual choreography. That's when I buckled." She snaps the ball point pen in half and pulls out the ink tube. "I can't risk that

399

pig messing up our $1300 Serta. I guess a $50 mattress cover is good insurance."

"Well, I don't like it at all. I'll be damned if I'm going to buy that s.o.b. enemas."

"He's putting $500 in an envelope under his door."

"Four you say? I'm on my way, Darling."

"And pick up some more strawberries and a tri-pod."

"What's the tri-pod for?"

"You don't want to know."

Sandy slaps around on the nightstand for her phone just in time to cancel the five-thirty wake up. With a breakfast to prepare and work left over from the previous day, she has set her alarm an hour earlier than normal. Buddy lies motionless and snoring soundly as she crawls out of bed. Dawn has yet to color the eastern sky as she and Scarlett begin their jog through the darkened city.

She seethes with anger about the demanding visitor and his companions camped out in the master suite. Trying to put a positive spin on the circumstances, she is thankful that he was at least concerned about the mattress. It could

400

have been much worse, she rationalizes. After all, she had committed to the rigors of serving the public. And of course, making money was the name of the game. But there always seemed to be something popping up. The news about the French drain was just added to the long list of surprises that had plagued them from the beginning.

As she and Scarlet approach the house, she sees Katherine's Cadillac parked in front. A red dot glows in the dimness of the veranda. The cigarette voice growls, "How was your run, Sandra Lee."

Sandy stomps off the wet debris from her shoes. "Good morning, Mother. Didn't expect you this early."

"Figured you needed some help. I swung by my place and brought over two pans of frozen cinnamon rolls. Got the coffee brewing."

"Oh, thank you so much. You must have read my mind. I'm afraid to ask, but was Taylor there?"

"Believe it or not, she was. Been behaving of late."

"That scares me."

"Me too."

Katherine holds open the door as Sandy and Scarlet walk towards the back of the house. Entering the kitchen Sandy says, "I'm having the cheddar grits and sausage casserole for the guests. Hope it doesn't spook anyone."

"Just tell 'em it's polenta. They'll love it."

"You left Joseph awfully early this morning."

"He got up an hour before me. Had to make calls to China. Got to get those pricks standing tall, you know."

Sandy laughs as she ties on her apron. "Mother, what am I going to do with you?"

"You worry too much, Sandra Lee." Katherine pours a cup of coffee.

"I've surely got enough material." Sandy begins to empty the Sub Zero. "At least Isabella's helping while Megan sorts things out."

"I didn't know she was going to be such an airhead."

Grating cheese, Sandy says, "And that jerk off in the Master has me treed. I think you were right about him being some kind of a porn mogul."

"How so?"

"I think they're making movies in the master."

402

Chapter 25

In The Air Tonight

Buddy is enjoying a quiet Sunday morning in his lab at Colorado Medicinal when he takes a call from his brother. "Mack, my man. What's happening, Bro?"

"All's cool on this end. How about you guys?"

"Same old, same old. A crisis a day keeps the cobwebs away, or something like that. Are you in this hemisphere or is that too sensitive to disclose?"

"Actually, I'm at MacDill working on an assignment. That's why I called. Might need a big favor if you're up to it."

"Sure, what do you have in mind?"

"Don't be so quick until you've heard me out. This is serious stuff and I want you guys to understand what you'd be getting into."

"You're starting to scare me, Bro."

"We've been tracking this guy all over the globe. He's like a ghost. Haven't been able to pin anything on him."

"What kind of a guy?"

"He has some associations that we're keeping an eye on. He doesn't seem to be affiliated with any specific group and we're not sure what his game is."

"But what does that have to do with us?"

"Was getting to that. We just got word he'll be coming to Denver within the next few days but we don't know exactly when or for what. If we can get him to stay at the *Pleiades* hopefully we can monitor what he's up to."

"You've never been much of a salesman, Mack. You're telling me to put up a terrorist and bug his room? Do we get free funeral plots with this agreement?"

"Never said he was a terrorist but it may be a little dicey."

"Dicey? It's fucking risky, Mack."

"We don't like that word, Buddy. He'll be under complete surveillance and there's no reason to believe he'll cause any trouble. It's not his M.O. He's very discrete and never draws attention to himself. If he had violent tendencies, we wouldn't be asking for such a commitment."

"Well, I don't like the idea at all."

"We do our job well, Buddy so we don't believe you or anyone will be at risk. Besides, you owe me one after that fuck-up at the Bellagio. You almost got me fired."

"You have to admit that was pretty funny. So let's say that we went along with this thing. How would we get him to stay here?"

"Good question. You've got a promotional brochure, right?"

"Yes, but."

"You'd offer him a deal he can't refuse. We know he loves his grass and is very frugal. No flashy cars or homes. He has no pattern as he moves around the world with burner phones. If he has a weakness, he's vulnerable to deals and discounts at nice hotels."

405

Buddy gives semi approval. "Maybe."

"We want to get that brochure in his mailbox. We believe he'll only be at this place in Vancouver for a short time."

"You think he's going to make a decision on a lousy brochure?"

"Not totally. At the same time, we'll make sure he gets a personalized offer from one of the hotel internet brokerage sites. A 50% off a one night's stay in your Master Suite. When he begins to search for a cheap room in the Denver area, he'll be the only one linked to your deal but he won't know it."

"How're you going to do that?"

"We have our ways, but that's not important. I hate to push for a decision, but this opportunity just came up and we've got to move fast. Need a court order, coordination, and..."

"Gee, Mack, I don't know. Sandy and Katherine are not going to be real keen on using our place to bait a terrorist."

"I never said terrorist, but there's something else. For your trouble, my company will pay you thirty grand."

An hour later Buddy and Sandy huddle in a booth at a McDonalds only a short distance from his office. As she slides in the booth, Katherine says, "Well this better be good. This was my last morning with Jo Jo."

"Good God, Mother. You've been shacked up for three days. Isn't it time for a break?"

"Break? Let me tell you girl, I haven't had so much fun since..."

Mortified at the prospect of Katherine detailing her sexual exploits, Buddy abruptly pleads, "Please, you two. Can we cut out the girl talk? We've got some serious decisions to make here."

Exhorting to her 'bug Buddy' routine, Katherine looks upward and begins to blissfully hum *Over the Rainbow.*

Sandy takes a sip of her diet Coke and looks around. "No one ever told us we'd become a casting call for Miami Vice." She holds her head down and quietly says, "I don't like it. Particularly coming on the heels of our current guests."

Ignoring Katherine's antics, Buddy says, "Honey, I know. But Mack and one of his associates will be in the adjoining room. He's not violent and doesn't even pack a gun."

"Not violent? Well, why are they so interested in him?" Sandy strums her fingernails on the table. "Plus we've got Mr. Big Shot in the master. What if he shows up before we can get him and his trash out of his room?"

"It's not going to happen according to Mack. Bianchi is leaving tomorrow morning and this fellow wouldn't be coming until the middle of the week."

Buddy looks to Katherine who is reading emails. "So where are you on all this? Mack needs an answer right away. Remember, he helped us bust up whatever Taylor had going with her probation officer."

She shrugs her shoulders. "We can surely use the money." And then she announces with her usual flare of confidence, "And, hey, sounds exciting as shit to me. I say let's do it!"

Buddy sticks his thumb up and says, "So Sandy, what say you? I vote with Katherine."

"That's a first." Swirling her Diet Coke with a look of indecision, she agrees. "Okay, surely hope we know what we're doing."

Back at the grow house, Buddy walks to the far corner of a patch of mature marijuana plants. With an exhaust fan humming above his head, he gets Mack on the line. "We're in, but very reluctantly, particularly Sandy. This wasn't to be part of our marketing strategy."

"Excellent and I understand. If everyone were happy about this, I'd think you were off your rocker."

"There you go again, you silver tongued devil."

"It's all cool. A lot of stuff has to happen for this to work out right. This is a long shot at best."

"Can we not use gun analogies? So what do we have to do?"

"First of all, we need to get one of those brochures. Make it five to be safe."

"Do you want me to overnight them somewhere?"

"That won't be necessary. I'll text Sandy to take them outside to Gene."

"Gene?"

"Yeah, he's there now. In a white Malibu. Our plane is ready to take him to Vancouver."

"You have one of your goons outside our house with a plane revved up?"

"He's not a goon and you'll get to like him. He'll be my roommate."

"What is with this bonding shit? You've got some guy named Gene that we're going to become pals with?"

"Maybe not pals but he'll be installing the E.B.D.'s."

"What the hell is that?"

"Sorry, we love acronyms around here. Electronic Bugging Devices."

"What's wrong with just plain old 'bugs'?"

"Can we stay serious here?"

"Stay serious? You already have a court order, you've sent a goon, uh, operative to our house...and a plane is on standby before I even said we'd commit to this act of stupidity?"

"Just calm down, Buddy. I had a feeling you'd cooperate so I needed to make a move. Time is of the essence with things like this."

"We do have this issue about the current guests in the master all week-end. So how's your guy going to bug the room?"

"As for the E.D.B.'s, it'll only take ten minutes. Wireless makes it easy these days. We'll do it when we come in tomorrow."

"And exactly when is this cat supposed to arrive?"

"Tuesday at the earliest but most likely it'll be Wednesday. It's not clear at the moment."

"That means you don't know. Do you guys ever say what you mean? Does this fellow have a name?"

"Not one that we're sure of but he travels under various aliases. His code name is 'Rana'. For all the hopping around he does."

"What does The Frog look like?"

"We're not quite sure."

"Wait! What?"

"I have to go, Buddy. If he doesn't bite in the next twenty-four hours, the deal's off. Gene and I will see you late tomorrow afternoon."

As Sandy drags the vacuum from the hall closet, Isabella comes to help. After plugging in the cord, she says, "Isabella, please start on the first floor and we'll work our way upstairs. We have a late check-out today."

She goes into the drawing room where Katherine is arranging flowers. "I remember when I used to get stressed about coming up with lessons for Bible study. And now I'm cleaning up after a porn shoot just in time for a terrorist to check in."

Tweaking the flowers in the vase, Katherine chirps, "Kind of exciting don't you think?"

"*No*. I do *not* think, Mother. Anyone who lives in that world is willing to die in it. And that means inviting all those around to join in."

"No one's going to die, Sandra Lee." Katherine produces a small pipe from a buffet drawer. She strikes a light, takes a draw. "Want a hit?"

412

"What? We can't be lit up when this guy checks in."

Exhaling, she says through the smoke, "Mack said he's not coming until later."

"I don't care. He booked it for today and we've still got to face that room clean up. That is if we can get our movie mogul out of the master."

"So what's up with that?" Katherine puts another flame to her pipe.

"He and his little tramps were to have been on their way by noon. But now he's asked for a late check-out. I tried to get him moving but he threw another wad of cash at me. I can't believe I'm turning into a whore for $100 bills."

Katherine takes another puff and says through her exhale, "I've done a lot worse for less."

Her phone rings. "Hold on, Mother. It's our friend calling. "Yes, Mr. Bianchi. That's good. I'll be in the parlor."

"Checking out?"

"Finally! If he calls me Missy one more time I'm going to kick him in the balls." Her phone rings again. "Now what does he want?" she complains before seeing its Mack. "Hi Mack." She answers.

"Sandy, we've got a little situation. Rana's coming earlier than we thought."

She looks at Katherine. "Don't tell me that, Mack. Just how much earlier?"

"Like any minute. We lost track of him. He might have taken another flight."

"But you're not here!"

"Gene and I are about to take off from Tampa. We should be at your place about six or so."

"*Or so?* I knew this was going to get screwed up. I just *knew* it." Sandy hurries to the front in time to see a black Escalade coming up the driveway. "Shit!" she says. "That's Mr. Bianchi's driver!"

"Who's that?" Mack asks.

"Hold on, Mack." She turns to Katherine, "Mother, please go check out Mr. Bianchi."

After taking one last hit from her pipe, Katherine casually taps the ashes into a potted corn plant.

Pointing out the room, Sandy anxiously whispers as Katherine cleans debris from her pipe, "Mother! Please!"

"Just a sec. Got to take a pee." Katherine says as she stuffs the warm pipe in her pocket and strolls away.

Sandy rushes into the foyer and opens the front door. She moves aside as the driver brushes by and hurries up the stairs. Back on her phone she says, "So Mack, what am I supposed to do when this dude shows up?"

"Treat him like a normal guest and don't do anything suspicious. Stay calm and everything will be okay."

As the chauffer passes by and leaps up the stair case, she exclaims, "Did you say to stay calm? Mack, I can't take this." Her head swivels to the sound of another car door shutting.

A moment later Sandy is shuffling papers when a thinly built man in his early thirties appears at her desk. Wearing dark sun glasses and a red Braves baseball cap, a stubby beard spots his pocked olive complexion. Casually attired, a plaid long sleeved shirt drapes over his loose white tee. Faded and tattered jeans fall an inch short of his grey Adidas Yeezys.

"Good afternoon, Madam. Checking in, please." he says in a thick Spanish accent. Handing her his driver's

415

license and an envelope he continues, "I prefer to pay in cash. There's more than enough to cover my stay." He and Sandy are startled at the boisterous voices resonating from the hall.

Mr. Bianchi pushes into the parlor with one of his companions tugging at the back of his shirt. He turns and begs in a placating tone, "Would you please calm down Crystal, darling and go get in the car. I have to check out. There's some champagne iced..."

She kicks his shin and shrieks, "You can't do this to me, you fat fuck!"

"Shit, that hurt!" He grabs her by the arm as she advances. "But Sugar, my agreement with Solstice gave her top billing."

She spits a wad of gum and spittle into his face. "Fuck you! It's only because she lets you do all that kinky stuff to her. Besides, if it wasn't for me we couldn't have gotten Benton."

He wipes his chin and laughs condescendingly, "We hardly have trouble getting studs to tap you babes."

She shouts into his face, "You *know* there's a shortage of BBC's in Denver. I saved your ass."

"Well, there ain't no shortage of dumb cunts." Bianchi chuckles rubbing his throbbing shin. He doesn't see her reach for the brass candlestick on the coffee table. After whacking him across the head, she crunches her right spiked platform into his sandaled toes. As he wails, she plants both hands onto his chest sending him reeling over the back of the sofa. His stumpy legs fly into the air as he flips backwards and onto his knees.

As Crystal grabs a lamp stand, Bianchi frantically pulls to his feet. Hobbling from the room with his assailant on his heels, he calls back to Sandy, "Bill my Visa, Missy. Had a great time."

Katherine pokes her head from around the corner and asks, "Do we have a problem here?"

417

Chapter 26

Rocky Mountain Hi

Sandy is sitting at her apartment's kitchen table staring at her computer. Surrounded by stacks of files and papers, she repeatedly clicks her pen. "Looks like we had another bad month, Mother."

Thumbing through a magazine, Katherine straightens out in Buddy's recliner. "That doesn't surprise me. We knew the first year was going to be tough." She gets up and looks out the window. "Hard to believe we're into Fall."

"And our second year." Sandy says as she enters more data into her spreadsheet.

"Yeah, seems like only yesterday when Gabe and I pulled out that box of coins. They really save our butts."

"Or cost us our butts. Without them, we wouldn't be having all this fun."

"You know you love it."

"I guess I do in a way but there's never a moment to rest. It's always something as Rosanna Danna use to say. Speaking of such, what do you think about Taylor working for Gabe as a paralegal?"

"I'm never sure about her. At least she's earning some money and sharing an apartment with her friends. I had it with her running around all night and sleeping all day."

"How she managed to fulfill her diversion probation without getting busted is beyond me. I tried to get her to help around here but she refused to change bed linens or clean baths." Sandy puts her hands together. "Thank God for unanswered prayers."

"Yeah. Gabe's taking a chance with her. After all, her skill set lies somewhere between a functioning sociopath and the Devil's hand maiden."

Sandy laughs, "Perfect for an attorney. At least he's gone into this thing with full disclosure. Plus, she's taking some on line paralegal courses. So that's a start. That's all

419

she's getting from us. We said we'd pay for any education and that's it. She had no choice but find some work. It wasn't easy keeping Buddy from buckling to her."

"I think that Las Vegas fiasco convinced him."

"I agree. He finally was able to see firsthand plying her trade. He always went to her defense, but she ran out of explanations. Or rather other people to blame things on."

"She'd put a contract out on us if she found out we were involved with that sting."

Sandy looks to Katherine. "Contract? She'd do it herself."

"I laugh every time I think about it. Taylor running naked down the hall with her probation officer hovering in the bathroom. Buddy's lucky he didn't get tangled up in that mess."

"After bungling the set up with the housekeeper? I guess. Who wouldn't have known the Bellagio has a turn down service?"

"Buddy." Katherine says dryly.

"Case rested. And speaking of Mack. What about that screw up with the so-called terrorist? He couldn't say a thing about Buddy. At least he didn't almost get us killed. I never wanted to stage that stunt from the get go. It was just too dangerous."

"He didn't almost get us killed, Sandra Lee. But he almost got us sued. That fellow was awful nice to back off after that Gene guy wrestled him to the floor."

"He shouldn't have reached into his back pocket."

"He was after his phone, Mother. It could have been much worse."

"The ten thousand cash to keep quiet didn't hurt."

"Mack was so embarrassed. He still hasn't figured out how their target managed to make that poor fellow into an innocent decoy. At least we got paid for our trouble."

"And they still haven't caught that guy." Katherine sizzles her cigarette butt in a water bottle. "So when did you say Mack was coming to town?"

"He's yet to confirm but in several days. I've already alerted the boys. Even if he doesn't show up, the mere thought of Uncle Rambo dropping by strikes terror in them. Always get good mileage out of it."

"Have they decided about college?"

"I can't even get them to talk about it. That's something I want Mack to push for. To get some type of commitment. All I know is that they're not staying around here."

Having entered the month's operating expenses and revenue, Sandy studies the Excel columns. "That leads me to my next question. These extra household surprises have just about killed us cash flow wise. We've got to do something. We're about to max out our line of credit."

"Can't we sell-off some of the stock we bought with the gold?"

"Don't think so. Our accountant wants us to cut back on expenses. At least until we catch up with the rare books. We're getting a lot more selling as singles on EBay than auctioning. It should only be for another two to three months."

"It'll all be fine, Honey."

"Mother, we need to talk about something...the noises in the house, the sightings...the guest complaints."

"How are bookings looking?"

"You can't keep ignoring this. I remember as a child. Things no one could explain. There was this time when..."

Car lights stream across the room. Sandy looks up. "I think that's Buddy." Checking her watch she says, "The time's slipped up on me. We've only got forty-five minutes before Happy Hour. I'll get Buddy to help us get set up."

The Henderson's have designated the larger of two parlors on the first floor of the *Pleiades* as the marijuana smoking room. The inviting space utilizes classical Victorian elements while delivering the panache of an upscale coffee house. A color wheel gradation of soft grey-green-blue hues is set off by woodwork marbleized by the ancient technique of fauxing. The inner wall has been crafted to resemble blocks of stone by the scoring of wet plaster. Works by prominent Denver area contemporary artists provide a fresh flare to the warm and inviting decor. Antique pewter tiles crown the twelve-foot-high ceilings. Soft yellow satin glass globes set off the 48-inch ceiling fan twirling above. The traditional sofas and chairs are upholstered with Barcelona bonded leather with period decorative embossing. Victorian patterned throw pillows accent the ample seating. Curving around the corner, the custom granite topped mahogany bar provides a spacious serving area.

As Buddy spins a bottle of sauvignon blanc in a wine bucket, Sandy arranges the assortment of imported cheeses and crackers across the bar. As part of their daily happy hour, they have prepared several easy-to-make but delicious appetizers. A selection of suitable wines and local craft beers compliment their offerings. In addition to the cheeses, today's features will be fig and olive tapenade, Vietnamese spring rolls, and crab stuffed deviled eggs.

It was often times difficult to predict how many guests might partake. However, they soon found that there would be few leftovers as the tasty treats were no match for the marijuana enhanced appetites.

The spread is completed as the first couple arrives. Sandy recognizes them as the Robert's from New Orleans and goes over and extends her hand. "Hello, guys. I'm Sandy. Welcome to the *Pleiades*. I hope you are comfortable with your room."

"Oh, yes." says the young woman enthusiastically as she clasps Sandy's hand. "Your place is magnificent."

"Why thank you so much." Gesturing to the bar, Sandy says, "Help yourself to the appetizers and drinks. And please let me know if I may be of any assistance." Seeing two men enter dining room, she politely dismisses herself and walks their way.

The older gentleman is lighting a light a pipe as she approaches. He passes to his friend as Sandy makes her gratuitous greeting, "Good afternoon, I'm Sandy. Welcome to..." As their eyes meet, she stops in mid sentence. A strange feeling sweeps over her.

Staring intently, the man says, "You look awfully familiar."

The statement takes her by surprise. "Katherine must have checked you in. I don't believe we've met."

"Oh, I'm sure of it." he responds. "I cannot seem to remember the circumstances. But I never forget a beautiful face. It'll come to me."

Sandy realizes that he is right. They have met, but where? Curiosity is soon overtaken by anxiety as she nervously shakes his hand and says in a broken tone, "Well, thank you, I guess. In the meantime, I hope you enjoy your stay at the *Pleiades*. And please let me know if I may be of assistance." Spotting another guest entering the parlor, she smiles and says, "If you would excuse me. Have a pleasant evening." Moments later she is at her desk flipping through the pages of her guest book. Her finger traces down yesterday's check-ins.

She jumps as Buddy appears unexpectedly. "Honey, there's a guy out here that seems to think he knows you." he says.

"Uh, I was talking to him earlier. I've never seen him before." She forces a laugh. "He seems to be stoned. Must be confused." She stands and walks past him towards the kitchen. "Would you mind running over to the apartment and getting some cocktail napkins? I'm short a few."

As Buddy leaves, Sandy rejoins their guests in the smoking parlor. It only takes a moment for the guest to again approach her. "Yes, now I remember you." he proudly proclaims.

"I'm sorry but I don't think we've ever met, sir."

"It was the night of the Snowmagheddon in Atlanta at the Waverly. I'm Charles Higginbotham, the general manager. I'm sure that was you with Yancy Collingsworth's daughter and that NFL player in the presidential suite. David Stark...that's who it was."

Sandy swallows hard and struggles to maintain her composure. "I'm afraid you are mistaken, Mr. Higgenbotham. I was nowhere near Atlanta then." She attempts a feeble laugh and says, "Must have a twin sister out there." Seeing Buddy enter with the extra napkins, she hurriedly excuses herself. "Have to run. Hope you enjoy your stay." She turns and exits the room.

The pitched ripping of chain saws awakens Sandy from her short nap. She goes to the bathroom and turns on the tub water. After unwrapping a Rodin bath bar, she drips in a portion Jo Malone's Pomegranate Noir bath oil.

She's had a busy morning in the kitchen preparing a feast for Buddy's birthday. She has taken a few hours to relax before the special evening. Her torturous routine of running the *Pleiades* has left Sandy little time for pleasure.

427

But tonight, she will enjoy one of her passions, cooking a gourmet meal for her husband. With an early winter storm on the way, they agreed it was a smart idea to stay in and celebrate. With the boys overnighting with friends, the small apartment is all theirs.

Sandy has orchestrated a classic English dish of Beef Wellington, a succulent preparation of steak filets coated with pate and wild mushroom duxelles wrapped in puff pastry. Accompanied with French beans and truffle fries, she knows it is sure to set the mood for a perfect evening. With carrot cake being Buddy's favorite dessert, Sandy has baked one the day before. She is not surprised to see that he has taken a big chunk out of it for breakfast that morning.

Tethered to a lamp, three brightly colored Happy Birthday balloons float aimlessly. Underneath, sits his birthday present. Wrapped in a foil blue box and tied with a gold ribbon, is a new Citizen's Titanium Eco Watch, a replacement for his fifteen-year-old Seiko.

Approaching the unnerving outside noise, she stretches the curtains and looks through the small paned window of the carriage house apartment. A grimace crosses her face as a huge oak trunk cracks and crashes to the ground, the last of five massive hardwoods that have been butchered. She has suffered for the past two days at the tree devastation, the first step in clearing a path around the main house for the French drain.

The thick rain harkens a cold front that will soon recolor the scene. Across the gardens and walkway, she eyes the backhoe delivered only hours earlier, readied for plowing up the century old root system that has strangled the home's foundation.

For the past year, most days have been overbearing with no semblance of normality that they had become accustomed to. Transitioning a family, coordinating a major remodeling and starting up a business, have taken their toll. A rare mid week lull has the *Pleiades* without any guests, providing her a much needed respite from the grueling chores of the Bed and Breakfast.

Anticipating the rising water, she returns to the small steaming bathroom. Taking luxurious baths is one of her few indulgences; stress relief baths, dead tired baths, sexy baths. Baths for every mood. She will sometimes soak for an hour or more with a variety of fancy soaps, oils, and potions. She inches herself in with care as the near scalding water seductively tingles her bottom. Stretched out as the line reaches the overflow drain, she pushes in the faucet knob with her big toe. With her head against a bath pillow, she shuts her eyes.

As if awakened from a Rip Van Winkle slumber, Sandy relives her once settled life passing through a wash, spin and dry cycle. Ruminations of the past fifteen months replay like a bad country and western song, churning through the inexplicable convergence of events that have reshaped her life. *How could things get so totally out of control? What uncertainties yet lie ahead? And what about the inexplicable coincidence of Mr. Higginbotham showing up and remembering me? I was so lucky to have dodged him during his stay. My secret can never be revealed. At least David is it bay and out of my life. This will pass with time...I surely hope.*

Her anxieties begin to abate as the warmth of the bath and aromatic oils envelop her. Rehearsed to perfection, the crafted routine triggers the exhilarating flashback of those

430

impassioned hours with David and Abby. Intoxicated like a rush of morphine, Sandy is seduced by the lived-out fantasy that has once again overtaken her senses.

Finished with her bath and donning her Capilene thermal jump suit and wool socks, she returns to the cramped living-dining room area. Begging for attention, Scarlett nuzzles against her thigh. Sandy reaches down and twirls a velvety ear and continues a few steps into the efficiency kitchen. She sparks the blue flame beneath her teapot.

Knowing how Buddy loves martinis, she's carefully arranged a station for him. Beefeater gin and blue cheese stuffed queen olives are set next to his shaker. A frosted stemmed glass waits in the freezer. Knowing the risks of Buddy and gin, she has measured exactly 3-oz. in a jigger. Add ice and stir. One ration would be okay she calculates.

Also to share is a bottle of Piper Heidseick, given by Gabe for the occasion. Sandy places it in the ice bucket next to two fluted glasses. The fine French champagne will soon be perfectly chilled. A serving tray of mini bagels, smoked salmon, cream cheese, chives, capers, and red onions sits nearby.

431

After brewing her chamomile tea, Sandy retrieves one of the saved first edition books from Uncle Billy's collection. With a quilt across her lap, she nestles in her Chintz covered wing back. The birthday meal prep completed, there's time to get in an hour's reading before Buddy's arrival from the grow house. Scarlett curls up at her feet as Wallis sleeps on the sofa.

Removing the place marker, she begins Chapter 14 of *Gone with the Wind*. It is July, 1863 and a great battle has taken place in a small town in Gettysburg. As the casualties are read in Atlanta's town square, many Southerners begin to accept that their lives will be forever altered. The parallel does not escape her as memories of the past year skirt about her readings.

Sandy closes the novel, recalling how she hung on every word as a child when Uncle Billy would read it to her, so many lifetimes ago it seems. Perspectives are starkly different now.

As she rests her tea on the coaster, the sight of the buckled veneer on the end table crashes the halcyon moment. Recalling sorting through their wet belongings in

432

the Kansas warehouse, she blurts out loud, "Damn it!". Scarlet's eyes flinch and her ears flatten. "It's okay, girl. It's okay," Sandy reassures, as she rehashes the move from hell. She closes the book on her lap and turns to stare at the freezing rain rippling down the window pane.

Sandy's day dreaming is halted by the ping of her phone. Her concern is confirmed as she finds it's yet another text from David. While never responsive, she always read his quirky and flirty messages. But this time it will just have to wait as she hears Buddy's car door shut. Home an hour early, he catches her by surprise. She jumps from the chair and carefully places her rare book back on the shelf.

"Honey, I'm home." he harkens as the front door swings open a moment later.

Sandy greets him with a hug and a kiss. "Happy Birthday, Sweetie. Didn't expect you for a while. I haven't gotten dressed and the kitchen is a mess. Dinner won't be ready for an hour or so, but I've got some lox and bagels. Even have a martini ready to go and Gabe's champagne should be chilled about now. I guess we can get started a little early."

After hanging his dripping rain coat on the rack, Buddy grins. "Martinis?"

"Mar-ti-*nee*! You know how you get with those things."

"Uh, okay. Maybe just one." Buddy half heartedly agrees as he painfully recalls the last time he tasted gin. "I already got started early when I attacked the carrot cake for breakfast. That stuff should be outlawed."

Knowing how Buddy craves her specialty, Sandy laughs, surprised he didn't take the whole thing to work with him. She removes the cellophane from the appetizers and shifts the chilling champagne bottle in its bucket. "Let me go get dressed and we'll get this party started."

Grabbing Sandy by the waist, he pulls her to him and gives her a warm kiss. "You're just fine as you are. I told you I'd have a surprise for us and there's no need to dress up for it."

After retrieving a glass pipe and Bic lighter from his attaché, Buddy presents a small snuff can from his pocket. He leads her to the sofa by the hand. "Come sit down. I've got the good stuff."

434

Seeing the rich green buds as he twists off the top, Sandy exclaims, "Is that the Stargazer? You sure we want to start with that?" She goes to get the appetizers.

"Just a hit or two and I'll relax and have my martini. You can have some champagne. It'll get us ready for the Wellington. Kind of whet our appetites."

"Like your appetite needs whetting." Sandy says approaching with the lox and bagels.

As she sits down the tray, he pinches a slice of salmon and throats it down like a seal with a herring. "Man, that's good. Haven't had anything to eat since the carrot cake this morning."

"No lunch?"

"Nope. Wanted to finish up at the grow house so I could get out before the storm hit."

"Looks like it's going to stall the work on the French drain. That's a good thing as we won't have to pay anything until it's complete, which will now probably be next Spring. But I'm just sick about losing those beautiful old trees."

"Me too. It's a double whammy. Never thought the cost of taking them down would be more than the drain itself."

"Honey, I want tonight to be special. Let's not talk about all this mess. So what are they saying about the storm?"

"After the freezing rain, they're calling for a 12 to 14-inch blizzard overnight with gusting winds."

The thought of a blizzard sends them momentarily into their own worlds as they recall the massive ice and snow storm that scrambled their moral compasses.

"Can't be as bad that that crap that hit us in Marietta." Buddy says with an uneasy smile.

"Uh, yeah. That was horrible. Hope we never have to go through that again. Well, at least we're at home and not stuck somewhere." Wanting to end the discussion, Sandy pushes the tray forward. "Yeah, it's safe and warm here."

Buddy seizes a half bagel, spreads on cream cheese, presses down a few capers, layers sliced red onion, and piles on a stack of smoked salmon. After finishing off the second creation, he's at the kitchen counter bringing together his martini.

With Sandy off to the bathroom, he sneaks the gin bottle from the pantry and glugs into his shaker another four ounces. After the ritual of 50 swirls through the ice, he pours. With the glass about to overflow, he quickly slurps the icy 90 proof down to the acceptable level. After another gulp, he plops in his skewered stuffed olives. Careful to avoid spilling the sloshing challis, he creeps back to the sofa with his second martini. Soon Sandy is by his side watching in anticipation as he preps their smoke.

Gently fondling a pungent bud, he takes a lingering sniff before stuffing the small ball of Star Gazer Indica Flower into the glass bowl. Giving her the honor, Buddy holds the pipe to Sandy's lips and lights his Bic. The flame darts into the olive-green lump. "This stuff is the bomb. Be careful, Honey."

Sandy takes a hit and sucks it to the depths of her lungs, setting off a convulsion of coughs. They both laugh as her hacking finally subsides, tears running down her cheeks.

437

"Here, got mine!" Sandy stutters, straining to hold her breath for the remaining smoke that burns her throat. She passes it back to Buddy and weaves her way to the champagne bucket on the counter.

Taking a large chef's knife from the block and stabbing into the air, she emits her best *Psycho* screech, "Eeeeek! Eeeeek! Eeeeek!"

"Yikes! Put that damn thing away before you hurt yourself." Buddy laughs. "You're already screwed-up, aren't you?"

She giggles as she gashes the foil neck liner. After unwinding the wire, she slowly twists out the cork. Seconds later the projectile jettisons from the bottle and bongs violently into the stove vent, ricocheting into Buddy's forehead. They laugh as Sandy sloshes champagne into her crystal flute.

Back on the sofa, she takes a gulp and points to the pipe on the coffee table. "Gimme another hit."

Buddy, having taken his second toke, passes the pipe back to Sandy. Holding his breath, he evokes a guttural warning, "Whoa there. You better be careful. This is bad stuff, I'm tellin' you."

She does not listen.

Clang, clang. Clang, clang. Clang, clang. Lost in the deep fog of sleep, Sandy has no sense of presence as her phone alarm resonates from a distance. Stuck in a dreamlike state and struggling to move, she's glued motionless to the bed. Finally poking her nose from beneath the coverings, frigid air bites her face. Next to her, naked from the waist down and snoring, is Buddy. A blanket is half pulled over his backside. *Why is it so damn cold in here?* She wonders, straightening the covers over him.

Clang, clang. Clang, clang. Clang, clang. Assessing her state, Sandy recognizes the daily alarm she had failed to suspend. It's 6:30 a.m....much too early to be rising. With her wits coming into focus, she wraps the goose down blanket around her bare body and shuffles towards the intrusive noise.

Holy crap, did we get screwed up last night. Did we even get to eat dinner? She wonders. Spotting the uncooked beef Wellington sitting next to the remnants of carrot cake, she shakes her head. *Well, that answers that question.*

Shivering, she makes her way into the living room. The source of the arctic blast becomes apparent as bursts of wind whistle through the half-opened window. The Happy Birthday balloons strain to stay tethered to the wobbling lamp. His birthday gift sits unopened. Several inches of snow have accumulated, tapering to icy wetness soaking the floor and rug.

She vaguely recalls Buddy needing some fresh air. *Damn!* She calls out clawing down the window pane with one hand while wiping away the snow. Her toes crimp shut as they squish into the freezing puddle.

Clang, clang. Clang, clang. Clang, clang continues the alarm as she hurriedly grabs towels and blankets from the linen closet. After dumping the bundle onto the wetness, Sandy searches for her annoying phone.

Crawling on her knees with her teeth chattering, she reaches under the dining table and retrieves her device. Finally shutting off the alarm, she repositions the quilt, goes to the dry sofa and tucks her numb feet beneath two pillows.

Deciding to check her messages, she remembers the text sent from David Stark the previous afternoon.

Will he ever stop this nonsense? She laughs to herself as she opens the text. An icy chill races down her spine...a chill worse than the winter winds that have whipped into the room. *Hi! C U soon. D*

Sandy clicks off the hair drier and studies her reflection in the mirror. A forced smile reveals her near perfect teeth as she contemplates another whitening treatment. Her eyes widen with a blank look that decries the tenseness of the moment. As she traces on liner, her queasy stomach churns, rattled by uncertainty and excitement. Midnight Mauve or Really Red? Definitely the Mauve she determines while twisting the tube. Combing through her blonde strands, she studies the sexy Navy Print Wrap hanging before her. Nope. Can't do the Lulu's...too skimpy. And screw the pumps. Too wet out there. It's definitely a Nike's day. On to Plan B.

She slips over a faded Bronco's sweatshirt and dons her paint stained comfort jeans. The meticulously applied makeup is hastily erased with a towelette. After positioning the slate

441

Polo cap, she pulls through her pony tail. With hands on hips she studies her look in the mirror, hoping for assurances that do not come. After a mist of Flowerbomb behind each lobe, Sandy leaves the apartment.

An unusually warm spell has come to Denver on the heels of the recent blizzard. Streams of icy salt water splash aside as Sandy glides her SUV into the strip center on the outskirts of town. Backed into a remote corner of the lot, she cases her surroundings.

Built in the late '70's, the out-dated mall is anchored by a K-Mart now in its final days. An unusual amount of vehicles fill the spaces by those flocking to the clearance sale banner strung across the store front. A few doors down she sees Kathie's Diner, a shopworn but warmly inviting eatery. It's 2:25 p.m. with a lull between lunch and dinner.

David Stark's text on the heels of Buddy's birthday dinner has sent Sandy into a tizzy. Comfortably separated by distance and her stand-offish attitude, she had envisioned no risk in their ever becoming involved again.

But here he is on her door steps. In town on business, David has pushed for a face-to-face. Deciding to play it safe

442

had won the tormenting confliction she harbored. Her plan is down pat. Frumpy attire and dreary day at a mundane venue. A perfect setting for a send-off. She would deliver a clear-headed message for David to go about his life and to leave her alone.

Across the way, a tall recognizable figure approaches the diner and enters. She downs the last of her Starbucks, closes her eyes and inhales deeply.

Chomping on a couple of Mentos, she dons her over-sized sunglasses and flips the hoodie over her cap. As she opens the door, her phone chimes from her purse.

The End...Maybe

Grow House

Buz lives in Marietta, GA with his wife of
forty-seven years and a cat named Wallis.
With a degree from the University of
Florida School of Journalism, he enlisted in
the Cola Wars. Dragging his family and
pets along the way, Buz worked in twelve
cities across North America. Fleeing the
corporate morass with a pink slip and a
package, he became a serial entrepreneur
chasing rabbits into the woods. Most got
away. Tiring of this futility, he wrote
Grow House...just for the fun of it.

444